THE
COLORADO
CONSPIRACY

VICTOR O. SWATSEK

VOS & Associates

PO Box 3887

Tustin, CA 92781

www.NovelsByVic.com

(657) 212-5021

First published by VOS & Associates

ISBN: 1482366509

ISBN: 13: 9781482366501

Library of Congress Control Number: TXu 1-779-839

Printed in the United States

This book is printed on acid free paper

In 1975, a plan was put in motion by a group of investors that would change the boundaries of the Pawnee Indian Reservation. Ten years of very careful planning and collaboration between factions in Florence, Italy; Las Vegas, Nevada; Cheyenne, Wyoming; and Fort Collins, Colorado, would ultimately give them access to a gold mine - but not mined by the Pawnee Indians.

It was a plan so cunning and daring that organization's in both the United States and Europe weren't going to let anything stand in their way. However, the timings of these events were extremely crucial to its success.

The Monarch Ranch was a key ingredient to its success. But when the new owner purchased the ranch two months earlier, they hadn't counted on Rick Benedict, a professor of European history, to be that fly in the ointment.

It was a race against time to mine the gold and distribute it to certain parties in Europe and the United States before the Air Force in Cheyenne, Wyoming, could mount a major investigation surrounding the seismic disturbances.

I dedicate this book to my wife Liz, who is also my closest friend and has been my inspiration from the very beginning of my writing career.

I would also like to thank my family and friends for encouraging me to continue my writing career.

PROLOGUE

In 1894, the Pawnee Indians received a large grant of land as part of the peace process from the Unites States Government. The Pawnees settled and prospered, even in the harshest of winters. They were the first settlers to own the land that ultimately became part of the Monarch Ranch in later years. Soon after settling, they discovered gold in the rivers running through their land.

The trapper who managed a small trading post on the outskirts of their reservation accidentally found out where their mine was located and mined enough gold to enlarge the size of his trading post and lived quite comfortably for many years. But as quickly as he found the mine, he just as quickly closed the mine – and never filed a claim.

Warren Air Force Base, originally established in 1867, was a cavalry post for the U.S. Army. Today it serves as the home of the U.S. Air Force Space Command's 90th Space Wing, located on the outskirts of Cheyenne, Wyoming, and just northeast of Colorado. It is responsible for defending America, with the world's most powerful combat-ready ICBM missile force. It is a heavily fortified area cut deep into the mountain and surrounded by the most advanced technology available to protect, attack or approach by any of the country's many enemies. From this mountain headquarters, it also closely monitors all seismic activity, twenty-four hours a day, three hundred sixty-five days of the year.

CHAPTER

1

As Rick stood on the tarmac waiting to board Walter's private plane, he thought about what Walter said last week, just before he flew out to Colorado.

"Rick, I recently purchased a company," his accent still strong, "and one of the assets is a cattle ranch in Fort Collins, Colorado. They used it as a weekend getaway where the owner took his clients. It's a working cattle ranch, and I have some ideas about expanding my restaurant business on the West Coast, but I'm not sure that the beef is up to my standards to launch a new chain of fine dining restaurants."

Rick thought that very interesting, because this was the first time Walter invited him to participate in one of his new ventures.

"Uncle Walter," said Rick with a shrug, "I don't know anything about the cattle or beef industry, much less the restaurant business."

"That is all right," said Walter with a slight accent. "I have someone in mind that may be able to help with that end of the business. The ranch consists of about twenty thousand acres and needs more management skills rather than an actual knowledge of the beef industry."

"What's this all about?" asked Rick.

"With your permission," Walter said, "I will transfer full title of the twenty- thousand-acre cattle ranch to you."

Rick was silent for a moment taking in the stunning news and finally said, smiling, "While I'm very grateful, you know, of course, I'm still angry that you didn't tell us everything the last time you got us involved."

"I understand, Rick," said Walter, "but there were certain issues that I also did not know about. Still, I was confident that you would find everything out on your own. That was a major accomplishment, and you should be proud that you were able to stop them from looting Europe and killing many innocent people."

Rick was considering Walter's generous offer. He figured that he would have to see what it looked like before he decided this would be good for him.

He still remembered what Walter said before he left. *Remember, you are destined for bigger things to come. I built my empire by taking some risks, but at the same time, I like to think I am also a visionary. I must say, though, that when I started building my empire, there were many opportunities, which were at that time not hampered by the regulations, we have today. You are getting an education you could never get from any university in the world.*

"All right, Uncle Walter," said Rick. "I at least owe you by flying out there to see the place, and then I'll let you know."

"That sounds reasonable," said Walter. "I think you will like it. While I have not personally been there, Leonard said it is in a beautiful part of the country. On a different note, I am sorry you and Liz could not work things out, but sometimes there is a good reason."

"Thanks," Rick said. "I guess that it just wasn't meant to be. She'll be okay though. She's strong, and she's doing what she loves best anyway… lecturing and cruising on her boat."

Knowing how his Uncle Walter operated, Rick got that strange feeling that there was more to the story. He was infinitely aware that Walter had special plans for him that for now were to take place in Colorado. He just wished that Walter would share more of what his plans were so he could better prepare himself. But that just wasn't Walter's way.

He figured this was just another test, but now he had to consider if he wanted to continue these adventures, because he really enjoyed teaching and missed that most of all. He also felt he owed Walter a huge debt for what he did for him and Liz and both their parents. However, at some time in his life, the bill would have to be considered paid – he just didn't know when that time would come.

It was now 1980, and he was at an age where he should start thinking about settling down and having a family. With Liz out of his life, he didn't know when that was going to be.

As Rick got into the plane, he leaned back in the plush leather chair and started to think of the previous two months. Being reacquainted with his father Jacob Teaubel was the highlight of his life. All these years when he drove up to visit his uncle he was actually Walter's gatekeeper. He just listened to him for hours talk about the days leading up to World War II, where they had lived, and how the war ended all that.

He was feeling nostalgic again, because he never got the opportunity to know his mother. All he remembered was that they shipped him off from Bremerhaven, Germany, on a troop transport named the USS General Ballou to the United States as an immigrant when he was five years old. He remembered the weeks he was on board the ship, sleeping in a sailor's hammock that would constantly sway and keep rhythm with the ship moving in the rough seas. He still recalled eating saltine crackers and sucking on lemons to reduce seasickness.

When Walter gave Rick the deed to the Monarch Ranch, he wasn't as excited as Walter probably had hoped. Rick felt like a duck out of water, since he hadn't been on a horse for years, and he knew nothing about working a cattle ranch.

Walter made the argument, "This was one of my new business ventures, and I wanted someone to manage it that I could trust. My two restaurants are doing well, and I am considering franchising and opening other high-end steakhouse restaurants from the Midwest to the West Coast area."

Rick knew he wouldn't be able to teach for a while, but was all right for the time being. He took a year's sabbatical from Brown University and notified Chancellor Martha Franklin that he needed some time off for a book he was writing.

Walter had made contact through Chancellor Ralph Mellon from Brown University with Allen Piermont, the President of Colorado State University, and asked for a favor. Walter felt that Rick might inquire about teaching at Colorado State.

"Would you give me a call if Rick contacts you?" Walter asked. "In return, I will create a full scholarship program for two people each year. I would make Rick the trustee to oversee and develop the criteria for receiving the scholarship."

CHAPTER

2

Rick Benedict arrived at Kingston, Rhode Island, in 1955 from West Germany when he was only five years old and stayed with his uncle, Walter Donleavy. He spent a short time at his uncle's home, but was quickly enrolled at Mount St. Albens, a military prep school in Providence, Rhode Island. He was a brilliant student and had the transcripts to prove it.

When he graduated, he went on to St. Basil's, also a private school in Providence. Again, he excelled in all the academic subjects and had a particular fondness for European history. He received his Bachelor's in history and completed his Master's in art and architectural history from Columbia University, majoring in the historical European era. He received his second Master's in engineering, also from Columbia. Rick knew he liked teaching and several excellent universities had courted him.

Walter visited Peter Billingsly, President of Brown University, and made a special request of him. He was hardly in a position to refuse, since Walter "anonymously" financed a new wing. As a result, Peter Billingsly personally asked Rick to teach at Brown University and made Rick a generous offer. Rick accepted.

However, after a year of teaching, because he was still single, Rick got the call from Uncle Sam and was promptly drafted into the Army. Since he had degrees in various subjects, he automatically applied to Officer Candidate School (OCS). After completing the course, he advanced to the rank of Second Lieutenant. After a battery of tests during OCR training at Fort Bliss, Texas, the Army felt he had a higher calling and gave him orders for AIT training at Fort Belvoir in West Virginia.

Rick's MOS was a Nike Hercules Missile Maintenance Repair Platoon Leader. Three weeks later, he shipped out to Zweibrucken, West Germany. Rick received his promotion to First Lieutenant as soon as he returned from his training. He was issued new orders to work for a private *think-tank* attached to the Pentagon in Washington, D.C.

His assignment was a cipher code expert, supervising ten other individuals. After six months in his new position, Rick received his promotion to the rank of Captain and head of the department. He became the best code breaker, as well as a great mentor to his group. But that quickly grew boring for him, and he wanted to do something more exciting and fulfilling.

Rick was handsome, with a chiseled jaw, blond hair, and blue eyes. After his classes, he often found notes on his desk inviting him to sorority parties. While he was single and unattached, he dated women that were not at the college. He always felt it was safer.

CHAPTER

3

Walter Donleavy lived on a 20,000-acre estate in a heavily wooded and secluded part of Northern Rhode Island. He had built an estate that would rival the Rockefellers and the Melons of their time. He went to great lengths to keep his anonymity and privacy. He made his fortune after the war by purchasing various newspaper companies, radio stations, and later television stations for pennies on the dollar.

While most people were still trying to recover from the Depression, Walter was very quietly buying companies. He would typically sell off some of the assets of the newly purchased company, reorganize the management team, and selectively lay off at least ten percent of staff in order to recoup some of his initial investment. This would almost immediately increase performance and profits.

He was a very distinguished looking individual, with his full coiffed silver gray hair. His beard and mustache were always perfectly groomed by his personal staff barber. He was five-foot-eleven, with steel blue eyes that could melt butter, but when needed, he could be very intimidating. He also had a smile that would light up a room, which he used sparingly and only when it had its advantages. Even when he was at his home, he always dressed impeccably and wore a three-piece suit with a royal blue silk kerchief in his outside pocket.

He was a long-term planner, always felt that information was the key to being successful, and was meticulous in everything he did. Over a period of forty years, he outright purchased over forty newspapers and magazines, twenty-five radio stations, and three television stations, including one in Belgium. Most of the executives running the company never met or knew Walter, but worked with his chief legal counsel and corporate lawyer. Every single one of his enterprises was doing well because he provided very lucrative incentives to his executives.

In those early days, as Walter accumulated his wealth, he also became more powerful and developed a reputation for throwing lavish parties, but never held them at his estate. It was always far away from prying eyes, and he never talked about his business, but always talked about their business. This is how he was able to buy companies, because they never knew that when they talked to Walter, they were talking to a very perceptive and well-informed executive. Nobody seemed to realize that when Walter gave a party, shortly thereafter he acquired the company. It was his way to evaluate the executives and their wives.

People knew very little about Walter, and that was how he liked it. In the financial world, he was almost invisible and went to great lengths to keep it that way. In some ways, he was a little insecure, except when he saw a company that would complement his other enterprises. He paid a little more for the companies he wanted. This eliminated the bickering and negotiating of the sale, which otherwise might expose Walter to scrutiny.

Most of the companies' executives didn't know each other or that they all belonged to the same holding company – Monarch Enterprises. He was secretive about himself and his business, but he had one business partner, Leonard Schultz. Leonard also functioned in a COO capacity when required and gave Walter weekly reports on their progress. He had recruited him from Yale.

Leonard was at the top of his class and single. His parents died during the Great Depression and his grandparents raised him. Leonard's parents were also German immigrants and came over to the U.S. in 1929. He studied international corporate tax and business law, and even though he had several very good offers from prestigious law firms in New York and Chicago, he finally decided to accept the exclusive position from Walter. In the coming years, Leonard became a very wealthy man with only one client – Walter Donleavy.

CHAPTER

4

Rick landed at the Loveland Municipal Airport in Walter's private jet, which caused quite a stir with nearby onlookers. As he walked off the airplane wearing his aviator-mirrored sunglasses, Grant Williams, the Monarch Ranch Foreman, met him.

Grant walked up and introduced himself. "Hi, I'm Grant Williams, did you have a good trip?"

"Yes, it was very peaceful," said Rick. "I even got in a few winks."

Grant was a rugged looking individual and looked like he spent a lot of time on the range. He was about six feet tall, with a muscular build from roping and living that ranch life. He always wore a black leather vest, with a gold watch and chain that crossed the front of his vest. His long handlebar mustache was black, with just a tinge of gray at the tips. He always felt it gave him character, and only he trimmed it. Grant had that western down-home drawl that most people immediately liked.

"We have about an hour's ride to the ranch," Grant said, "so just sit back and relax."

As they drove away from the airport, Grant said, "Maybe we ought to stop in town and get you some *ranch-style* clothes."

Rick sheepishly looked over at Grant, nodded, and they drove over to the Peabody Mercantile, which was one of the largest general and clothing stores in Colorado. As they walked in, a very statuesque girl in western clothes greeted them. She was dressed in a red-checkered shirt and very form-fitting jeans right through the waist, with a tightly cinched wide belt and a big silver buckle in the middle. It was a typical buckle, but you couldn't help but notice it.

She wore a pair of red and white, eagle-wing designed, stitched Tony Lama boots, with silver tips and heels. She had long auburn hair that hung simply at her shoulders and gently swayed from side to side as she walked to greet them. Rick also noticed that her red checkered blouse was probably two sizes too small and showed her great cleavage, which he didn't mind.

Grant introduced Dale Honeycutt, the general manager of Peabody Mercantile.

"Hi, Rick," she said smiling. "It's a pleasure to meet you. Grant thought you two might stop by to pick out some clothes."

Rick, fascinated by her looks, was staring because Dale reminded him so much of Liz.

"I'm sorry to stare," Rick finally said, "but you look so much like a woman I was dating."

"Why, thank you," she said. "I'm flattered. A few shirts and jeans will help you over the rough spots. In addition, of course, you'll need at least two hats and two pairs of boots ... one for everyday wear and one for special occasions."

Grant was listening to all of this and just rolled his eyes and smiled. Rick purchased all these clothes and almost didn't have room in the pickup truck. He decided to get in the spirit and wear his new hat and everyday boots driving to the ranch. He also wanted to see how they felt.

Grant had been the general manager and ranch Foreman of the Red River Ranch for the past eight years, which was then sold to a private investor in Rhode Island, who quickly renamed it the Monarch Ranch. He was concerned about the ranch and his men who worked there.

He'd had several conversations with Leonard Schultz, who assured him that this was an investment and there were no plans to change anything. The only thing Grant was worried about was his personal investment in a venture that was worth millions and had taken a long time to set up.

Grant tried to make small talk, but Rick answered with no elaboration. After a while, Grant stopped talking and figured Rick was not going to be a problem at the ranch.

As they finally pulled off the main highway and started up the road to the ranch, they drove directly up to the main house. Mildred Conklin, the housekeeper and chef, met them on the front porch standing by the front door.

She smiled and said, in her genuine Texas drawl, "It's a pleasure to meet you, Mr. Benedict. We've heard a lot about you and hope you'll be comfortable here at the ranch. I see you've already been shopping at the Peabody Mercantile. Let me show you to your room."

Rick turned around and casually said, "Thanks for the lift, Grant. We'll get together later today to talk about the ranch."

Grant tipped his hat and said, "Just give me a call."

Rick followed Mildred through the front foyer and up the stairs. Along the way, Mildred pointed out certain things, and he made a mental note to look at them later. She opened the door, and Rick was surprised at the size and plush look of the room.

"My other things are being shipped," Rick said, "and should be here this week. I'll unpack and come down later."

"I hope you'll be comfortable," Mildred said. "Come on down when you're ready and I'll cut you a piece of my wild cherry and pecan pie."

"Thanks. I may just take you up on that offer," Rick said, as she left and closed the door.

CHAPTER

5

Walter had told him that the main house had about twelve thousand square feet of full living space. Eight bedrooms for guests; a movie/TV room that seated twelve, with satellite TV; a billiard room, ten-seat bar, with two card tables, and enormous elk antler chandeliers over the pool table; the foyer; and the dining room. It also had a twelve-foot-wide balcony that encircled the entire house, furnished with chairs and tables for all. This allowed all the guests to meet for cocktails. Also, at the northwest corner of the balcony, there was a full bar that when not in use rolled into a space in the outside wall.

There was separate housing for the ranch hands that, unlike the Old West, gave each one their own room and bathroom. They lived in spacious surroundings and had separate rooms for the twenty-five ranch hands needed when the time came for the cattle roundup and branding.

He put his things down and just lay on the bed to catch his breath. As he was looking up at the ten-foot ceiling, he wondered how Walter accomplished all he had done. Now he wanted to convert all this to a cattle ranch to service the new restaurants he was planning to open soon.

Within minutes, Rick was fast asleep. He woke up with a start, was sure he had been asleep for hours, but saw it was only twenty minutes. He got up, unpacked some of his clothes, and wanted to try some of the cherry and pecan pie that Mildred was raving about.

He went downstairs into the kitchen and saw the pie waiting for him.

Mildred turned and asked, "How about a fresh cup of coffee to go with that?"

To that, Rick smiled and said, "That sounds great."

"Now dinner is usually at 6:00 p.m.," Mildred said. "Is that all right for you?"

"That's just fine," Rick acknowledged. "And by the way, what are we having tonight?"

"T-bone steak, baked potato, and corn on the cob," she answered.

"Call Grant for me and ask him to join me tonight for dinner here at the house," Rick said. "I want to go over some things about my plans."

She made the call and confirmed that Grant was coming.

Rick finished his pie and coffee. "That was outstanding. Thank you."

"You're welcome," said Mildred. "Let me show you your office."

It looked very impressive, with a massive carved desk, several PCs, printers, and file cabinets. In one of the corners of the room, there was also an eight-foot-tall carved grandfather clock, with two large bears wrapped around from either side of the door. He couldn't figure how the previous owner ever got it in the room.

Yep, it looks like an office all right, he thought.

He started going through some of the ledgers labeled "payables" and didn't know if these were good or bad numbers, but he knew someone who could easily help him. After all, he owed him for the time he got him out of a speed trap jail in a small hick town that was always looking for this type of individual.

When the Grandfather clock struck six, Rick looked up and found it was time for dinner. He was so involved he hadn't taken a break since he sat down at his desk. Grant also showed up.

"Hi, Grant," Rick said. "Let's go over some things at dinner. I know that Mildred has already made a great meal, and it'll give us a chance to talk a bit."

"That's sounds great," said Grant. "I've been wondering how soon we could find out what your plans are for this ranch and how much you actually want to be involved in the day-to-day operation."

Rick looked at Grant and thought it was odd asking him how much he wanted to be involved in the operation. But maybe this was how they operated, since the previous owner wasn't involved at all. As they ate, Rick outlined in very simple terms what he hoped to accomplish, including some general timetables for achieving his goals. Grant listened very intently, but gave no sign of concern.

As Rick was talking, Grant appeared more relaxed.

Rick casually mentioned, "I'd like to take a ride out and tour the ranch tomorrow."

"That's gonna be difficult," Grant said, "since there're just a little over twenty thousand acres and no real fencing in some of the areas."

"Then we'll rent a helicopter," Rick said, "and see it from the air. This way I can get a quick bird's-eye view of the surrounding country."

Grant frowned slightly, but quickly said, "That will be just fine. I know a fella that has a helicopter, and I'm sure he'd be willing to give us a ride around the property, because he owes me a couple of favors. I'll go into town early, set it up, and stop by to pick you up around nine in the front yard."

"That sounds great," said Rick. "Also, is there anybody else we should take with us that may appreciate an aerial view of the ranch?"

"No, can't think of anybody offhand," said Grant. "See you in the morning."

After Grant left, Rick went back to his office and tried to familiarize himself more with what was there. After a couple of hours organizing it his way, he went off to bed.

❖   ❖   ❖

Rick got up the next morning feeling refreshed and started to get excited about seeing the ranch from the air. It'd been a while since he'd been in a helicopter and felt it should prove interesting. He did remember, however, the slightly petrified look on Grant's face when he mentioned what he wanted to do. He was concerned, but decided he might just be overly cautious.

When he took his shower, it reminded him of how Liz used to shower with him. How the glass enclosure and all the mirrors would steam up. That was a couple of months ago, and he still couldn't get her out of his mind. He felt a loss, but if she were happier with Steve, then he would have to get over it.

He dressed in his new *western duds* with his *daily* hat and went downstairs to have breakfast. As he walked on the second floor landing, he stopped to admire the detail and design of the room. They seemed to have spared no expense in building the house.

As he walked down the wide curved stairs, they sounded solid and didn't creak. He walked towards the kitchen, but stopped to admire the massive river rock stone fireplace that was almost thirty feet tall. It had four openings: to the living room, the formal dining room, kitchen area, and the front door. Each side had a massive mantle with western style corbels. As you walked in towards the front door, the first thing you saw was this fantastic, massive fireplace.

"Good morning, Mildred," Rick said.

She looked up and said, "Good morning," and continued cleaning the counter.

"How about some bacon and eggs, no toast, and just coffee?" Rick asked.

"It's almost done," she said. "I figured when I heard you moving around upstairs, that you'd be down soon enough."

Very perceptive, Rick thought. *She's going to work out just fine.*

While he was sitting enjoying breakfast, he called Grant on his mobile phone to see how he was doing with the helicopter.

"I'm working it out with him now," Grant said, "and should be back at the ranch in about forty-five minutes."

"That's great. See you then," Rick said.

Rick looked back at Mildred, who didn't seem as friendly as she had yesterday.

He thought that maybe she was just preoccupied with other things. Rick grabbed another cup of coffee and headed to his office.

In order for this to succeed, thought Rick, he had to understand how and why the ranch operated the way it did. He was still curious about this interesting opportunity from Walter, but he agreed to it partly because he felt he still owed him a lot for helping him and his parents and partially to clear his head and try to stop thinking about Liz.

He stood on the front porch in his new ranch clothes, like a billboard out of a cigarette commercial, just gazing and admiring the beauty and majesty of the Black Mountains, which seemed to reach for the sky on one side. On the other side, were tall Aspen tree groves, with White Ponderosa Pine trees surrounding them.

The house itself sat on a slight hill in the southwest corner of the property, with a commanding view of the Rocky Mountains and alongside the banks of the Cache la Poudre River. His new home was just northeast of Fort Collins close to the Wyoming and Nebraska borders.

After a few minutes of enjoying the view, he suddenly realized he should look like a seasoned cowboy and that his clothes looked too new. He quickly rushed back into the house and asked Mildred what she could recommend to do with his clothes so he wouldn't look like he just stepped out of a cowboy movie.

She turned, laughed, and said, "I was waiting for you to ask me that."

Rick, looking embarrassed, smiled and thought *what a relief that was*.

"I actually have some other clothes that may fit you," she said, "while I take your clothes and beat 'em up a little."

Mildred walked over to a small closet off the kitchen and handed him a shirt and pair of jeans.

"I'll take your clothes and wash them a few times and have them ready for you by the time you get back," she said still smiling.

With a big sigh of relief, Rick grabbed the clothes, ran into his office, and quickly changed. As he buttoned his shirt, he was surprised how well it fit.

He rushed back to Mildred's kitchen and said, "Thanks a lot," and handed her his new clothes and shot out to the front porch, just as Grant flew in with the helicopter onto the front lawn.

Grant looked up at Rick, smiled, but didn't say anything.

They took off and headed north to where the cattle grazed the majority of the time. As they looked down, Grant pointed out that there were four grazing areas and that he was looking at about ten thousand head of cattle. The other fifteen thousand were in the eastern corner of the ranch.

Rick asked, "Why do you need four areas to graze?"

"Because the grass has to re-grow," said Grant, "so we alternate where they graze. This allows us to have good grazing land almost all year round. Only time it's a problem is in the winter, and that's because the snow covers up the grass. They still graze, but not as much, and that's the main reason we have dried hay back at the barn for them."

Grant continued to describe the operation for another several minutes; then Rick's eyes glazed over. Grant stopped talking

Rick had zoned out, because he suddenly thought about Liz and the great times they shared together. He was hoping she was doing well and still loving the lecture circuit. It was strange to think that just five months ago, they were deeply in love and in Prague trying to save the world, or so they thought. It took him a month to get over Liz. But in the end, you never got over someone like Liz. You just had to let her go.

CHAPTER

6

Liz came to Kingston Rhode Island in 1956 when she was five years old. She was an immigrant from Linz, Austria, when her parents shipped her to the United States to live with her uncle and to get an education. She spent a little time with her uncle and was quickly sent off to *Sister of Passionate Sorrow*, an exclusive school for girls in upper New York.

She had very good school transcripts from St. Gaudins, a private school in Vienna, Austria. She did very well in all her academic subjects, but had a particular fondness for languages of European countries.

She graduated with honors from Sister of Passionate Sorrow and excelled so highly that she had offers from ten top universities. She settled on Radcliff because they had the best classes for her long-term goals. By the time she graduated from the university where she received her Bachelor's degree, she was proficient in six foreign languages, including German, Hungarian, Romanian, Italian, French, and Latin.

Liz went on to Columbia University for her Master's and PhD in languages. She had offers to work at the UN as a multiple language translator. They were well-paid positions and in high demand, but she felt a different calling. She didn't want to live in only one place and wanted to be free to select her assignments.

Upon graduation, her Uncle Walter drove her down to the Conanicut Harbor and presented her with a Ferretti 74 yacht, complete with a full-time captain named Steve Weisen. The yacht had twin diesel engines, traveled at twenty knots full speed, and included a complete kitchen and cooking system. It even had a washer and dryer and could easily sleep six.

"There's no cost to you," Walter said, "except you have to buy your own clothes and food. Steve Weisen is your full-time ship's captain and will take care of everything, including all maintenance requirements."

Within weeks, Liz came to love that boat, as she had never treasured anything else in her life. She would see boats at the marina but had never had the urge to buy one. But she quickly found that she loved being on the ocean away from the hustle and bustle of city life.

She decided that she would teach. With her credentials, she could have taught at any of the universities, and she decided on Georgetown University in Washington, D.C. Over the next few years, she gained a certain academic notoriety and as a result received continuous requests to lecture elsewhere. She recognized a personal need for this more challenging role, which also turned out to be financially rewarding for her as well. Liz took her job seriously and ultimately moved onto her yacht full time.

She loved lecturing, which made life much easier on the lecture circuit. Several universities in Europe asked for her, so she finally planned the trip aboard her boat. She spent a year in Europe, traveling up the Adriatic and Black Sea, the Rhine River in Germany, and the Danube in Germany and Austria.

It was while Liz was in Europe that she took up painting. She started with postcard size paintings. Some of them she kept and others she sent to Walter. When Walter received them, he was so elated that he had them framed and hung them proudly in his study. All of her paintings were just signed "Liz," with only a date.

It was only a few months earlier in 1979 when both Liz and Rick learned of their relationship to Walter. Each had a living parent working on Walter's estate. Both Liz and Rick had deep mixed reactions and both needed time to adjust – and to heal.

CHAPTER

7

Captain Steve Weisen graduated from Annapolis in 1973, served several tours of duty in Vietnam, Korea, and finished his service in Germany. When he finished his tour, Walter was waiting for him with a special job. He'd excelled in all the techniques of managing a ship. He was also an expert in hand-to-hand combat, knew how to use almost any weapon, and became proficient in electronic surveillance and counter-terrorism. He was well paid, and he owed Walter since he also helped his parents flee from Austria.

At first Steve didn't think he could live and work in such a mundane environment after doing three tours in Viet Nam and two in Korea, plus multiple *blackops* missions. He felt this might be too tame for him.

"Give it a try for a couple of months," Walter told him, "and if you are still having trouble adjusting, I will understand and will get someone else."

But after being at sea, he decided he liked it a lot more than he'd expected. He felt he was on a permanent, long-term vacation and after three months told Walter, "I've got to be crazy not to do this. Thanks, Walter, for the opportunity."

"Now you know," said Walter, "this is a special job being a bodyguard for Liz. I consider all of you as my children and as such you must take care of each other."

Steve's parents also lived on Walter's estate. He had no real personal life and felt it was his duty to watch out for Liz. Plus, he loved sailing, especially in the Mediterranean. Unbeknownst to Liz, Steve's job wasn't only being the captain of her yacht, but also a personal bodyguard to Liz. He was always around, but stayed in the shadows and not visible. Sometimes he attended some of her lectures, sitting in the very last row to keep an eye on her.

Liz and Steve got on famously. However, he realized early on when they had a good relationship, that if he had emotional ties to Liz, he couldn't function properly. He would be too distracted as her bodyguard and would potentially put Liz in danger. He was in a quandary, because he loved the job he was doing and getting to travel, but he also wanted to start having a family and settle down. He knew that he would have to put that part of his life on hold for a little while, and he knew the relationship he and Liz entered into last January was wrong.

CHAPTER

8

In 1864, Fort Collins was originally founded as a U.S. military fort and, in 1873, incorporated as a town. It was also home to Colorado State University. Across the state line in Wyoming was Warren Air Force Base, which opened in 1867 as a cavalry post for the U.S. Army. Today it serves as the home of the Air Force Space Command's 90th Space Wing, which is responsible for defending America with the world's most powerful combat-ready ICBM missile force.

One of the critical aspects of this U.S. Air Force location was that they had to be constantly alert, especially for seismic disturbances. In the past two years, they often felt slight tremors that lasted about fifteen seconds and then went still. Initially, they just chalked this up to small earthquakes, because anything less than two points on the Richter scale gave no cause for alarm.

But what did concern them was the frequency of these tremors, and they had been going on for quite some time. They checked with Caltech Seismology Laboratory in Pasadena, California, but they had no recordings in that area.

Captain Albert Peterson, who was the watch commander, would make out his usual daily report and send it to Lieutenant General Lawrence Alexander.

Captain Peterson went to deliver his report to the General and said, "General, in my reports, I've indicated that while I'm not worried at this point, I am concerned that the frequency of these tremors is consistent with possible dynamite blasting and heavy moving equipment. I recommend sending out a reconnaissance patrol in the general area to confirm exactly what's causing these tremors."

"Hold off on the mission," the General said, "and I'll look into it."

The General had seen these reports for the last eighteen months and didn't know how long he could hide this. When he prepared his quarterly report to the Pentagon, he left that part out.

After the Captain left, the panicked General made a quick call on his secure line to Judge Jack Thornton in Fort Collins.

The Judge picked up the phone and said, "Hi, Larry. What can I do for you?"

"I've got my watch commander," the general said, "Captain Peterson monitoring all seismic readings. He's getting a mite too close and forcing me to launch a full-blown investigation with people from Washington. You have to stop using dynamite for a while. These tremors are registering on our seismic charts at the mountain, and we don't need any type of investigation going on anywhere around here, not until we're finished with the job."

"Understood," said the Judge, "and I'll take care of it. By the way, when are you coming down to the Cheyenne Country Club to play some golf with us? How about next Friday and we can make a weekend of it?"

"Sounds good to me," the General responded. "I'll see you then."

When the Judge hung up, he started having concerns about the General and wondered if he could keep it together.

Captain Peterson left the General's office still concerned, because in the past the General had always taken more interest, especially since this could potentially affect national security. He decided to perform his own study into what was causing these tremors and how long they'd been going on, including the frequency, and try to pinpoint the locations of the tremors.

When he had all the detailed facts collected, he could better present them to the General for review. He was going to keep this particular task to himself until he could figure out if he should be concerned about anything. He knew of a couple of people who tried to find out if there was something going on and ultimately ended up ice fishing at the North Pole for the rest of their military duty. But Captain Peterson was now concerned about finishing the report.

Captain Peterson called a friend of his at the Pentagon. "Hi Fred, how are you? Can you give me some advice, on the Q.T., on how to handle a delicate matter?"

"The General has been around for a long time," said Fred, "and you don't become a General by just doing your job. You tend to know where the bodies are buried and use it as a *chit* in later years. You need to be very careful. The General is well connected at the Pentagon. Your best bet would be that you do this off the books and try to do this alone. But if you find out something, then you have a different problem. What will you do with the information and to whom will you give it? I'll do a little unofficial digging here, and I'll get back to you. In the meantime, just be careful."

CHAPTER

9

The Judge hung up the phone and called Grant, but his mobile phone went to voicemail. He left a cryptic message that he knew Grant would understand and would take care of the matter. After all, they were so close to completion that they couldn't afford to have any problems, especially not at this final stage of the game plan. The Judge sat back in his chair and pulled out a nugget from a black leather pouch in his desk, reminding him how big this project actually was.

He'd had this nugget for many years and received it as payment from the Pawnee Indians over forty years ago when he was working at the White Feather Trading Post. That's when he got the gold fever and never got over it. He tried to make the Indians like him and tell him where the mine was, but to no avail.

One night, years ago, when he was getting ready to go home from working at the trading post, he spotted Jesse packing up three burros at the back of the trading post and silently riding off. He'd decided to follow him because he knew that Jesse was interested in the gold that the Indians were trading.

As he followed at a safe distance, he became aware that it was getting darker and it was harder to see in front of him. It was late at night and with no moon to help show the way, he was concerned he'd lost him. Suddenly an arm reached up and pulled him off his horse and threw him to the ground.

As he rolled over several times, a voice said, "Why are you following me?"

"I know you found the location of the Pawnee Indian gold mine," Jack shot back startled, "and thought you could use some help in mining it."

Suddenly Jesse lit a match and saw it was Jack Thornton.

"I don't need a partner and surely not you," Jesse said, "because I know you're as crooked as they come. Now get out of here."

Jack got to his feet and slowly moved towards his horse, and then suddenly he slapped the rear rump of his horse. It reared up and fell on Jesse, crushing and killing him.

"Oh, my God," said Jack aloud. "What have I done? How am I going to explain this to Harry?"

Jack panicked because now he had to explain the death of Jesse to his brother, Harry, and he wasn't looking forward to that. He just sat down trying to figure out what to do.

He thought for sure that they would probably blame him for Jesse's death, and he couldn't have that. After all, he was only sixteen, just starting out, and ready to go to law school in the spring. He picked Jesse up, carried him to the edge of the rock, and leaned his limp, bloody body against it. He sat there next to Jesse's broken body and cried until daylight peeked over the horizon. Both the burros and horse were still here, so he took the saddles and blankets off and let them all go. Then he got on his own horse and went back to town.

Unbeknownst to him there were several Pawnee Indians watching from a higher rock who had seen everything. There was a concern that if the Sheriff found the body, he might also accidentally discover the mine. After Jack left, the two Indians made their way down the large granite boulder to where Jesse was propped up. They decided that they would hide him in the mineshaft since it was close by.

They found the horse and burros and let them go free in the hills close to the reservation. As they carried Jesse's body, they went deep into the mineshaft, where they were sure no one would find him. They took all of his camping and mining gear, including the kerosene lamp, laid them down around Jesse and left.

They went back to their camp and told the Tribal Chief. The Chief now had some concerns someone might find him and think the Indians killed Jesse. Even though they were on their own land, they still had an occasional Sheriff try to find something or some reason to harass them. They knew if they discovered the body, there would be consequences and many questions asked. He decided to leave Jesse propped up against the wall deep in the mine.

CHAPTER

10

In earlier days when the West was young and still a vast wilderness, settlers came from the Eastern part of the United States, as well as from Europe. They were all in search of the dream of owning their own land. In those days, property rights generally weren't a big issue unless something of value was found, like oil, gold or other precious minerals.

The Pawnee Indians settled on land given to them as part of the peace process with the Unites States Government in the late 1800s. They settled and prospered, even in the harshest of winters. Later on, the Pawnee Indian tribe discovered gold in rivers running through their land and found they could trade this, along with their fur pelts, for food and clothing from the local trapper who managed the trading post. They were friendly to the trader, and he in turn gave them a fair price for their beaver pelts, buffalo hides, and their gold.

But when the Pawnee Indians started bringing in nuggets and not just gold dust, William Jackson was intrigued and got *the gold fever*. He knew that the Indians didn't know that the gold they were bringing to him was very valuable, and so he kept it quiet. The Pawnee Indian Chief Running Bear got along well with the other settlers. One day William received an invitation to their reservation to share a meal with them, which he eagerly accepted.

William arrived around dusk at the Pawnee camp and was greeted by the Chief. He was asked to sit on the right side of the Chief, which he later found out was a great honor. Soon the entertainment started with the young braves in headdresses dancing a welcome dance in honor of William. This went on for hours and all the while the Chief was looking at William, satisfied he'd found a friend.

It was while they were eating freshly killed roasted venison and feeling unusually happy that one of the elders told him a story of how they found the gold they had been trading with him. At the end of the evening, they gave him the name of *White Feather*. While he knew this was a great honor bestowed on him, he still felt a personal and strong desire to find their gold mine. They never disclosed the location, but always kept him as a close friend.

After a few years of trading with the Indians, new settlers started buying provisions. William prospered and his trading post turned into a general store. Traveling settlers stopped to buy their supplies for their continuing journey.

He finally married and had two boys named Harry and Jesse. They grew up in the store and learned how to manage it well. William died in 1938, but not before he told them the story of how he got the name *White Feather*.

Harry and Jesse took over the store and renamed it *the White Feather Trading Post*. After hearing the story of the Pawnee gold mine and things settled down a bit, they decided they were going to find where the Pawnee gold mine was actually located.

Jesse was always getting into trouble by gambling, drinking, and carousing with women. He was greedy and wanted the good life, but wasn't willing to wait or work for it. One night after he spent most of his money, he decided he was going to find that gold mine on his own. He purchased some mining equipment and food and water for a week in another town so as not to attract any suspicion to himself. He didn't tell anyone else in town where he was going and so nobody missed him for a while. With a full moon and under cover of darkness, Jesse rode out and wandered onto the Pawnee Indian Reservation.

Jesse told Harry before he left that he was going on a camping trip, but didn't tell him where. He just said he would be back in four days. After the sixth day, Harry was getting worried and went looking for him, but didn't find him. He assembled a search party, but they couldn't find any trace of him either. Harry went out several more times but never found Jesse ... or his body.

Now Harry was alone to deal with not only the loss of his father, but now the loss of his brother as well. He went on trying to run the trading post, but people that knew him saw that his heart wasn't in it anymore. His mother had passed away a short time later, which made it all the more difficult. He had difficulty accepting the fact that his brother might be dead, and it took him a while to get over it. Years passed, but from time to time, he still wondered what had happened to Jesse. He hoped that maybe Jesse just kept traveling because he wanted more out of life than just running a trading post.

One very cloudy day, with only the moon to guide him, Harry was coming home from a friend's house when a sudden cloudburst caught him by surprise. He knew he had to take cover. As he sat hunched under a dense pine tree shivering and watching the lightning flashing, he caught a glimpse of what appeared to be an opening in the side of a mountain.

He thought about making a dash for it to get better cover. As he got closer, he saw that it was actually large enough that he could duck inside, along with his horse, to weather out the storm. As he got in and sat down, he looked around and noticed it was an opening to an old deserted mine. Lanterns were lying about, and some picks and shovels leaning against the wall.

He found one lantern that still had some kerosene left in it. He lit the lantern and rested on the wall of the cave to dry off. When he finally got his bearings and his eyesight adjusted to the low lighting, he looked around. He noticed that the cave looked deep. Since he hadn't anything else to do and the storm was getting worse, he started walking down the path that seemed worn the most. As he was walking, it came to him that maybe this was the Pawnee Indians' mine.

He was excited, with his heart pounding in his chest. He remembered what he had promised himself in the past – that if he ever found the mine, he would never disclose the location. He wasn't sure, but it looked like it was abandoned and forgotten, probably because all the gold had been mined – or so they thought.

After walking another three hundred feet, he came to a much larger clearing and found there were two smaller shafts going off to the right and left. He decided to take the left shaft; but it stopped abruptly, so he came back and took the right shaft. About fifty feet ahead, he found a hat that he recognized – it was his brother's. It was sitting on top of his skeletal remains, dusty like he'd been sitting there for a long time. The bones looked broken, and there were marks from some creature that must have eaten some of his remains. He sat down and cried, because he knew his brother died trying to find the Pawnee gold mine.

Harry waited in the mine until the weather cleared up. The following morning, he took Jesse's remains, wrapped them in a blanket roll, took him back to town, and buried him next to his mother and father. He suddenly felt resentment, because he thought the Pawnee Indians killed his brother. And so he decided that this was going to be his mine. He started thinking about working the mine, even though it might actually not have any gold left in it. But today he had a new goal: It was to mine for gold and not file a claim.

He had Albert Butler, one of his trusted employees, manage the trading post while he was gone. Harry told him that he was going scouting to see if it was worthwhile opening another trading post in Wyoming. Over the next several weeks, he discreetly purchased the equipment needed and, in the dead of night, packed up two mules with mining equipment and provisions and left town quietly.

He slept inside the mine, worked day and night, and slowly began finding the little bit of the gold that the Pawnee Indians had left behind. It was hard work from sunup to sundown, but he felt it was worth it.

He thought about registering his claim, but decided against it because he wasn't sure if the Indians still had a legal claim to the land, and just in case he discovered a lot of gold, he didn't want people nosing around the property.

After about a week and while he was resting, he thought, *If this is the Pawnee gold mine, why haven't they come around and stopped me?* Like all gold mine claims, there were always unscrupulous miners who would try to steal it the *legitimate* way.

He also wasn't sure where the Pawnee Reservation actually started or ended. In any event, Harry cautiously started mining for gold. After about a month, he felt he had enough gold dust and nuggets to take into town and start cashing in. He didn't go back to the town that knew him, but instead went to Cheyenne, Wyoming, to cash in his gold.

Harry opened several bank accounts in neighboring bigger cities to avoid people thinking he was rich. This gave him the financing necessary to expand the White Feather Trading Post. After several years, he sold the trading post to Albert Butler, the person that was managing it while he was prospecting. He then left the area and settled in Fort Collins.

When Harry stopped working the mine, he had decided to hide the entrance with local brush and fallen tree branches. He never went back to the mine, even though there may have been more gold to dig out.

Harry felt he had enough to live very comfortably and built his home in Fort Collins and opened a general store, calling it the Peabody Mercantile. He never married, but many women were aware of his eligibility and knew he was wealthy. Over the years there had been numerous newspaper articles written about Harry's accomplishments. Now he was able to expand the size of the store and live the life he had always dreamed of having. Everyone knew he had found gold and tried several times over a fifty-year period to have him divulge the location, but he never did, and the location died with him.

CHAPTER
11

Rick and Grant continued to head north in the helicopter and then northeast to the edge of the property.

Grant smiled out of the corner of his mouth and said to Rick, "You're awful quiet for a fellow who just inherited a major cattle ranch. Most people I know would be partying all day and all night."

Rick looked over at him, smiled back and said, "You're right. And I do love a good party, but I also don't want to run it into the ground. I'm interested in expanding and having the ranch grow. But since you mentioned it, why don't we get everyone together tonight and have a country-western style barbeque to get to know one another and let them all get to know who I am and what I want to accomplish."

Grant grabbed his mobile phone, called back to the main house, and talked to Mildred.

"Mildred, Rick would like to have a get-together. Let the entire ranch know that we'll have a barbeque tonight and everyone is welcome. See if we can get the Dusty Pioneers on short notice to give us some music."

"That sounds great," Mildred said, and hung up the phone with a happy look on her face.

That's when Grant discovered a voicemail from the Judge. He made a mental note to call the Judge back later.

They flew around about another thirty minutes into a thickly populated forestry area with tall Aspen and Spruce trees. As they flew a little further, they saw a cow lying down on the side of the road.

"Take us down there by the road," Rick told the pilot.

They immediately landed in a clearing, and Rick was already out and running towards the steer.

Grant saw from a distance that it was dead as its tongue was hanging out to one side. As they got closer, they couldn't see any visible signs of what had killed it or why it died. Grant thought it peculiar that it was all alone in this part of the woods.

Grant went back to the helicopter, called John Hammond, the ranch veterinarian. "John," said Grant, "can you come out with your flatbed truck? We found a dead steer on the road. See if you can figure out why this steer died."

"Let's walk a little further," Rick said. "Let's see if there are any other strays around here."

They didn't have very far to walk when they spotted another cow and suddenly spotted five more. Grant cursed to himself because he already knew what caused this.

"This is the most mysterious thing I've ever seen," Grant said. "Tomorrow morning we'll perform a cattle headcount to see how many others we may have lost."

They headed back to where they spotted the first cow and saw John Hammond just coming up the road. He got out with his black bag and started examining the carcass.

"The best I can determine right now is that it was poisoned," he said, "because of the color of the tongue. I'll know better once I get it back to the ranch. I can't determine if this is contagious or not, so I'm having our flatbed truck driver pick up the carcasses and take them all back to the ranch."

He added, "Be sure to wear gloves if you touch it."

John had gone to veterinary school when he left the service after the Korean War. He'd worked at various places, until the day he attended a trade show demonstrating the latest and greatest applications and equipment available to a veterinarian. He was especially drawn to devices used to track animals. At the time, the idea had not caught on for cattle, but he felt there was definitely an application for the cattle industry. He knew most cattle ranches in the Southwest were large, so he focused on getting a job at some of the biggest ranches to sell this as a special service.

Things were not progressing well, so John decided it would be best to become a full-time, in-house ranch veterinarian. That's when Grant found John.

Rick looked at Grant bewildered. It was only around noon, so they decided to go on farther.

"John," said Rick, "we're going to borrow your Jeep to drive a little further and see if there are any other dead cattle around. We'll be back shortly."

They drove another several miles but found no other dead cattle.

"Did you notice that these cattle didn't have a brand on them?" Rick said.

"No, I didn't, but we don't always brand the cattle," Grant said. "Believe it or not, we still have cattle rustlers in this day and age. We actually have several options to identify the owner. One is the typical outside brand on the left rear flank. Another is to tag them through the earlobe. And lastly, we have ours electronically tagged with a chip in their shoulder. Electronically tagging and serial numbering is still the best way. We can always find out exactly where they are at all times, because they're serial numbered."

"I'd like to see that list," said Rick, "after you run an updated report."

Now I have something else to worry about, said Grant to himself.

They got back in their helicopter and flew back to the house.

CHAPTER

12

As they flew back to the house, Rick began wondering if this was what Walter meant by "managing" his new venture. So far it seemed to have problems, which weren't easily explainable. They landed in the large yard in the front of the house and Rick got out, preoccupied by the day's events.

As he walked up the steps, Grant said, "Don't forget the chuck wagon barbeque tonight at dusk."

"I won't," Rick said. He turned around and went inside to check how Mildred was doing with the barbeque for tonight.

He went into the kitchen and found her busy baking pies.

"Have there been any strange or unusual things happening on the ranch in the last two to three years?" Rick asked, getting himself a cup of coffee.

Mildred stopped for a moment, looked up and said, "Other than the dead cattle you found today? I'm told we occasionally have cattle go missing. There are still cattle rustlers in this part of the country. And I'm sure there are mountain lions in these parts as well."

"What about some of the other ranches around here?" he asked.

"You'd have to ask Grant," she said. "He's been around here for a long time, and I'm sure he would know. He and the Sheriff are in-laws and they talk all the time."

She turned around to put her pies in the oven.

Rick thought she was a little too tense, but now he knew that Grant was related to the Sheriff, so he changed the subject.

"What kind of food do they normally prepare at one of these barbeques?" he asked.

"We already butchered a cow this morning and made about twenty-five man-size T-bone steaks, twenty-five rib-eye steaks, and enough half-pound burgers for the next two weeks. Then we have corn on the cob, giant baked potatoes with butter and chives, and, of course, three kinds of my special pies. Top all of this off with about ten kegs of beer and soda."

Rick was pleased and thought, *this was a completely new world to embrace.*

"Thanks for the information," he said smiling, grabbed a cup of coffee, and went into his office.

There was also a small library just off his office, which was lined with books that he was sure were for decoration only.

He sat down in the plush covered, thickly upholstered chair made of smooth cowhide and started going over the books. He looked at them for a while and still didn't understand most of it, but he knew someone who might. If by some chance the books were *inaccurate*, then he didn't want to sound any alarms.

He put in a call to his friend, Fred Tremane, who had a very successful reputation for finding hidden assets. He turned his business into a very lucrative forensic analysis practice and found that it paid very well. Maybe this was just a coincidence, but Fred was at Walter's party when he and Liz had returned from Prague.

The more he thought about it, though, and knowing how Walter operates, the more he didn't believe it was just a coincidence. Fortunately, he'd known Fred when he was in the Army, so it had been great to catch up and find out what he had been doing.

"Hi, Fred. This is Rick Benedict …... Aare you still busy uncovering bad guys?"

"Hi, Rick. Actually I'm just winding up a job," Fred said laughing, "and ready to pick up my bonus check and head for Hawaii. What can I do for you?"

"It sounds like you need a vacation," Rick answered back. "How would you like to spend some quality time at my new ranch in Colorado? You'd be doing me a huge favor."

"How can I refuse an offer like that," Fred said. "Okay, I'll be there next week. I'll call you when I get ready to take off so you can meet me at the airport. See you soon."

Fred currently worked as a consultant to a major litigation law firm, performing forensic analysis on a company that appeared to be hiding assets through multiple shell companies and offshore corporations. They wanted to water down the stock to drive the price down and then purchase enough back in order to have fifty-one percent or majority ownership of the company.

He was also a law school graduate with an MBA from the Wharton School of Business. Well before he graduated, some of the *Big Ten* accounting firms had already courted him.

He got himself into trouble when the company he first worked for set up what amounted to a Ponzi scheme to create nonexistent revenue and hide profits. Unfortunately, the three executives who concocted the scheme had been secretly wire-transferring millions of dollars to a bank in the Cayman Islands, and before Fred knew it, they just didn't show up for work anymore.

Fred was the only one left, and since he was the CFO, they assumed he knew all about it, and he took the fall. Walter heard about the case and knew some of the principals, hired the finest lawyer for Fred's defense, and luckily Fred was acquitted on a technicality. After the trial, Fred wanted to get even, and he knew the only way to hurt them was in their wallets. In addition, he felt he owed the good people of the company who had lost their life savings.

He went after them with a passion and within a week, working night and day, had traced the money back to a bank in the Netherlands. He had one of his friends, a whiz computer hacker, tap into and transfer all the money to a bank in Lichtenstein. They could no longer pay their own bills. A note was anonymously sent to the hotel indicating what they had done, and with no money to pay their bills, they flew back to the U.S., where the U.S. Marshals were waiting for them.

Fred returned what was left of the money back to the company's own business accounts. He never told the company's personnel what he'd done, but the new CFO knew and was very happy. Fred Tremane now owed Walter a huge debt.

In the coming years, he worked with Leonard Schultz, Walter's lawyer, and performed very detailed forensic analyses for some of the companies Walter purchased. Fred was able to save Walter a lot of money and, in return, was handsomely paid for his analysis. From that point on, Walter found another specialist to add to his arsenal of professionals.

Rick was happy that things worked out for Fred the way they did, because he'd found a new profession and was now in high demand.

CHAPTER

13

Rick was still concerned about the dead cattle but now had to focus on what he was going to say during the barbeque, where he knew he would undoubtedly be the main topic of conversation. He was already figuring it out when his phone rang.

It was John Hammond. "Rick, I just thought you ought to know that the dead cattle died from cyanide poisoning."

"Have you ever had this problem before?" Rick asked, with a frown on his face. "I asked Grant if it's possible they may not be part of our herd, because they had no brand."

"Well, they're definitely ours," said John. "They had that electronic chip in their shoulder, which matches our inventory. In addition, we've had this problem before, ever since they purchased that additional ten thousand acres of grazing land north of the property. I understand they got it at a great price. It has Boxeleder Creek running right down the middle of the place, which connects all the way north to Wyoming."

"Thanks for the rundown," Rick said. "See you at the barbecue John," and hung up.

Rick now wondered why Grant looked so surprised that they found dead cattle due to cyanide poisoning, since according to John, it had been a problem before.

49

Rick thought that all of this happened at the northeastern end of the property, which was downhill from the ranch itself. Tomorrow he'd go on a scouting trip on his own and see what was around there that could cause this type of problem.

He quickly peeled out of his clothes and jumped into the shower. He looked down at the shower floor and was surprised at how much dust and dirt you could accumulate on just an afternoon outing.

As he dried himself off, he was again reminded how he and Liz would take showers together and run right into bed, make mad passionate love, and fall asleep in each other's arms. He hoped Steve was taking good care of her, because he sure missed her. He made a mental note to call her next week while he was driving down to the new area.

When he got out of the shower, he saw that Mildred had brought up his daily clothes. No pressing, just tumble-dried, lying on the bed.

CHAPTER

14

Liz was on the Mediterranean Ocean basking in the sun on her boat and wishing this day would never end. She had to remember that Steve needed to stay alert because, after all, that was his real job. But lately he had been somewhat distant, and she couldn't understand why.

It was noontime and both had lunch on deck of freshly caught lobster, with a bottle of Ca De Rocchi Valpolicella Montere Ripasso, one of the local wines of Naples.

She could tell Steve was preoccupied so she asked, "What's on your mind, Steve? You seem to be off in another place. Is everything okay?"

"No, not really," Steve finally confessed. "Everything is not okay. When Walter first asked me to take on this task, I was ecstatic to have such a dream job. Falling in love with you was never my objective. I'd actually put that part of my life on hold for a while. Don't misunderstand me, the job is great, but I'm concerned that I'll let my guard down and then something may happen to you, and I'd never forgive myself."

Liz's fork stopped in mid-air as she listened to Steve.

After a moment, she quietly put the fork down, looked at her plate for a few seconds, and said, "I've also felt you've been trying to distance yourself, and now I know why. What would you like to do about this? You've been just great about everything, and I guess I understand why and how you feel, but there must be some way we can work this out."

"I've spent the better part of ten years," Steve said, "in various deep cover and dangerous military positions. I was told long ago that in order to be 100% effective, it's very difficult if not almost impossible to have a personal relationship, let alone with the same person I'm supposed to protect. I thought I could make it work, but I was wrong. I'd like to call Walter and tell him about our situation and ask what he recommends we do. I can still stay on as your yacht captain or maybe he could recommend someone else to fill my position. I can always go back into the service."

Liz understood how he was torn between the two problems. She was very sad and holding back tears. "Okay... give him a call, but my vote is to at least have you stay on as my boat captain, unless you feel this would be too hard for you."

Steve wasn't handling this well. He'd been in many tight situations before, made split-second decisions, and was always right. But with Liz, he just couldn't seem to function as he normally would. He had a responsibility to Walter, but at the same time was trying to have a personal life that was fulfilling to him. He was at an age where he wanted to settle down, be married, have children, but not while he felt guilty for not being able to perform his job well.

Steve got up, went into his stateroom, called Walter, told him the situation, and asked what he would recommend.

"Steve," Walter answered, "if you think you can do your job as the yacht captain in the same capacity you were in last year, then that would be my recommendation. But if you feel that it would be a problem, let me know and I'll make other arrangements. Let's talk about it again in about thirty days."

"Okay, Walter," said Steve. "But I'm not sure it's going to be any different in thirty days. Thanks, Walter," he said, hanging up and staring at the phone.

He thought back at all the difficult situations he'd been in over the years and never had a problem making a decision. But this was the first time he felt out of his element and couldn't figure out a solution that wouldn't hurt Liz.

Steve had to make a decision and then talk to Liz about it. He went up on deck to find her.

"Walter thinks we should give this about thirty days," said Steve, "and then we'd talk again. If I still have a problem performing my duties, then we'll figure out what to do."

By that time, Liz had tears running down her cheeks, because she already felt she knew the outcome, and sadly said, "Okay," then left the table. Liz liked Steve a lot and hoped he would stay on. After this, Steve probably would always look at her differently, but he would still be close by. In addition, he was a great captain of her yacht, and if he left, she might have to put into port for a time. She would miss the sea and all it had to offer …. and Steve.

Liz went back to her cabin, curled up in bed, and stayed there the rest of the afternoon. Absentmindedly, she started thinking of Rick, wondering what he was doing and if he missed her. She decided to stop thinking about Rick, because it wasn't fair to him or Steve. She stayed in her cabin through the night and didn't come up to have dinner, even when Steve called down to her. She felt it too difficult to sit at the same table across from Steve pretending as if everything was all right.

CHAPTER

15

Rick came downstairs to meet with Grant and so he could introduce him to everyone, including the ranch hands. He was wearing his other hat and had to admit that it did make him look taller.

Grant looked at him as he walked down the stairs, smiled and asked, "Are you going to church?"

Rick smiled back and said, "I learned a long time ago that when you're the new kid on the block, you get one chance to make an impression, and the first time they see and hear me, they'll remember for a long time."

Rick was dressed like a *gentleman* rancher, with a western jacket, a necktie lariat with a hefty turquoise stone in the center of it, and, of course, his hat.

"Well, I'll be," said Grant. "You look like you're gonna give us a lecture rather than just introducing yourself. I told everyone that this was your idea and that you wanted to get to know everyone. It would also be real helpful if they knew a little about you as well."

"I can sum up me in about thirty second." Rick smiled and said, "But, I'm more interested in hearing about them."

"Well, let's go and join the party," Grant said.

As they walked across the expansive lawn in front of the house over to the area staged for the barbeque, Rick noticed Dale Honeycutt.

"Is she seeing someone from the ranch?" he asked Grant.

"Yeah ... me," Grant answered, staring at Rick.

Rick thought, *Well, that was awkward.* He tipped his hat in her direction to acknowledge her, walked over to the bar, picked up a beer, and continued to the makeshift stage.

He grabbed the microphone and said, "Good evening, everyone. I'm so glad we could all get together on such short notice. I'd have done this sooner, but I had to wash out the dust in my throat, beat up my jeans so they looked used, and stomp on my shirt a few times to get the creases out. I also didn't know how difficult it was to beat up a pair of boots."

They all had a good laugh.

"As you can tell, I'm not from around these parts. I actually spent most of my adult life in Rhode Island and New York. In those areas, they make you press your clothes or they don't let you back in town. I'm not sure, but they may even have a regulation about this."

"For those of you that don't know who I am, my name is Rick Benedict, and my last job was as a professor of history at Brown University. I spent about five years in the Army, but I got out because I wanted to teach."

He left out many things, because he was still under classified status from the government. As he looked out, he counted roughly eighty-five people in the crowd. Some had their kids with them, which he thought was somewhat strange, but maybe they did things differently out here.

"I know that you're probably wondering what I'm doing here as the new owner of the Monarch Ranch. My uncle and I feel that the cattle can support a series of restaurants we're planning to open. They're going to be located from the Midwest to the West Coast. Actual numbers and locations will be decided sometime later.

"We plan on opening one in Fort Collins and in Cheyenne within the next six months. The key is that we want absolutely the best beef to support our new business, and all of you are a big part of this plan."

They all clapped because it was good news to hear finally.

"As we move forward, we may want to have a trout pond on the ranch that will also support the local restaurants. We may also buy some more land and increase the size of our herd as our restaurants grow. And now you know everything I know. I've got a lot of work ahead of me just to understand the cattle business, but with your help, we can make this into a first-class cattle ranch."

He asked if anyone had any questions that he could answer and few did. It appeared everyone was mostly there for the free food and beer.

"Now I want you to enjoy yourselves, and I'm looking forward to getting to know each of you," said Rick.

Rick went over to the area where the steaks and burgers had been cooking. You could smell the barbeque sauce from across the road. He started milling around the various ranch hands and their families. He had a feeling from some of them that they were going to keep him at arm's length until they got to know him better.

But he also recognized that some probably resented that he was here and wished it could go back to the old days. In this part of the country, if you weren't born and raised here, they all just assumed you were a tourist and only here for the food and sightseeing.

The Dusty Pioneers started playing, and everyone was dancing, drinking up a storm, and forgetting that for the moment tomorrow was only about eight hours away.

Meanwhile, Rick kept mixing, introducing himself, and carefully asking what they specifically did at the ranch. When things started to shut down, he had a good idea of who did what, and first thing in the morning, he and Grant were going to sit down and develop some new guidelines.

Rick didn't think anybody noticed that he'd been carrying the same bottle of beer around for the last four hours. By midnight, Rick was almost the last to leave. He said good night to Grant and Dale and walked up to the house, towards the kitchen, and thanked Mildred for making this a success.

She turned around, looking tired, and said, "You're welcome. We haven't had a real good barbeque like this in quite some time. I gotta tell you, though, it was fun." She said goodnight and went to her room.

As he walked upstairs, his thoughts were again on the dead cattle. He reasoned that if it were just cattle rustlers, they wouldn't have killed them. He was sure there must be more to this problem and maybe Grant wasn't telling him everything.

He took a quick shower and went to bed. As he lay there, he was wondering what was really going on at the ranch. He knew that some people were almost afraid to talk to him, but he initially thought he was just overly concerned.

As the lights went out in Rick's room, Grant was about a hundred yards away leaning against one of the big oak trees and smoking a cigarette. He thought, *Well, it's time to get to work.*

CHAPTER
16

The next morning Rick got up around six in the morning so he could get a jump on the ranch hands, or so he thought. What he didn't realize was that the ranch hands actually got up before dawn, and three roosters reminded them of that every morning. Grant made a Jeep Cherokee available to Rick, and he decided to use this time to do some investigating on his own.

Rick still found it hard to believe that Grant either didn't remember or didn't want to admit he'd seen any dead cattle before. He surmised that John might be lying, which meant Grant might also be in on it, but why? The more he thought about it, the more he felt that Walter knew there were some problems on the ranch and that he wanted Rick to find and resolve these problems. He needed to be careful of what he accused anyone of, since he still didn't have any facts and wasn't sure whom he could trust.

Grant watched from a distance as Rick rode off in his Jeep. He was getting concerned, because he could accidentally stumble onto something else that he would have to explain, and at this particular time – he didn't want to.

He made a call on his mobile phone and said, "Watch out for Rick Benedict. He may stumble into your area, and if he does, you know what to do."

The other end of the line went dead. Grant jumped into his truck and headed off to town to talk to the Judge.

Rick drove to the area where he first saw the dead cattle and saw that John had picked them all up. He decided to drive a bit further and off the road to try to find out where they had been. According to John, the dead cattle definitely came from the Monarch Ranch.

He found the small river in the ten-thousand-acre parcel that the previous owner purchased. He walked on foot for a ways along the riverbank. As he was walking, he noticed that the river was running north towards Cheyenne, Wyoming, and in some areas was very fast and wide.

As he looked around, he saw that quite a few trees were cut down, and only stumps remained with some of the branches. And as he looked closer, it looked like it happened just recently. He wasn't aware of any logging rights on his property. He made a mental note to ask Grant when he got back to the ranch.

As he walked through the tall Aspen grove, he eventually came to a large clearing with tall green grass. He guessed it was where the cattle had strayed. But as he started going into the clearing, he suddenly felt himself walking in mud and discovered that the area was more of a swamp than grassland.

Rick wanted to know where the water had come from, so he walked around the swampy area. As he was walking, a rifle shot suddenly rang out. It hit a large rock close by and Rick quickly ducked. He was crouched below the grass line, but was afraid that he was the target, so he crawled toward the grove of trees for better cover.

He was almost there when another shot rang out and this time hit a tree. When he looked where the shot came from, he decided that either the shooter must be a bad shot or he was just trying to warn him. In any event, without a gun he was outclassed, so he slowly crept back through the grove to his Jeep, leaving the way he'd come.

As he drove off, he became more than ever convinced there was something suspicious going on at the ranch, and he was going to find the underlying cause. He called Grant's mobile phone, but it went right to voicemail. He left a message asking to see him back at the ranch in about an hour.

About forty-five minutes later, Rick got back to the ranch and went into the kitchen to talk to Mildred.

"Did Grant call while I was gone?" he asked her.

"No, he didn't," answered Mildred and kept cleaning up the kitchen.

"If he does call," said Rick, "tell him I want to see him," and went into his office.

He sat there for a little while going through all the drawers to see if he'd missed anything earlier. As he did this, he confirmed his earlier conclusion that this office had been really just for show. It didn't have any of the normal office items. He told himself that he'd stop in town and pick up some supplies when he got a chance.

It was now eight o'clock at night and still no word from Grant. This just made him more suspicious. He called John, the veterinarian, and asked, "Have you heard from Grant today?"

"I talked to him early this morning," said John, "but not lately."

"Thanks," said Rick. "I guess it'll have to wait until tomorrow."

Rick made himself a light dinner and sat in the kitchen bewildered by today's events. Finally exhaustion set in and he went upstairs to bed.

CHAPTER
17

The next morning Rick was up even earlier, just had coffee, and headed to the front door. As he stood in the doorway of his house, he stopped again to take in the majestic splendor of the view. Standing there, slightly shivering, it reminded him to get his jacket and take his mobile phone. He checked his mobile phone and still no word from Grant. Grant hadn't shown up or called the previous night, so Rick was worried, but mostly angry.

He jumped into the Jeep and took off again in the same direction he and Grant had gone two days before. About an hour out, he passed the place where they had seen the first dead cow and just kept driving. About thirty minutes later, he was in the forest on a two-lane dirt highway that seemed to be in good condition.

Suddenly he heard a shot in the distance and slowed down. He knew he was still on his property, so why would there be any shooting and especially at him again, unless he was getting too close to something he shouldn't see. He drove on a little further, turned the engine off, and glided to the side of the road.

He heard more gunfire, and now he wished he had a handgun instead of his rifle with him. He started walking into the thick forest, careful not to step on any dry twigs. As he moved further, he heard people talking, but couldn't make out what they were saying. He walked closer and saw in a clearing a cabin with smoke rising from its chimney.

Several people came out from the cabin that he didn't recognize. All were carrying guns and looked as though they had just woken up from a bad hangover. He now more than ever needed to find Grant. He wondered why there was a cabin with people wearing guns on his property. Nobody said anything about a hunting lodge.

He got back in his Jeep, drove a little further up the highway when he saw the *No Trespassing* chain blocking the road. He got out, started walking, and came to another clearing that was just incredibly beautiful.

There were sheer cliffs on one side, with a five-hundred-foot waterfall coming out of a hole on the topmost part of the mountain. The grass must have been three feet high and so green it hurt your eyes. The trees on the outskirts of the area were spectacular.

Now he wasn't sure if he was on his property, and if it wasn't his property, he was going to recommend to Walter they buy it, unless it was part of a National Forest. He thought, *Maybe we can develop this part to be a dude ranch in addition to the cattle ranch.*

As he continued further, he saw a small road that veered off to the right and followed it to see where it would lead him. He came upon rusty railroad tracks, but the tracks were closer together than standard train tracks. They didn't look like they'd been used in a long time. He followed the tracks on foot for about two hundred yards, when suddenly they weren't rusty anymore but instead looked as if they'd been used recently.

He walked further and ran into dense brush, which looked like it was used as camouflage. That's when he discovered a mine opening. As he walked closer and cleared the brush, he was reminded of some of the old cowboy movies he had seen where large beams were used for a mine opening.

It was dark and he was reluctant to go in without a flashlight, but then he noticed a small metal cabinet inside the mine, hidden from view slightly. It was a typical electrical panel used on exterior walls of houses, but looked new. He opened the panel door and, as he did, a small light came on in the cabinet. It had two columns of circuit breaker switches that looked like they were in the *on* position, but the main switch was *off*.

He wondered what would happen if he turned the main switch on. His second thought was that he might be trespassing. Now that his eyes were focusing on the dark tunnel, he saw what looked like ore carts sitting on the rail line and a faint light in the distance.

Rick decided it would be best to check with the City Clerk's office for a copy of the property registration. He closed the electrical panel, turned around, and carefully left the tunnel. He put all the shrubs back as he had found them and walked back to his Jeep. As he was walking back, he noticed another rail line veering off to the right side and started following it.

After about a hundred yards, it stopped at a newly created gravel road that emptied into a much larger parking lot area. This area can't be seen from the highway because it winds downhill and is hidden by trees. He saw two trucks that were hauling large rocks or gravel and a skip loader.

These skip loaders were noisy, but he figured the dense forest and being downhill from the road helped muffle the sound they made. *This is interesting,* he thought. But again, maybe this wasn't his property, so he left.

CHAPTER

18

Rick drove back towards the ranch and decided to call Walter before he went into Fort Collins to check with the City Clerk's office about the exact boundaries of his property. As he drove along the highway, he saw a pickup truck in his rearview mirror. At first he wasn't concerned, and it seemed to stay at a safe distance so he couldn't read the license plate number, but he could make out that it had Wyoming plates. He rounded a corner, stopped and got out, but the other driver kept going straight. Rick waved to him.

He drove into town, went to the City Clerk's office, and said, "Hi, I'm Rick Benedict. I would like a copy of the Monarch Ranch site map. It was missing from the title search escrow papers."

Judd Stewart, the Clerk, stared for a few seconds and, with an arrogant grin, and sarcastically asked, "What do you need this information for?"

Rick answered back sharply, "Because I want to check the boundaries of my property since it's over twenty thousand acres and has no fencing to speak of. I'm thinking of increasing my herd size and don't want my cattle to graze on someone else's land."

"You'll have to fill out this form," Judd said. "We'll verify you own the property, and you can come back in three weeks for the copies."

"Why does it take three weeks?" Rick demanded. "Why can't you just get the document and make a simple copy? As far as proof of ownership is concerned, anybody can get a copy of this information. It's available to the general public!"

Seeing that he was caught, Judd quickly said, "Yeah, that's true." His brow glistened in the noonday sun. "But these things take time because all the information is not archived at this building."

With that, Rick filled out the form, paid the fee, said, "I'll be back in three weeks," and stormed out of the place.

As soon as Rick left, Judd made a call and said, "Hey, it's me. Rick Benedict was just in here asking for a copy of his property's site map so he could determine the boundaries. He said something about expanding his herd size."

"Thanks," Grant said and hung up.

Grant now had a new concern and needed to plan another diversion. He called the Judge and let him know about Rick's request.

"We have to be careful about this and not let him get suspicious," the Judge said. "Have Judd pull the original survey maps right away and make him a copy. Then have Judd give Rick a call within the next two to three days and tell him they're ready to pick up anytime. Is Judd aware of what we're doing?"

"No," Grant said. "I just told him that if anybody came asking for information on the Monarch Ranch, to call me."

As Rick sat in the Jeep, he thought it somewhat odd that the Clerk was so flippant about his request and wondered why it should take three weeks. Then he remembered that he should have a copy of the ranch property map with boundaries attached to the title company's deed to the ranch. It should also give him a complete description of the property, including the house size, and might even show the cabin he saw in the woods.

He took off back to the ranch in time for a dinner. He decided to mingle with the ranch hands, have dinner with them, hear and see how they thought and operated. Maybe if he ate with them, it might ease a little of the tension. He knew they had a tough job, which sometimes required you to work all day and half the night.

As he walked in, the room got deathly quiet. When he walked over to get a plate, they stopped eating and reduced talking to a low murmur.

"Listen, guys," he finally said, "if it makes you feel uncomfortable for me being here, I'll be happy to leave. After all, I know you guys work hard all day and you need to blow off some steam, but I just want to experience what you're all doing at the ranch. I'm not looking to be an accomplished wrangler I just want to understand."

Billy Haddock stood up, slightly drunk, and said, "We don't have any problem you being here for dinner with us. We're still wondering what you're actually doing here at the ranch."

With that, he walked over behind Rick and pushed him down by his shoulders. Rick fell backwards, and they all had a huge laugh.

Rick got up, dusted himself off, walked right up to Billy only inches from his nose, and said, "You're fired."

As he walked away, Billy roared out and said, "You can't fire me. Grant hired me and only he can fire me!"

With that, Rick turned around, walked back to him, and said, "As long as I own this ranch, I'll fire anyone I want ...... You've got two hours to get out."

Billy was a big man, with fists the size of baseball gloves, and he stood almost a head taller than Rick. He took a swing at Rick, who heard the swooshing sound and ducked. Rick took two steps back, then quickly stepped into Billy and hit him hard just below the rib cage, right in the stomach. As Billy doubled up, you could see he was in pain. All the air exhaled from of his mouth, and he fell to the floor. Billy rolled over several times to try to catch his breath. Part of Billy's problem was pure shock that anybody would dare to hit him. The other was – Rick did it with one punch.

The room suddenly went quiet, but clearly they were impressed. Nobody ever took on Billy, because he was always picking on the other guys, especially the new guys. Some even smiled and figured he had it coming. The only problem was that he was a workhorse and could do the job of two men.

"Just so you all understand," Rick said. "I don't take any crap from anybody, and while all of you obviously know more about the cattle business than I ever will, my job is not to be an expert at your jobs; it's to manage this ranch, and I aim to make sure it successfully grows to what my plans are, and you already know what that is.

"Just so we're all clear, I typically categorize people into two buckets: Either you're part of the problem or you're part of the solution. You each decide which bucket you want to fit in. But I can tell you this: You can make a lot more money being in the solution bucket."

He walked out of the bunkhouse and toward the main house. As Rick left, some of the men's mouths hung open, and it didn't take anybody long to figure there was a new marshal in town.

Grant looked on from a distance and wasn't happy, but figured he would have a talk with Rick when he cooled down. He scratched his weathered chin and thought that maybe he'd underestimated him. Now he was going to have to tell Billy's mother, Mildred, that Rick just fired her son Billy.

Grant was standing in the shadows of the trees but finally emerged and went into the bunkhouse.

"Get Billy cleaned up," said Grant. "Put him to bed, and I'll go talk to Rick."

With that, he turned around and walked towards the main house. He called out to Rick that he wanted to talk with him.

Rick was heading to the main house and was already on the first step of the porch when he stopped, turned around, and said, "Yeah, Grant," in a brusque voice, "what can I do for you?"

"That was quite a display you put on back there," Grant said. "Billy didn't really mean it. He gets a little drunk and carried away and sometimes forgets whom he's talking to. I think you need to give him another chance."

Rick walked closer to face Grant and said, "I don't think so ......
All I've heard from some of the other men is that he bullies them when nobody is looking, and as far as I'm concerned, that reduces the efficiency of this ranch. I've only been here a short time, but I get the feeling that a lot more work could be done if people weren't afraid of their co-workers. Frankly, I'm surprised that you didn't see it or maybe you tolerate it – I don't. That means that Billy stays fired and should be out of here in less than two hours.

"By the way, why is your mobile phone turned off? I want to be able to talk to you anytime. The next time you're going to be gone for any length of time, give me the courtesy to tell me. I wanted to talk to you about a cabin in the forest and some timber cutting I discovered. Also, where have you been? I've been trying to call you."

Grant was flustered with all the questions and said, "I was playing cards with a friend of mine and my mobile phone battery died. I don't know about any cabin in the woods or any timber cutting.

"Also, Billy is Mildred's son," Grant said. "Do you want me to tell her he was fired or do you want to let her know?"

"I'll tell her in the morning," Rick said, and turned around and headed back to the house.

Rick hadn't known Billy and Mildred were related, but that shouldn't make a difference. He knew that Grant was also unhappy about what he'd just seen and heard, but Grant merely shrugged his shoulders and said, "Okay," and casually turned around and sauntered back towards the bunkhouse.

Rick knew there was more to this than Grant was willing to discuss, so he let it ride for the moment. Rick went to his office, still pumped up about firing Billy.

He found a note on his desk that Fred Tremane called saying he would be flying in on Colorado Pacific, the 11:30 a.m. flight, and could he meet him at the airport. He left his mobile phone number. Rick wondered if anyone else had seen this note and went to see Mildred, but it was late and she was probably already asleep. He wondered if he should wake her up, but decided to wait until the following morning.

CHAPTER
19

As he sat in his office, he thought some more about Grant's attitude and what he tolerated from his men. He finally found the deed for the ranch and started looking for a document that showed the complete property boundaries. As he went through the mountains of paperwork produced by the Fort Collins Title Company, he found a picture of the house, but nothing about the property boundaries.

He found that odd, since he knew Walter would never have bought this place without having all the proper paperwork. He would call him in the morning and find out if he had a copy, or possibly the title company would have a copy. In any event, he was exhausted and needed some rest.

He went into the kitchen and peeked in the refrigerator to see if anything was left to eat. He found some cold chicken and potato salad and then had a few beers to wash it all down.

As he sat in the kitchen staring out the window, he suddenly felt alone. When he was teaching, he never had that feeling, even when he was just sitting in the quad and watching people walking by. It was so quiet he could hear a pin drop. Finally he got up, put the dishes in the sink, and walked back to his office. He pulled the note that Fred had called and tried calling him on his mobile phone, but it went directly to voicemail. He surmised Fred was already on a plane to see him.

He planned to call Judd, the City Clerk, in the morning and find out if he made the copy for him yet. He was tired of having to wait to get answers to simple questions. He knew there was definitely something wrong at the ranch. He went upstairs to his bedroom, and to be extra cautious, he slid a chair under the door handle just in case he had unwanted visitors. He lay down and, within minutes, was sound asleep.

CHAPTER

20

Rick had a restless night wondering what was actually going on at his ranch. First, they find some dead cattle that appeared to be poisoned, and then he finds a cabin hidden in the middle of the woods that looked like it was being used. Then he is shot at, accidentally runs across an old mine, and now he has a run-in with a bully while Grant appears to want to look the other way.

He finally got up, showered quickly, and went downstairs to have breakfast and talk to Mildred.

He saw a note taped to the door going into his office.

Dear Mr. Benedict,

I'm sorry to give you such short notice instead of the normal two-week's notice, but I cannot work at the ranch anymore. I took all my personal belongings with me. Thank you for the opportunity to work here.

Mildred.

Rick didn't know what to say and gave Grant a call to find out if he knew anything about this.

"Billy called her last night," said Grant, "and told her he got fired, by you. She called me last night and told me that she was going to be leaving," he said.

"Why didn't you say anything last night?" Rick asked.

"She wasn't going to stay, no matter what you would have said to her," said Grant.

Rick hung up and went out to his truck. As he drove off the ranch, he noticed there was no movement in the cattle pen where normally all the crew would be. He turned around and drove back up to the bunkhouse. He opened the door to the bunkhouse and saw there were six people still eating breakfast, plus Grant.

"Where is everybody?" asked Rick.

Grant spoke up and said, "I sent some of the boys to the northeast corner of the property to look for strays and to see if there are any other dead cattle that may have wandered off last night. I sent the other group over to the southwest corner to look for strays."

"I thought that the cattle in the fenced in area," Rick said, "are only let out for grazing?"

Grant laughed a little and said, "You don't know much about the cattle business. We can't be bringing in all the cattle every night and let them out in the morning. That's a mountain of work and unnecessary. That's one of the reasons we went to the expense of planting chips in their shoulders."

"So that must mean that you or John," Rick said, "performed the electronic headcount and found they were in those areas?"

"Yep, that's right," said Grant.

"When am I going to see this list?" Rick demanded. "I told John that when it was generated, I wanted to see it!"

"Yeah, he mentioned that to me," said Grant. "Right now we're missing about a hundred head of cattle."

"When were you going to let me know?" asked Rick. "How long has this been going on? It would appear that this isn't a good way to utilize our wranglers. If we once and for all find out where the holes are in the fence and fix them, just possibly we'll learn that we have too many ranch hands and maybe we should be cutting back!"

Grant was now getting red in the face. He stood up, walked over to Rick, and said calmly, "You're right. We should find out where the holes in the fences are and fix them .... I'll get on it today."

Rick also controlled himself and just quietly left. He went to look for John Hammond.

He opened the door to John's office. "Hello, Rick," John said. "What can I do for you?"

"Have you found out anything else about the dead cattle?" Rick asked. "Have you conducted that electronic headcount of all the cattle you told me about?"

"Yeah, I did," John said, "and gave it to Grant. I assumed he'd get together with you."

"The next time," said Rick, still angry, "that I ask you for information, give it to me personally and don't worry about Grant."

John, looking a little nervous, said, "Nothing more on the dead cattle, except that it was a commercial grade of cyanide. The reason I say it was commercial grade is because there was so much of it."

"Cyanide!" Rick exclaimed. "Where could that have come from?"

Rick wondered how a commercial grade of cyanide could get into the water system and only at the northern edge, which is downhill from the major portion of the ranch.

"What do they typically use commercial grade cyanide for?" Rick asked.

"Primarily, the larger mining companies used it years ago to separate the gold ore from the granite," John said. "Plus there may be some military uses. But other than that, I don't know. I don't think that we've seen any major mining done in these parts for quite a few years.

"I ran an electronic headcount of the cattle and found there were one hundred and two roaming around in two places on the ranch. I gave the information to Grant this morning, and he said he would send some of the boys to bring them back."

"When they get back, run me another report and send only me a copy," Rick said.

"Okay," said John, with a concerned look on his face as if he had done something wrong, because for most ranches, these are everyday occurrences.

Rick looked at his watch and said, "I've got to go. Thanks for the info.

"By the way, are you aware that Mildred left last night without saying good-bye? Is there something I should know?"

John smiled slightly and said, "I guess you're not aware that Billy Haddock was her son from her first marriage. When you fired him, she got angry."

"But all I hear is that Billy bullies some of the crew around," Rick said, "and has total lack of respect for probably most of the men, me probably, and anyone in authority."

John said with a smirk, "Somebody should have told you that they were a package deal. You need to watch yourself with Billy; he's a mean guy."

Rick, now more infuriated, said, "Thanks," and walked out.

CHAPTER

21

Rick headed to the airport to pick up Fred Tremane. As he drove, he thought some more about the *package deal* and convinced himself he could do without it. He pulled up to the curb and was early, but he waited by the Jeep at the curb.

While he was waiting, he gave Walter a call from his mobile phone.

Walter picked up after the first ring and said, "Hello, Rick. How do you like the Wild West?"

"I sure do miss teaching," Rick answered, laughing, "but other than that, it's fine."

Then Rick got more serious and said, "I discovered some strange things going on out here. After the second day, I had Grant give me a helicopter tour of the property and ran across at least half a dozen dead cattle that appear to have ingested cyanide. What's interesting is our ranch veterinarian said he thought it was a commercial grade."

"That's very interesting," said Walter.

"Tell me a little more about this ranch you gave to me," said Rick. "Were you aware there are some problems out here? I don't think I'm being paranoid when I say that there's something going on that they seemed to be hiding from me."

"It was just one of the assets," Walter said, "of a business I bought several years ago. The company was almost bankrupt before I bought it and liquidated most of the assets. The ranch was one of the items I decided to keep. I hadn't had an opportunity to assess the ranch, because the business didn't cost me much. But as I told you before you left, I'm very serious about opening additional steakhouses in the U.S. and serve only the finest beef, pork, and fish. I'm in the process of looking at an existing chain of restaurants that may also fit into our business plan."

"Well, that sounds great," Rick said, "but there are some additional things that I don't understand. For example, I looked at all the paperwork associated with the deed you gave me, and I can't find a survey map to show where the property starts and stops. Those pages are missing in my copy. The City Clerk's office gave me the run-around, and the local title company has theirs in off-site storage. I get the impression they, whoever *they* are, want me to stumble around till I get tired and leave."

"That's very interesting," replied Walter, "and sounds somewhat frustrating."

"Yesterday I fired a guy named Billy," Rick said. "Billy was a problem because I feel it affected the performance of the entire ranch. Tonight I'm going to sit down with the ranch hands and see if they have any problems with me."

"By the way, I can't remember when I had so much fun, unless you count the time Liz and I were in Prague. I also invited Fred Tremane to come out and go over the books to see if he can find anything out of sorts. I know you and Leonard Schultz went over the books, but I wanted to perform a forensic analysis on what has happened for just the last two years. Hope you don't mind?"

"No, I don't mind at all," Walter said and hung up the phone.

Walter was troubled at what had been happening at the ranch in the last two years. Leonard assured him that all the employees were on board when he took over the ranch. He knew that the cyanide was a commercial grade and that this confirmed what he already knew when he received a copy of the original water sample two years ago.

He made a few calls. One was to Jeffery Knowland, the president of the Superior Mining Company in Georgia. The other was to Leonard, bringing him up-to-date about the activities at the ranch. He had Leonard call the City Clerk's office in Fort Collins.

CHAPTER

22

As Rick was talking on the phone, Fred Tremane walked out of the terminal and waved to him.

Rick gave Fred a big bear hug and asked, "Where are your bags?"

"I figure this is the West," Fred said, "and since I don't have any western clothes, I thought we could stop somewhere and pick me up a few things."

"I know just the place," Rick said.

As they were driving over to the Peabody Mercantile, he brought Fred up-to-date about what had been going on at the ranch.

"I thought you said this would be a vacation," said Fred. "I gave up Hawaii to catch bad guys?"

They both had a good laugh, but Rick knew Fred would come help him whenever he needed it.

Rick had also called his friend Esther Parsons, a recruiter that he knew in Rhode Island, and asked if she knew of a reliable company in Northern Colorado where he could hire a head of household and cook for his ranch house. He'd helped her on many occasions with her son's schoolwork while he was at Brown University, so she was glad to return the favor.

Rick felt removed from city life and wondered if he could ever go back to the previous way of living he'd come to enjoy. That reminded him to call Liz later in the day and see how she was enjoying herself in the Mediterranean.

"I just talked to Walter," Rick said to Fred, "and told him some of what's been going on here. I'm not saying the books are not right, but I want someone of your caliber to sift through them with a very fine-tooth comb. We only need to go back two years, because everything should be in sync before that."

"It sounds as though there may be a problem," said Fred, "if you're discovering other things. Generally if you find visible problems, then there are other issues brewing under the surface."

"Walter got this place as part of an acquisition of a company he bought," Rick said. "This was one of the assets in the company's inventory. Everything may be all right, but look anyway. I'd prefer you to only talk to me about any findings, since I'm not quite sure who I can trust yet."

"Okay," Fred said. "I also brought my computer with me. It's not very pretty, but it is very functional. It was originally developed by the U.S. Government to house all the maintenance records to support their equipment. I was lucky that they let me have one."

Rick looked over at how Fred was dressed and said, "Blue seersucker suits are not the rage in Colorado, but we can fix that."

They stopped at the Peabody Mercantile, and as they walked in, Fred saw Dale Honeycutt and said, "They sure do grow them well out here."

Rick had to agree, and today she looked even better. They finally purchased some clothes, using similar criteria that Grant used with him when he arrived.

"If this is how the country people look," Fred said, "I may have to stick around a little longer, because I think I'm in love."

Rick just smiled and would probably let him know tomorrow that Dale was Grant Williams' girlfriend. Fred had a tough time with the boots, but finally managed to get them on.

"I'll introduce you as an old college friend who wants to get in the restaurant business and is here for some R&R, fishing, hiking, and so on. You do know how to fish, don't you?" Rick asked.

"Oh, yes. I'm an experienced fisherman," Fred said. "It's just that I happen to like deep-sea fishing. I suppose it can't be that much different in a lake or stream, is it?

Rick rolled his eyes, smiled and said, "Just a little bit."

They drove for a while and it seemed that Fred was too quiet.

"How come you're so quiet?" asked Rick.

"Every once in a while I reminisce about our Army days," said Fred, "and how simple life was then. It also led me into a completely new world of forensic accounting. Nowadays, it's much more difficult to try to hide things, because we have computers available to us. But that just means that it's now a lot more sophisticated and the *average country bear* will never find the problems."

They finally turned off the main road onto the ranch road and within ten minutes were parking in the front of the ranch.

"Wow," exclaimed Fred, "this place looks great!"

They walked up the front steps and into the front foyer.

"This is a great room," Fred said.

Rick smiled, walked Fred upstairs into the Redwood room, and said, "Why don't you go ahead, get unpacked, and come on downstairs into my office when you're ready."

"Okay, see you in a bit," Fred said.

As Rick sat in his office, he wondered if he should really call Liz. After all, he was sure she was happy with Steve, and he didn't want to create any problems for her or him. But they were friends and brought up by Walter, so he felt it should be okay.

He called her and surprisingly she answered.

"Hi, Liz. This is Rick. How is life on the Mediterranean?"

"Well, hi there," Liz exclaimed. "I had it in mind to also call you and see how you're doing on your new ranch."

Rick tried to control his enthusiasm and said, "I've been busy trying to figure out cattle and ranch life, with limited success. I've wanted to call and see how the lecture circuit's treating you."

"The work is just fine," Liz said, "but I must admit that the last time we were together trying to save the world was much more exciting, but exhausting."

With that, Rick had to ask, "How are you and Steve getting along? I don't mean to pry, and I really wish you both all the best in the world."

She finally said, "Well, Steve is still the captain of the boat," and let it hang in midair like an icicle waving in the wind.

Rick thought he understood what she meant and let it alone. They talked for over half an hour, just bringing each other up-to-date on what they're doing.

Feeling bold, he finally said, "If you have some time between lectures, maybe you and Steve would like to take a break and come and visit me at the ranch. It's just beautiful up here."

"Let me check my schedule," she cheerfully said, "and I'll call you back in a few days."

They each said good-bye and hung up.

As Rick hung up the phone, he was both happy and sad at the same time. He knew that Steve was a great guy, and if things didn't work out, it must be only because of his job as her bodyguard. Now he didn't know how he should act if she did come to the ranch with him. Maybe it was a mistake calling her. It might open up some old feelings, and both might be worse off, but he still wanted to take that risk.

Fred finally came downstairs, and at that same moment, the phone rang.

Esther Parsons was calling. "Rick, I made contact with an old schoolmate from Radcliff who said she would be happy to recommend a new live-in chef and housekeeper. Her name is Sandy McNamara, has excellent credentials, and generally only deals with high-end clients."

They talked some more, and Rick found out her son was now going to medical school, and thanks to the talk Rick gave him four years ago, he had turned his whole life around. She thanked him and said good-bye.

"Let's take a walk around the property," Fred finally said, "so people will see me as the new beef buyer."

They walked through the front door and stood on the porch so Fred could take in the panoramic view.

"Later I'll take you into town," Rick said, "and we'll visit the City Clerk's office to see if the information I asked for is available yet."

"Okay," Fred said, and they drove over to visit John, the ranch veterinarian.

"I think there are people watching us," Fred said. "Is there any special reason for that?"

Rick didn't answer but gave Fred a look that meant *yes*.

Rick told him about the general layout of the main house, the various cattle pens and what they are used for, where the ranch hands lived when they are on the ranch, and the fifty-thousand-square-foot barn that housed all the farm equipment.

They walked into John's office, but he wasn't in. They went back outside, drove back towards the house, and then headed towards town. Since he currently had no cook, Rick decided to go to town to eat. After all, this was one way to check out the competition.

CHAPTER

23

As they drove into town, they spotted Grant coming out of the City Planning building with rolled-up drawings under his arm. Rick wanted to confront him and his excuse would be to introduce him to Fred Tremane, the potential beef buyer.

"Hey, Grant," he called out to him.

Grant spun around, looking startled.

"Hi, Rick," Grant quickly replied. "Just doing some work for my mother. She wants to move closer to town and asked me to see if there was any land for sale in the area."

Rick knew he caught him off guard, but let it go for the time being.

"This is Fred Tremane, an old friend of mine," said Rick, "who turned to managing restaurants in Texas and may be interested in buying some beef from us. I'd like you to join us for lunch."

Grant hesitated but said, "Yeah, that would be great. Nice to meet you, Fred."

"Since I'm new here," said Rick, "can you recommend the best steakhouse in Fort Collins?"

"How about we meet up in an hour at the Chuck Wagon Grill," Grant said. "It's just up the street. Turn left on Third Street. You can't miss the wagon wheel sign over the doorway."

"Sounds good," said Rick. "We'll talk some more about our plans as well. See you at twelve-thirty."

"See you then," Grant said and rushed off to his truck.

Smiling, Fred said, "He sounds like a man who has a secret and isn't going to share it with anyone."

Rick nodded his head in agreement.

They walked into the Peabody Mercantile and were greeted by Dale Honeycutt.

"Well, hello, Rick," Dale said, "It's good to see you again. What can I do for you this time?"

"Not for me but for my friend Fred Tremane, who you met earlier," Rick said. "He's a beef buyer from Texas. Can we get him fixed up with some more working clothes and then something fancier in a western suit, shirts, and, of course, some really snazzy boots?"

"Sure can," said Dale. "Just follow me, Fred, and I'll personally get you squared away."

As they both left, Rick wandered over to the bulletin board and started reading some of the old newspaper clippings of old time cowboy stories. That's when he found out that her great-grandfather was Harry "Billy" Jackson. He read that he never made out a claim, that no one ever found the mine, and he abruptly had a heart attack right in the middle of the very store he founded over seventy years ago.

Rick thought that it was too much of a coincidence that he happened to find some type of mine on his property and then this article. Other newspaper clippings said there was a massive gold rush because of the gold that William Jackson brought into town. People in those times made big assumptions, and for a while, they all had *gold fever* and dreamed of striking it rich, but nobody ever found any gold or even the mine. Rick now wondered who actually owned the Peabody Mercantile today.

As Fred and Dale were walking back to the checkout counter, she noticed Rick reading the old newspaper clippings and said, "In 1905, my great-grandfather Colonel Harry "Billy" Jackson came into town and brought with him a lot of gold dust and some gold nuggets. At the time, folks around here thought that this was going to lead to another mother lode, but, of course, it never happened."

"I don't recall ever hearing about this," Rick said. "In all that time, this was the only gold found and no other since then?"

"None that we're aware of," said Dale.

"You know," said Fred, "today gold and diamonds are very carefully monitored by the government and any huge finds would be reported."

"My great-grandfather," Dale continued, "was very crafty and a shrewd businessman. I figured he found just enough gold and brought it with him to show he got his share. That was when he opened up the Peabody Mercantile store. Six months later, he started selling food that miners could eat out on the range, like flour, bacon, and beef jerky. Later on, he started selling whiskey, because he knew they'd get depressed if they didn't find much gold or any at all. He was selling at top dollar and made a fortune."

"That's what's called an opportunity," said Rick, "and sounds like he was smart enough to realize that. I also happen to know someone else like that."

"The only trouble was," Dale said, "since the miners never found any gold to speak of, they got very angry. They thought he lied about what part of Colorado he found his gold and he wanted to keep it all to himself. Since he never registered a claim, nobody ever found it. At the same time, the Peabody Mercantile grew from one room to a block-long structure, because by then he was selling everything, except mining equipment."

"How did you decide to expand," asked Rick, "and sell general western clothes and souvenirs?"

"About forty years ago," Dale said, "we started selling western clothes, and as Fort Collins grew, we also started selling more expensive clothing, with all the trimmings."

"It's impressive," said Fred, "that this person who started a trading post store in the middle of nowhere grew his business primarily from the local Pawnee Indians and ended up a very wealthy man.

"Are you the sole owner of the store?" Rick asked.

Dale blushed and said, "No. It was actually bought about ten years ago by Grant Williams, your ranch foreman. I've wanted to buy it back, but he won't sell it. The store is now very profitable, and he plans to retire in about another ten years and use this as his retirement nest egg. Since it originally belonged to my great-grandfather, he lets me manage it, and I rather think it's mine. He lets me do pretty much what I want with little or no interference."

"When you were at the barbeque last week at my ranch, he said that you're his girlfriend. Is that true?" Rick asked. "And if you tell me it's none of my business, I'll understand."

"Yes, I guess you could say that. We've been going out off and on for quite a while," said Dale, "but nothing really serious. He takes me out when he meets some friends. Other than that, I don't spend a lot of time alone with him."

"Thanks for the history lesson," said Rick.

Fred went to the counter to pay for his clothes.

"Do you think that maybe we could have dinner," Fred asked coyly, "a little later after I rest up from my plane ride and trying on my new clothes?"

Dale walked up closer to Fred and said with a mischievous grin, "I don't see why not. Here's my card. Give me a call whenever you're ready for a second fitting."

Rick had never seen Fred blush; but then again, Fred hadn't had many girlfriends either.

Grant was watching from across the street and was curious what they said. As soon as Rick and Fred left, he slowly came out of the shadows and walked across the street to the Peabody Mercantile to see Dale.

"Dale," Grant called out, "what did they want?"

"Nothing," said Dale, frowning. "They just bought some more clothes."

"I saw Rick reading the news clippings on your bulletin board," said Grant. "I told you a long time ago to get rid of those clippings. I don't want anybody snooping around."

Grant got closer to Dale, grabbed her arm, and squeezed it.

"Hey!" Dale winced. "You're hurting me."

"I know it," said Grant. "Just don't forget who owns this place. I can take it away as quickly as I let you run it."

"Okay, I get the point," said Dale.

"Good," said Grant and walked out the front door.

CHAPTER

24

"It's about that time," Rick said to Fred. "Let's stroll over to the Chuck Wagon Grill and see if their steaks are as good as Grant thinks they are."

"Yeah," said Fred, "I'm starved. You make me fly all the way out here and don't feed me."

They drove over, found the place, walked in, and asked if Grant Williams had arrived.

"I'm sorry, he hasn't come in yet," said the hostess.

"There will be three of us for lunch," Rick said. "I've heard a lot of great things about your steaks and just thought I'd see for myself just how good they actually are."

The hostess smiled and said, "Why thank you. This way, please."

Fred walked behind Rick and said, "There's another one I could fall in love with. Boy, I just don't see me leaving here anytime soon."

Rick turned slightly and hadn't noticed until now that Fred had become a ladies' man. They sat down, ordered a beer, and waited for Grant.

"You know," said Fred, "I like it here. This is beautiful country and probably still affordable. My business takes me all over the country and sometimes out of the country, so I could live just about anywhere."

"That's true," said Rick, "since you're seldom working in the same area you live in."

Grant finally arrived, and the hostess showed him to where Rick and Fred were sitting, right in front of the big picture window looking out at the main street.

"Hi, Rick …. Fred," said Grant. "Did you get done what you needed to get done?"

"Peggy," Grant said, "tell Nansie I'll have a cold beer.

"By the way, Fred, what's the name of your restaurant chain and where are they located, in case I've got to use a refrigerated truck?"

This caught Fred off guard and he stammered around. He finally excused himself and went to the bathroom.

Rick could see that Grant knew what they were doing. If Fred were truly going to buy beef for his restaurants, he would have given him a business card and started talking about the beef business in general.

Grant then turned to Rick and asked, "Who is this guy, because it sure doesn't sound like he understands which end of a steer is up?"

"The truth is," Rick said smiling, "he just inherited a lot of money from his parents, and he's trying to sound like he knows what he's doing. I went to school with him Back East, and he did well, but he didn't have to work for a living, and so he just lived like the rich and famous, without a care in the world. I was the person that talked him into getting into the restaurant business. He needs a lot of help in managing it. You're right. He doesn't know which end is up. But he does have money, and his business may help turn this ranch into a real cattle ranch."

That seemed to satisfy Grant, and just then Fred came back to the table, less flushed.

"Let's order," Rick said. "I'm starved."

"Sorry if I caught you off guard," said Grant. "Rick filled me in, and if you're truly interested, I'd be happy to have one of the boys give you all the information you need."

"Thanks, Grant," said Fred. "I think I'll take you up on that, since Rick talked me into the restaurant business."

That seemed to settle everyone down.

"I was recently at a restaurant in Rhode Island," said Fred, "and ordered a bone-in rib-eye steak that was so delicious and tender that it just melted in my mouth. Later I found out it was actually Kobe beef from Japan. The owner had it delivered to the restaurant daily, and they ran out every day, I was told."

They all ordered, but Fred ordered first.

"I think I'll have the twenty-four ounce Porterhouse, with one of those giant baked potatoes with lots of butter and chives, and throw in a small bowl of chili. Don't forget the chopped onions and cheese."

Grant looked at Fred, with eyebrows turned up, smiled and said, "You're gonna eat that whole steak, a little guy like you? You better ask them to bring you a big doggy bag at the same time."

Rick looked over at Grant and said, "He is going to eat the whole thing, I promise you that. In college, he was the guy that always entered the pie-eating contests and the all-you-can-eat hardboiled egg contest, and, by golly, he would always eat the most of anybody. He almost never had to pay for dinner because back then he was famous."

"Fred," asked Rick, "do you still eat as much as you used to?"

"No," Fred retorted. "I've cut back a little, because it was affecting my drinking time."

They all had a good laugh about it.

"By the way," Rick finally asked Grant, "are you aware of any logging going on close to where we found those dead cattle the other day?"

"Why, no," said Grant, with a surprised look on his face, "I didn't authorize anything like that. I'll check into that when I get back to the ranch."

After several more beers, lunch arrived. Fred's steak was definitely big, and the baked potato was nearly as big as a loaf of bread. Fred's eyes got as big as silver dollars and without waiting for anybody else, started right in.

True to form, Fred ate the whole steak and almost all the giant baked potato, put down about four mugs of beer, and finally admitted he had to stop.

Fred sat back and said, "I don't think I'll need a doggy bag for only a small baked potato," and laughed.

"Where did you go to school?" Rick asked Grant. "Is there a school that actually teaches you how to become a wrangler or ranch foreman?"

Grant had to dance around that one, because they didn't teach ranching at Oxford.

"In order to be a good ranch foreman," said Grant, "you have to be raised on a ranch and almost live on a horse. I spent my summer months on cattle drives going up and down the state. There are harsh winters where you might lose a toe or two because you didn't take care of yourself properly. In addition, you have to learn all you can from the best in the business. I've been in this business for over twenty years, and I've seen lots of guys come and go. It's definitely not for everyone."

"That's interesting, and I'm sure very true," said Rick.

"Come on, Fred," said Rick. "You look tired from your long flight. I need to get you back to the ranch."

Rick paid the check, and they all got up to leave.

"It was nice meeting with you, Fred," Grant said. "We'll probably see each other around the ranch."

"Thanks for lunch. I'll see you back at the ranch, Rick." Grant said. "I'll check on that timber cutting you mentioned tomorrow."

"Okay, that sounds good," said Rick and watched Grant leave.

"Except we're not going back to ranch – not just yet," said Rick.

Rick didn't bring up that he'd found the opening of a mine, just in case Grant was involved. He looked at Fred and said, "I bet if we try to find out about Grant Williams' past, we won't find he existed more than maybe ten years ago."

Fred looked at Rick, nodded and said, "I'll do a little searching."

CHAPTER

25

Fred and Rick rode around town a little and didn't say much. Finally Fred asked, "What's really bothering you, Rick?"

"It's Grant," said Rick. "There's just something off about him that doesn't ring true."

"Like I said earlier, let me do a little research on Grant," said Fred, "and see what I can find out about him before you get yourself all worked up."

Trying to change the subject, Fred said, "I sure do like these new clothes. Can you see me in my new western suit? I'll be the envy of everybody in Florida. Wait till I get back home and parade around in this for all my old girlfriends."

"But I thought you said," Rick said smiling ear to ear, "that you wanted to stay here?"

"Yeah, I know," said Fred, "but I'd go back to Florida and tease them just a little bit first."

Rick laughed aloud but didn't have the heart to tell him that when they got back to the ranch, he'd have to take off his clothes, tear all the labels off, beat' em up, and wash all the clothes except the suit.

They rounded the corner off the main street when Rick spotted a car he thought had been following them from the time they left the ranch that morning.

"Did you happen to bring a gun with you?" asked Rick.

Fred looked startled and said, "No. My gun is my computer and calculator."

Rick needed to find a couple of handguns and some ammunition. He had rifles back in his office, but they were too cumbersome in close quarters. He'd get them later.

They drove up and walked into the City Clerk's office. Judd was filing some papers. When he saw Rick, he looked flushed as if he'd just swallowed something he shouldn't have.

"Do you have the copy of my property records yet?" Rick asked casually.

"Why, yes, I have them right here," Judd answered. "But this must be a coincidence, because you're the second person today to ask for a copy."

Rick shot back a cold look and said, "Who else has been asking and why did you give them a copy without first asking me?"

"As you yourself said yesterday," Judd nervously answered, "they're a matter of public record and anybody can get a copy."

"Give me the name of the other person," Rick asked.

"His name is Howard Fraser, a real estate developer from Boulder, Colorado," Judd quickly responded. "I just shipped his copy this morning."

Rick was curious why Howard Fraser wanted a copy, but he was going to find out.

Rick said, "Thanks," and left. They drove back to the ranch in silence.

As they drove up the road to the main house, the car that Rick thought had been following him drove past. He couldn't get the license plate number, but made a mental note of the type of car and the color.

When they walked into Rick's office, he showed Fred the accounting ledgers.

CHAPTER

26

When Rick had met with Walter at his home several months earlier, Walter told him, "The previous owner of the ranch established it as a write-off business expense, because he wanted a place to take his clients."

"That sounds normal," Rick said.

"Yes," said Walter. "Quite a few companies have similar types of deductions, and as long as it's within reason, the IRS is okay with it."

"But the question that I had," said Rick, "was if that was the case, why would you need twenty-five thousand head of cattle, and why just before they sold the company did they purchase an additional ten thousand acres of land?"

"What's even more interesting," Walter said, "is the land at the northern part of the property has much better soil and grass. The added feature is that it has the Platte River running through that part of the property. Something doesn't make sense."

"It appears that the original plans for the ranch may have changed," continued Walter, "and after about a year, the owner didn't frequent the place much."

"I'm actually more interested in the cattle than the ranch. I think that the cattle can be bred to produce high quality meat," said Walter, "to be sold to restaurants like the ones we're going to either buy and convert or build. We do have some things in our favor, and one is that we don't need any financing to do this."

"This is all well and good," Rick finally said, "but I don't know anything about ranch life, let alone what makes up good beef versus just okay beef."

"I am aware of that," said Walter, "and that's why, to help you out, I'll temporarily move Aki Watanabe to your ranch. He takes care of my prized Kobe cattle at my estate and supplies my two restaurants. Even though your cattle are not Kobe beef, he can tell us how to get from just *best beef* to what makes *supreme beef*."

At that point, Walter said to Hilda, "Ask Aki Watanabe to join us in my office."

Minutes later, Aki walked in wearing traditional western clothes. He first bowed to Walter and then to Rick. He wasn't a tall man, but looked as though he could take care of himself.

Rick introduced himself, smiled and said, "Hello, Mr. Watanabe. It will be my great pleasure to work with you. How soon can you come out to the ranch?"

Aki looked at Walter.

"By the end of the week," Walter said, "he will be there. Can you arrange to have him picked up at the airport?"

"Yes, I can take care of that," Rick said.

"Well," said Rick, "I'm still not sure I'm going to be much good to you on this ranch."

Walter sat back in his chair and smiled at Rick.

CHAPTER

27

Walter had brought Aki Watanabe over from Japan in 1975. He'd met him at a trade fair when he was looking to purchase Kobe beef for his own two restaurants. He invited him to lunch to discuss his plans and make him an offer. Aki was surprised and curious at the same time but listened.

They sat down at the Golden Dragon Restaurant and Walter said, "I currently have about fifty head of Kobe cattle, and I'd like to increase the size of my herd in Rhode Island. Many of my patrons revere my Kobe beef dinners. I currently serve it at my two restaurants, and it has always been a big hit. And I want to increase my herd size to make sure I can continue to support my two restaurants. I may want to open another one or two on the East Coast. Your compensation will be very good, and you can bring your family with you. You will have your own house and can come and go as you please."

Aki was surprised with such a generous offer from a man he had just met. This actually came at an opportune time in Aki's life since his parents had both passed away and his wife was an orphan with neither brothers nor sisters.

Aki also had a Master's degree in business and political science. He had trained and learned from the "masters" and was always on his guard. But he had a feeling that this was going to work out very well.

Aki thought back to his younger days when he was responsible for the life of a very powerful real estate developer in Kyoto, Japan. His father and his father before him were all ninja warriors, with only one goal in life, and that was to protect. He had trained in all the martial art techniques. He went on to learn all of the secrets of the ninja assassin. He used his skills only on rare occasions, but was ready if needed.

After a period of time, his master passed away, and the family didn't see a need for his services, so he was no longer obligated to serve the family anymore. His previous master also had a small Kobe beef ranch outside of Kyoto, and he began to appreciate how they raised them. He quickly found that he liked ranching. He now had a new *master* to protect who had similar ideas. He liked that.

Aki smiled and asked, "Would you mind if my wife and I first come to your ranch in Rhode Island and see firsthand what's expected of me and the surrounding area?"

"That would be just fine." Walter smiled and said, "If you'd like, I have my own private jet that will fly me back in two days. You and your wife are welcome to join me. But once you're there, if you feel that you'd rather pass, I'll fly you and your wife back first class whenever you like."

Walter felt confident he would come over and manage his ranch. He found out from a close friend, who had been a military advisor in Japan, that Aki's previous occupation was as a very elite bodyguard. Many in the martial arts circuit knew and highly respected Aki. Walter also knew he could be a valuable benefit if the time ever came to use him in that capacity.

Aki called Walter at the Crowne Plaza Hotel the next day and said, "My wife and I would be honored to fly with you to your home."

"That's wonderful, Mr. Watanabe," said Walter. "Why don't we meet in my hotel lobby tomorrow morning at 9:00 a.m. and go from there."

The next day the three of them took off for Rhode Island. After they were in the air for a while, Aki sat across from Walter and asked to speak with him.

"Of course," Walter said. "What can I do for you?"

"I'm most appreciative of the offer you made me," Aki shyly said, "but it's a lot more than we dreamed of."

Walter leaned forward and said, "Aki, I'm not hiring you only to manage my cattle; I want you to be a long-term partner. I realized long ago that a paycheck is not what drives good men. In order to achieve bigger things, you have to give them an opportunity to grow. You and I will do great things together."

"Money is not necessarily a motivator for me," said Aki.

"I realized that when I first saw you," said Walter. "In order for me to be successful, I need someone who is the best. Now you may say there are others that are better than you are, and I would have to disagree – because I have the best sitting in front of me right now. I just have one basic rule: I always want to know the truth. Whether it's good or bad news, I still want to know. If it's bad, let me know as soon as possible so we can fix the problem. Please do not be afraid to make mistakes. We all make them, but many people make the bigger mistake of not learning from them."

Aki said, "Thank you for being so candid with me."

Aki thanked Walter with a traditional bow and returned to the seat next to his wife with a big smile on his face. They both sat back to enjoy the flight.

CHAPTER

28

Rick was sitting in his office the following morning at the ranch going through some things with Fred and said, "Aki is coming out from Walter's place to look at the cattle at Monarch Ranch. Using his experience handling Walter's Kobe cattle Back East, he'll be a great help to me. Walter has two restaurants in Rhode Island where he serves Kobe steaks, and they're both doing very well."What are the names of the two restaurants Walter owns?" asked Fred, looking surprised.

"He owns the *Matterhorn* in Manhattan and the *Alpinhoff* in Providence," said Rick.

Fred was ecstatic. "Walter owns The *Matterhorn* restaurant in Manhattan? Do you have any idea what the waiting list is like? Basically only A-list people can ever get in."

"Yes, I know," said Rick. "I was invited to have dinner there before I knew it belonged to Walter, and I thought I was at an after-Oscar party with all the celebrities I saw. No wonder he's so hot to make sure this ranch can produce great beef. He's going into the restaurant business in a big way, and knowing Walter and his high standards ...... only the best will do."

Rick looked over at Fred and thought about what he just said. *Do I want to do this for the rest of my life, to be a cattle rancher and sell beef to my own string of restaurants? Maybe this is what Walter had in mind for me.* Opportunities to grow personally as well as financially only came along once or maybe twice in a lifetime. Recognizing an opportunity was one thing – but doing something with it was another.

Fred started to go through the accounting ledgers and got out his adding machine with lots of tape, yellow pads, and pencils. He was old school and liked to use these tools.

After a couple of hours, Fred stopped and asked, "How many head of cattle do you think you have on the ranch?"

"I was told there are about twenty-five thousand," Rick said, "give or take some dead cattle and some strays."

Fred came forward in his chair and said quietly, "According to my calculations, you've been buying various cattle feed for at least a hundred and seventy-five thousand cattle. The costs started to grow dramatically over the last two years. Someone has been buying hay and oats for a lot of cattle over the last two years."

Rick turned with a look of shock on his face and said, "Are you kidding me?"

"No, I'm not kidding," Fred said. "The reason this didn't show up as a red flag is that each invoice had been for less than ten thousand dollars, which was under the radar of normal accounting processes. There are three companies involved, and one may be legitimate, but I'm guessing the other two are not, and both are in league to defraud you. The paid invoices go to two different PO Box numbers in Fort Collins."

"Who's been signing the packing slip that they received the feed?" Rick asked.

"It looks like some were signed by John Hammond," Fred said, "but most seem to be signed by Grant Williams. It also looks like Grant created the original requests for the feed."

Rick thought a little and said, "Why don't you create a spreadsheet of the requests for feed and the companies that had been paid. Maybe we should also look at all the vendors and suppliers we've been paying for the ranch."

"That could take days," Fred said, "but I feel it's a good exercise to see what actually has been ordered and paid. You may also want to include the salaries of all your employees. I also noticed that all of this bookkeeping was going through an agency in Fort Collins called Peabody Land Management. It looks like they're the bookkeeping service for your ranch."

"I thought the books that are here were the only records," said Rick. "I'm surprised that Walter didn't know it, or maybe this changed just after they bought the ranch. He probably wanted me to find out. Let's take a ride into town tomorrow and look up this Peabody Land Management Company and see what they're all about," said Rick.

Suddenly the phone rang and Rick answered. It was Liz. "Well, hello there. This is a pleasant surprise."

"Yep, it's just me," said Liz. "I wasn't sure I should be calling you."

"You can call me anytime day or night," said Rick, "and I hope you know I mean that and not just saying it."

"I'm so glad to hear that," Liz said. "I've a big favor to ask. How would you like a visitor for about a week?"

"Anytime you want to come," Rick said, "you have an open invitation."

Liz stammered. "That's great, because I'm already here … right now at the Loveland Municipal Airport."

With a big smile on his face, Rick said, "You're kidding! Wait there and I'll pick you up in forty-five minutes. See you then."

He hung up the phone and told Fred, "Let's go … now we have two stops to make and two people to pick up. I'll tell you on the way."

Grant was listening on the other phone that he had installed in his office. Nobody knew about it, but after the ranch changed hands, he thought that maybe he needed more insight into the new owners, and now it had paid off. He made a call to Eldon Johnson, the manager of the Peabody Land Management Company, to alert them that Rick Benedict was going to be visiting them and to look busy.

Now Grant had something else to consider. Maybe it was time to stop the problem side of the cattle ranch business. He then called the Judge and told him that Rick was going to the Peabody Land Management Company.

"This isn't good," said the Judge, "especially when he finds out there are two sets of books. How much money have you taken out of the Monarch Ranch by buying the nonexistent hay and oats and whatever else you bought?"

"Almost two million dollars in the past two years," Grant said.

"Are you crazy?" gasped the Judge as he stood up. "There's no way we can hide that type of cost. You're getting greedy, Grant, and this may have jeopardized the entire operation."

"Don't worry. I'll take care of Rick," Grant said.

"Get back to the mine," the Judge told him. "Tell them to increase the work schedule. We may have to shut down sooner than we thought. And for the time being, don't submit any more funny invoices."

"Don't forget," Grant said, "I used the money to pay for all the trucks, machinery, and those guards your cousin the General sent me, which by the way weren't cheap either," Grant angrily said and hung up.

Grant started thinking about the Judge. This was Grant's operation. That pompous, arrogant bastard's part was so small and did little to help him. He doesn't even have any of his own money invested. He had been planning this for over ten years. For the Judge's contribution, he was grossly overpaid, and if he thought he was coming along, he was sadly mistaken. Grant might just have to eliminate him, but make it look like an accident. Heart attacks always worked well.

The Judge put down his phone and calmed himself before he made the next call to his cousin .... General Alexander.

"Larry," the Judge said, "just to give you a heads-up, we may have to increase work in the mine, which means we need to use dynamite."

"What?" the General said. "This is drawing a lot of attention, and there is only so much I can hide. But I might have an idea. I'll send the Captain on a training class to Washington, D.C. I'll talk to you later," and hung up.

Later that day the General sent for Captain Peterson.

"Captain," said the General, "I had special orders cut for you to attend a seminar in Washington, D.C."

"Yes, sir," said the Captain. "When do I leave?"

"Tomorrow morning at 0600 hours," said the General. "Since you'll be in D.C., I am also giving you a special three-day pass for a little R&R."

"Thank you, sir," said the Captain, saluted, and left the General's office.

As the Captain left, he thought, *This will work out perfectly.*

CHAPTER

29

Fred and Rick drove directly to the Peabody Land Management Company, which happened to be around the corner from the Peabody Mercantile and right in the middle of town. It was a small building across the street from the Peabody Savings and Loan Bank, which both thought odd.

They walked in. "Hi, I'm Rick Benedict, and this is Fred Tremane. We'd like to see Mr. Eldon Johnson."

Eldon, with raised eyebrows, came out of his office, introduced himself, and said, "I've been expecting you ever since you became the new owner of the new Monarch Ranch. I have been out of town for several weeks on vacation. What can I do for you?"

"I'd like to have a copy of all invoices," Rick said, "that have been paid over the last two years, including all salaries paid and to whom. Also, effective immediately, I'm suspending your rights to access the accounts for the ranch."

Eldon looked angry for a split second, then said, "Is there something wrong that we should know about?"

"No, but this is now my ranch," Rick said, "and I want to make sure I understand what it actually costs to run this place. After all, it may cost more than the ranch is worth, and I may even sell it if it can't make a profit. How long will it take to collect all of the information?"

"I'd need at least several weeks," Eldon said, "to make copies for you."

Rick didn't want to wait even a day. "I'll tell you what, why don't I just take all the original invoices that have been paid, and when I'm finished, I'll bring them all back. I also need the last two years' tax returns. And …. we'll wait for them, if you don't mind. Also, give me the checkbooks and all information on the various accounts."

With that, Eldon started to perspire a little and looked concerned, but said, "I'll get those right away."

As he went back to his office, Fred said quietly to Rick, "I think you opened up a hornet's nest. I've done countless accounting audits, and when they turn white and start sweating, it's not because they've eaten bad sushi. There must be underlying problems of mega proportions."

Rick thought so as well and nodded, but watched Eldon to see if he was making any telephone calls. He appeared to make none.

A few minutes later, he brought the checkbooks, the authorization for bank withdrawals, and said, "Here they are."

"From now on," Rick said, "hold all invoices and don't process them for payment. I'll be back in a week, and then you can continue."

Rick thought Eldon seemed worried, but probably only that he'd lose the business.

"One other thing," Rick asked Eldon. "Who authorized that your company be responsible for all the bookkeeping for the ranch?"

"Why that would be Grant Williams, your ranch foreman," said Eldon. "All accounts are processed through the Peabody Savings and Loan Bank located across the street."

Rick thanked him and left. He left Fred at their office to wait for all the invoices and packing slips he wanted. He went across the street to the Peabody Savings and Loan Bank and asked to speak to the bank manager.

Mike McAllister came out of his office smiling, wearing a three-piece suit you could see was too big for him, and introduced himself.

"Can we talk in private?" Rick asked.

Mike nodded and ushered him into his office.

"My name is Rick Benedict. I'm the new owner of the Monarch Ranch, and I'm reviewing the expenditures for the ranch, which include all paid invoices and payroll. I couldn't find any bank statements at the ranch, so could you give me a copy of all bank statements for the last two years? I've been trying to figure out what it costs to run this ranch and wondering if it's worth keeping."

Mike looked flushed, but signaled one of the tellers and said, "Print out a copy of the bank statements for all the accounts associated with the Monarch Ranch."

Rick turned to the teller and said, "We'll wait for them, if you don't mind."

"How do you like ranch life?" Mike asked, trying to look relaxed. "I understand you basically spent your years in the city, so this way of life must be very difficult for you to adjust to."

"Yep, it's a challenge all right, but an exciting one," Rick said, trying to sound enthusiastic.

Ten minutes later, the teller brought over a box containing all the bank statements.

"Thanks so much," Rick said. "Just one other item .... how many accounts are there for the ranch?"

Mike turned to his computer and said, "Well, let's see. There are two checking accounts, plus one just for payroll, and another savings account."

"Collectively," Rick asked, "how much money is in all of those accounts?"

"Exactly $290,234.11," Mike answered, "not including the last deposit, which is being processed as we speak, for another $112,000."

"Was that a wire transfer or sent by check?" Rick asked.

"Wire transfer," Mike answered, "from the Sugarland Plantation Company in the Cayman Islands."

Rick looked at him with a stare that could kill and thought ......
Interesting, an offshore account.

"Is there a problem we should know about?" Mike asked.

"No, not at this time," Rick answered, "but we may call on you later this week. In addition, I want to change the authorization to sign and deposit any checks to me only. If there are any checks coming in, whether they're wire transfer or paper check, I want to see them."

Rick quickly signed an authorization slip naming him and taking Grant off the account.

"Thanks again," Rick said. "You've been very helpful. And from now on, I'll be a lot more involved in the expenditures of the ranch."

As they left, Mike McAllister was sweating so profusely and was so nervous he walked into a desk before he came out of his trance. He called Grant on his mobile phone, but it just went to his recording. He wondered if now would be a great time to take a much longer vacation.

Later, as Rick got into the truck, he saw that Fred had about ten boxes of various invoices and ledgers in the truck. He just remembered that he had to pick up Liz at the airport and was already running a little late. As they drove to the airport, Rick told Fred about Liz. How she came from Germany when she was young and went to school in the United States. He told him how he found out about Liz and that both their real parents were still living and right on Walter's estate.

"Wow," said Fred, "that's fantastic. To think Walter planned and dropped it on you guys, that gives a completely new meaning to the term *long-term planning*. It also sounds like there are still sparks between you two, which may be rekindled with her visit?"

"I don't know," Rick smiled briefly. "But something was bothering her. I could tell, because she wasn't her normal, happy, bubbly self. So we'll just have to see."

CHAPTER
30

Aki Watanabe, who had just flown in from Rhode Island, met Rick in front of Terminal 2 and again bowed to show respect for his boss.

Rick, feeling a little awkward, casually walked over to him and whispered in a low voice, "Mr. Watanabe, while I appreciate the gesture, you don't need to bow each time we meet."

Aki turned and smiled at him and nodded.

"I've a tremendous amount of respect for you, Aki," Rick said, "having seen firsthand how you managed Walter's Kobe beef herd. As I told you when we met, I don't know very much about the cattle ranching business and even less about the beef industry. But I'm hoping based on your years of experience in that industry that you can make some recommendations that will help us."

"Thank you so very much," Aki said. "You are too kind."

"I know Walter mentioned to you that our goal is to open restaurants from the Midwest to the West Coast, but we don't want to just sell steaks and ribs. We want people to eat and remember forever what that steak tasted like. I already know that as we figure out how good these cattle are, I'll probably have a slaughterhouse built with refrigeration units on the property.

Next we'll hire some excellent butchers and hopefully develop signature steaks that will exceed everyone's expectations."

"First, I want to congratulate you on this very exciting venture," Aki said. "High quality meat and the perfect seasoning are crucial to being number one. I also brought my own saddle that Walter had made especially for me in Wyoming. It just fits perfectly to my size."

Rick smiled and said to himself, *Of course, he did.*

"We also have to pick up one more individual that flew in today, and then we're ready to head back to the ranch."

Rick already felt they were going to get along well. As they all piled into the truck, it suddenly didn't feel so big anymore. Rick secretly hoped Liz didn't bring many bags or he would have to make a second trip. As they pulled up to Terminal 3, he saw Liz standing by the curb with just one small bag and he sighed rather loudly. She was wearing designer blue jeans with fancy western style red leather boots, a multi-colored western shirt that emphasized her ample breasts, and was carrying a leather jacket with the traditional western fringe on the sleeves.

Rick was watching her from the distance, and while he was happy to see her, he still needed to find out why the sudden visit.

When she saw him, she smiled, waved, and started running towards the truck. Rick sat mesmerized in the truck and watched. As she ran towards him, her chestnut colored hair was swaying from side to side, just like when he saw her running toward him on the Brown University campus last year. Several of the men waiting for a taxi couldn't take their eyes off her either.

Rick finally got out of his truck, walked up, embraced her, and said, "You've no idea how good it is to see you."

Fred was watching and finally cleared his throat to say, "All the people are watching you guys hug and you're holding up traffic in the middle of the street."

Blushing, they both came back to the truck. "Fred … Aki, this is Dr. Elizabeth Hildebrand, or Liz.

Liz, meet Fred Tremane and Aki Watanabe.

"We have been friends since we recently found we shared the same uncle."

"It's also a pleasure to meet you both," Liz said, and got in the truck right next to Rick.

Aki bowed to her and said, "It's both a pleasure and an honor to meet you."

As Aki said that, he noticed a car across the parking lot with four people sitting in it. His senses told him they were not there to pick up anybody. He's wasn't going to alarm Rick just yet. They finally started their car and left.

"Let's go, boys," said Rick. "We found out what we came for. I'll call Grant and let him know."

Rick got quiet suddenly, thinking about meeting his father again after twenty-five years just six months ago.

"Rick, can we get something to eat before we go to the ranch?" she asked. "I'm starving."

Rick snapped out of his momentary thought. "Now that you mentioned it, I almost forgot that it's almost two in the afternoon, how about a big steak? I know this great place. But, I'm sorry, it won't taste as good as Hilda's cooking," and in his best western drawl, "but we make do Out West."

Everyone laughed. It was great to hear a little laughter again. They drove over to the Chuck Wagon Grill h as usual was crowded. As they were seated, Rick noticed there were a lot of men and women dressed a little better than the average western clothes, and they only had drinks on the table. He guessed that probably many *power lunches* were in process, and that made him feel more at home.

They ordered lunch, and all ordered steaks except Liz, who ordered rainbow trout, the special of the day, with boiled golden potatoes and sautéed spinach. They had the locally brewed beer and talked about what each had done for the last three months. Liz spoke first but seemed reluctant to talk about Steve, other than he was fine and taking the boat back to port for minor repairs and maintenance.

"Rick, how do you like being a rancher," asked Liz, "now that you've almost given up that quiet life of teaching? By the way, I love the hat and western outfit...... and where did you get that large belt buckle? Were you in a rodeo?"

"No rodeo." Smiling, Rick said, "Out here, it's important to find the largest belt buckle and wear it proudly. We can get you one in town before we go out to the ranch."

"That would be great," Liz said, "and some more clothes. I bought this jacket in Monte Carlo when I was cruising in the Mediterranean, and now I can wear it without looking out of place."

"So what have you been doing so far at the ranch?" Liz asked.

"I've only been out here about a week," said Rick. "There seem to be some irregularities going on at the ranch. That's why I asked Fred to come out. He's a forensic accountant and can literally find a needle in a haystack."

Just as he said that, he noticed two individuals looking suspiciously like they were trying to listen to their conversation. Rick wasn't sure, but one of them looked familiar. He tucked it away for future reference.

Aki excused himself to go to the men's room. As he walked to the back, he scanned the room for any suspicious people. He saw the two that Rick had looked at and remembered one of them was in the car he saw at the airport. It was too much of a coincidence they happened to pick the same restaurant. Maybe their car was bugged.

Lunch finally came. Rick looked at Aki and felt this was a perfect opportunity to ask him what he thought of the steaks.

Aki cut into his steak, smelled it, chewed it, and finally swallowed it.

"When we start serving our own steaks," Aki said, "besides good seasoning, a steak should never be cooked more than *medium.* In this way, the meat will retain more of the flavor. These steaks have a good flavor, but are a little tough and should be of higher quality. Even if they ordered it cooked *rare*, the steak would still be tough. There is also a process when you cook the meat to create a juicy and tender steak. That will be as important to teach the chefs. "

Rick was impressed with Aki's assessment. This was his first lesson about beef.

They continued eating and just made small talk until they were ready to leave.

The check came and Rick said, "I got it. Why don't you three wait outside for me in the truck while I pay the bill?"

Liz looked puzzled, but left with Fred and Aki.

As Rick got up, he walked in the direction of the two men who appeared to be listening to their conversation and asked, "Did you hear everything you wanted to, because I can always write it all down for you in case you missed anything?"

They both looked startled, but one said, "We weren't listening to you. We were just looking at your girl … She's gorgeous. Sorry if that bothered you."

Rick slowly looked them over from top to bottom and finally said, "You guys have a good day," and left.

They all got back in the truck and left the parking lot. As soon as they were in the street, Liz asked, "What did you say to those guys?"

"I just asked them if they heard everything we said," Rick said with a grin, "or should I write it down for them."

Fred just smiled and said, "Just paid the bill, huh?"

Aki smiled too.

They drove out of town, and Liz was stunned at how beautiful this part of the country was. At the same time, Liz was having a hard time sitting so close to Rick. She secretly was hoping that she could talk to Rick about her situation, but didn't want to push it. After all, this would be the second time she wanted to be with Rick and didn't know how he would react to her.

She told herself that she'd talk to Rick tonight, but then wondered if she should say anything at all, since she now knew he had his hands full with the problems at the ranch. She was going to think this through a little more and then decide whether she should. She was now more confused than when she got on the plane in Rome.

CHAPTER

31

Fred met Rick several years ago when he was in the Army in Kitzingen, Germany. At the time, Fred was just a pencil-pushing bookkeeper working as an orderly to the Supply Sergeant. The job was mundane, but it kept him out of KP and guard duty, and in the wintertime, you appreciated that the most. He was also a carpenter of sorts, and when the CO asked for anybody who had carpentry experience to dress up the mess hall to look like a Bavarian restaurant, Fred jumped at the chance. It was while he was working in the mess hall that he noticed something that didn't seem right. He couldn't quite put his finger on it, but he felt something was amiss. Two days later, he found out.

The menu for dinner was Salisbury steak and chicken as entrees. As he went through the mess line, he asked for the steak and all looked fine, until he sat down and tried to cut it. As he cut through, he felt some parts that were still frozen and the gravy was as thick as molasses. *Either he's a lousy Mess Sergeant or something is up,* thought Fred.

Later that evening he saw the server on the back porch, which was also one of the regular cooks, and asked him, "Why was the steak so tough?"

The cook laughed and then looked from side to side and said, "That's because you weren't getting steak. It was a frozen roll of liver, heated up but not completely thawed out on purpose to seem like tough beef, and then smothered with hot gravy. The Supply Sergeant took the real steaks home or he traded them to another Supply Sergeant for something else he wanted."

"Are you kidding?" said Fred. Fred was mortified that the Supply Sergeant would do this. "Didn't you think to ever turn him in?

"This is one guy that has connections," said the cook, "and you want to be careful what you say about him to anybody. On top of that, I'm a *short-timer* and I do not make waves, because next week I'm gone, back to my home in Texas."

Fred decided to investigate this on his own, because one of his other duties was to keep track of the food the Mess Sergeant was ordering.

One day he had little to do and had no money to go to the PX or into town, so he decided to develop a spreadsheet to see exactly how much they paid for food. It was a simple process, because he knew how many men ate at the mess hall; subtracted the officers, because they paid out of pocket for their food; then compared that to the posted menus to see when they substituted certain items.

He went back three years and found the average dollars spent per headcount seemed reasonable for three meals per day. But he started to notice an increase in beef costs after year two. As he finished year two, the average per day food costs almost doubled, but the headcount actually was slightly lower than in previous years due to soldiers rotating to other military assignments.

He didn't know what to do, because it might involve high-ranking officers. He went to his room after dinner and thought about this some more. As he was walking back to the barracks, he happened to pass Second Lieutenant Rick Benedict, who had just recently returned from a training seminar at Vilsec, West Germany. He needed to tell someone or he was going to go nuts, so he asked if he could talk to the Lieutenant in private.

"Sure, let's go to my room, Corporal," Rick said.

Over the course of the next hour, he told Rick everything and showed him the spreadsheets to support his findings.

"I was afraid to tell the First Sergeant," Fred said, "because I knew he didn't like me, and he may be involved."

Rick couldn't believe what he'd just heard.

"No, you did the right thing," said Rick. "I'm pretty sure the CO is not part of this."

"I know I'm taking a risk," said Fred, "by even bringing this up. If you tell me to drop this, I'll forget the whole thing."

Rick suggested he let him first talk to the Company Commander, Captain Bayhurst, and see how receptive he was.

"Go back to your billets," Rick said. "I'll tell the CO what's been going on here."

The Captain, who was a West Point graduate, was also very unhappy upon hearing the news.

"Lieutenant," said the CO, "have Corporal Tremane give me all the information he has, along with any supporting documentation, and let's meet tomorrow in my office at 15:30 hours."

"Yes, sir," said Rick, saluted, and left his office.

Rick left and later told Fred about the meeting and that he could present his story directly to the CO.

Fred was thrilled but also hesitant and concerned and said, "I've heard of these *GI parties* given to other members of the platoon causing their group in some cases to pull additional duty. When this gets out, I'll be ostracized from the rest of the men."

"Don't worry about this," Lieutenant Benedict said. "And if you have any problems with any of the men, let me know about it and I'll deal with it. These little bars on my shirt may seem small, but they pack a powerful punch."

"Thank you, sir," Fred said, saluted, and walked out.

Fred still agonized throughout the night over possible retaliation, but he resigned himself to facing the possibility. After all, he only had four months left in the service and then he'd be out of here.

The next day went by very slowly, and about noontime, the First Sergeant said he was leaving for the day. Fred didn't know if he should be relieved or worried because of the way the First Sergeant had said it.

At exactly 15:30, both Rick and Fred knocked on the CO's office and went in. They could tell the CO was angry. Both saluted the CO. The CO asked them to sit down and asked Corporal Tremane to tell him exactly how he concluded there were problems. Within thirty minutes, Fred showed the CO in detail what he felt were potential glaring inconsistencies.

The Captain was surprised and disappointed at the same time, because he took it personally. It was a reflection on him as well.

The CO simply said, "Thanks for letting me know. I want to keep all this as a package for my files. At this point, I don't know what my next step will be, because as you said, there may be other NCOs involved."

Fred saluted both Rick and the CO and left the office, with a sigh of relief.

"I am so disgusted," said the CO, "that my own NCOs can't be trusted."

The CO looked at Rick and asked, "What do you think about all of this, Lieutenant?"

"Well, sir, I went over the numbers," said Rick, "and it looks like they're legitimate."

Over the next several weeks, the Mess Sergeant quietly resigned his position and left the Army, the Supply Sergeant went to prison, and the First Sergeant abruptly retired.

As it turned out, Captain Bayhurst received a commendation from the Post Commander, Lieutenant Colonel Burwell, for discovering and correcting the problems. The next day, Corporal Tremane received a promotion to Staff Sergeant and was sent to a military accounting school in Vilsec, Germany. After graduating, he transferred to Third Infantry Battalion Headquarters in Wurzburg, Germany, reporting to General Theodore Anderson.

Fred had decided to stay in the Army for another four years and see if he could uncover other little issues, because this was quite exciting and even fun. Over the course of the next four years, he uncovered other discrepancies, and when he finally left the Army, he held the rank of Master Sergeant.

He left the service to pursue a career in forensic accounting. With the contacts he'd made in the Army, he knew he'd be very busy for a long time.

CHAPTER
32

Rick glanced at Liz off and on while driving to the ranch and wondered what was really going on with her. He remembered their visit to Kitzingen, Germany, last year and the showers they'd shared, the steam engulfing their room, and making love until all hours of the night. At night, the snow had fallen, creating a white blanket over the town. He missed those times, but quickly caught himself. He didn't want to get carried away.

They drove along the highway and finally pulled onto the road going up to the ranch.

"This is beautiful country," Liz smiled and said." Everything is so green and lush and obviously a big change from being on the water almost twelve months out of the year."

"Yeah, I'll bet it's a little different from sailing on the Mediterranean," Rick chimed in.

Fred, I'll help you get these boxes inside, and we can take a look at them as soon as I get Liz and Aki settled in their rooms."

Fred said, with a smirk, "Okay."

Grant was watching all this through binoculars from a window in his bunkhouse office. He had a worried look on his face. He couldn't afford to have Rick find anything wrong with the bank financials, but it may already be too late.

He made a phone call, said what he needed done, and the person on the other end said, "Okay, but this time it'll be ten grand."

Grant knew he had to be careful because if those papers suddenly were destroyed, then it might throw suspicion on him. He made a call to Dale and asked her to meet him in town. With that, Grant went to his wall safe, pulled out his gun and a silencer, and left the bunkhouse.

Rick told Aki that he could stay in the *Pine* room. "Go ahead and unpack, relax, and we'll see you downstairs later."

Aki said, "Thank you so much, Rick. I will see you shortly."

Rick carried Liz's bags and put her in the *Aspen* room, which just happened to be across the hall from the *Oak* room, Rick's bedroom.

"Well, here is your home away from home," Rick said, "which doesn't have any nautical themes so I hope you won't be bored. Why don't you rest up a bit and come down when you're ready."

With that, Liz rushed up to Rick, pushed him back against the wall, and kissed him hard.

He responded, when suddenly Liz stopped, and blurted out, "I'm sorry. This isn't fair to you. I need to explain something to you about Steve and me."

She sat down on the edge of the bed and almost crying said, "Steve said he felt his ability to act as my bodyguard would be jeopardized if he was emotionally involved with me. While I understood how and why he felt that way, it still hurts, and that's why I wanted to see you. I thought you could help me sort things out, and I could temporarily avoid the problem."

"I'm sorry it's not working out," Rick said, "because I think that Steve is a terrific guy, and I only want the best for both of you. Yes, I was a little jealous. But in the end, it is what it is."

With tears running down her check, Liz got up and went over to look out the window, with Rick following her.

"Maybe we can talk later," Rick said, "after I go over some things with Aki and Fred. Go unpack and try to rest up a bit, and we'll get together for dinner later."

He put her bags down, quickly turned around, closed the door behind him, and left.

Liz felt paralyzed and alone, and blurting out about Steve and her problem didn't help any. She didn't know what to do, so she decided to go ahead and take that shower and relax. Afterwards she would get dressed and go downstairs to check out the main house.

Rick hadn't moved away from the outside of her door and almost rushed back in, but caught himself. He finally walked down the hallway and downstairs to meet with Fred.

CHAPTER

33

Fred was going through the banker boxes, organizing them by year and month. He pulled out his laptop computer and started entering numbers into a generic database he'd previously created.

He stopped in midstream, looked around, and said aloud, "This is gonna take me forever. I've got to find a better solution."

He decided instead to hack into the Peabody Land Management's mainframe computer. Rick didn't need to know about this, he thought, and rather than spending days inputting data, he could pull the information directly from the bank statements, create and merge spreadsheets in one-tenth the time. Within an hour, he had a listing of all invoices paid by check number, which account number, and by month and year.

Just then Rick came downstairs, clearly in a better mood than when he went to take Liz up to her room.

"Well, how are we doing?" he asked Fred.

"I started to see a pattern," said Fred. "There were actually three companies receiving checks but sent to different PO Box numbers right here in Fort Collins. The interesting thing was that the companies had different names, different PO Box numbers, but the same main postal address. Each was selling various feed, hay, and so on and so on, which coincides with my previous assessment that you're feeding cattle you don't have."

"That sounds a little too coincidental," said Rick.

"The amounts of the checks didn't attract attention because they were always paid at different days of the month and were always under ten thousand dollars, which didn't require a second signature from the branch manager. But two of the companies were sending invoices several times per month. The comparison between the paid invoice and packing slips weren't questioned because Grant Williams signed them, as well as ordering almost all of the feed."

Fred used this awkward moment to say, "Rick, it's what I suspected and maybe even a little worse. All the receipts we looked at were incomplete, but there's definitely a pattern of fraud. We need to find out who owns the three PO Box numbers."

"One of these companies must be legitimate and that should be easy to find out," said Rick. "Let's look up each company's actual address to see where they're located."

"I've already done that," said Fred, "and you're right, only one is actually legitimate and that company is located just outside of Fort Collins. The other two I can't find anything on, so I assume they're not legit."

"You've already completed the analysis?" Rick said, "How'd you do this so quickly?"

Fred winced and said, "It may be better you don't know."

Nevertheless, Rick insisted.

"I hacked into the Peabody Land Management Company's main frame," said Fred, "and did a little cut-n-paste. By the way, how is Liz doing, if you don't mind me asking?" He was hoping to change the subject.

Rick, with a big sigh, said, "It's a long story, but the short version is Steve broke up with her, so she just needed to get away and clear her head. Right now, though, I have to concentrate on finding out what's going on here."

"Okay." Fred continued, "I also found out that you have nine telephone lines you're paying for monthly."

"Let's find one of the telephone bills and see where they're all located," Rick said.

Over the next hour, Rick also discovered excessive telephone line charges and car, truck, and farm repairs that were astronomically high for this size of a cattle ranch.

"How do we find out who owns these PO Boxes in Fort Collins"? Rick asked.

It was now approaching nighttime and getting dark. Liz came bouncing downstairs after overhearing them and blurted out, "I know how."

Both Rick and Fred looked at Liz in the doorway. Liz had changed into a simple white sweatshirt, along with her with jeans that fit like a glove. Her hair was in a ponytail, with a slight curl at the end, and swayed from side to side as she walked.

"We mail a package to the PO addressees," said Liz, "with the box wrapped in brightly colored wrapping paper and some telephone books inside for weight. When the person goes in to collect their mail, we'll just wait outside in the car and see who comes out with the colored box."

They looked at each other and Rick said, "That's a fantastic idea."

"I'll put the packages together and mail them tomorrow morning," Fred offered.

"I feel great after a little rest and a good shower," Liz said. "Is anybody hungry?"

"The chief cook decided to leave two days ago because I fired her bully son," Rick said, "and I haven't been able to get a new chef. I did make a contact with the local employment agency to see if they could help me, but so far she hasn't called with any prospects. Should we go out for dinner or I can probably still rustle up something? How about it, Fred, are you up for it?"

"We just ate four hours ago," said Fred. "I'm still full from lunch. I'm not very hungry. Why don't you two go and have dinner. I want to work with these numbers, and I still want to wrap the packages for tomorrow."

"Okay. We'll make it a quick one," Liz said. "Anything we can bring you back?"

"How about a double cheeseburger with fries and a chocolate milkshake," said Fred.

"You got it," said Liz.

She grabbed her jacket and got in the truck, just as the sun was slowly disappearing over the horizon.

"I just love it here," said Liz.

"Yep, it is pretty spectacular country," said Rick.

It suddenly got very quiet at the house, with only the chirping of the crickets and the hoot of a lone owl to its mate in the background. Fred was working on his laptop intensely and didn't notice he had unannounced company. Two guys wearing ski masks crept up, peeked in the window, and saw Fred working at the kitchen table.

"This ought to be a piece of cake," one said as he looked at his partner.

They came through the kitchen door and crept up quietly behind Fred. One of them smashed him in the side of his face with his gun before he knew what was going on. Fred crumbled and fell to the floor, with blood spewing from the gash on his temple. The taller one quickly grabbed his laptop and poured kerosene all over the boxes they had collected that afternoon and lit it. The flames instantly engulfed the area, with Fred lying on the floor just steps away from the fire.

One of the men let out a loud coarse laugh and said to the other, "This'll teach Rick not to fire his hired help," then left.

Unbeknownst to them, Fred was starting to come to. He'd stayed quiet and heard all of this. His head was throbbing. As soon as they left, he stumbled around, trying to put out the fire, but it caught on the drapes, but quickly passed out. Just then Aki, hearing the commotion, ran downstairs and into the kitchen. He rushed back to the living room, picked up one of the area rugs, and used it to try and smother the fire, which helped a little bit. He ran back into the kitchen looking for a fire extinguisher and found one in the walk-in pantry. After another few seconds, the fire was out. That's when Aki noticed Fred was lying* on the floor moaning, with blood trickling from his forehead.

Fred tried to reach a phone to call Rick and tell him what had happened. That's when he noticed Aki standing over him. After that, he passed out on the kitchen floor.

Aki picked Fred up, put him on the couch in the living room, and went to work cleaning his wounds. He used one of his special poultices to stop the bleeding. When Aki applied the special cream, the bleeding stopped almost instantly. Fred started to moan a little, holding his throbbing head.

Aki called Rick and told him about Fred and the fire.

CHAPTER
34

Liz and Rick had been having an enjoyable dinner at the Whale Watch Inn. Liz had ordered the orange roughy and Rick the halibut. Now that Rick was almost in the restaurant business, he analyzed what other successful restaurants were doing to attract customers, besides the nice menus and décor. He noticed that the kitchen was not in sight, which he liked, rather than staring at it while eating. Just then Rick got a call on his mobile phone. It was Aki.

"We'll be right there," said Rick.

After hanging up, he filled Liz in. "There was a fire at the main house," Rick said, "and Fred was hurt. We need to get back to the ranch, pronto."

As they walked quickly back to the truck, Rick felt he knew who was behind this. Within thirty minutes, by running a few stoplights and signs, they drove up to the front of the house, ran up the front steps, and found Fred lying on the couch with his head bandaged.

Aki bowed to Rick and said, "I must apologize. I was not able to be here in time for Fred."

"Don't worry about it," Rick said. "He's had worse beatings on the streets where he grew up."

"Liz, call for a doctor," Rick said. "Then call John Hammond, our ranch veterinarian, in the bunkhouse to get over here right away."

John was there shortly and treated Fred's head wound as best he could.

"It looks like his wounds are already dressed and very nicely done," John said.

That's when Rick introduced John to Aki. About then, Fred started to moan and wake up.

"Are you okay to talk a little bit?" Rick asked. "What happened?"

Fred was groggy but managed to explain. "After you and Liz left, two guys with ski masks jumped me, took my laptop, and tried to destroy all the records we were working on. It looks like you're getting a little too close to the truth. Something else was peculiar too. As I was lying on the ground, I overheard one of them say, *This will teach Rick not to fire his hired help.* Does that mean anything to you?"

Rick knew exactly what it meant and who he thought it was. Now he was concerned they had listening devices either on the phone or in other areas of the house.

"By the way," Fred asked, trying to smile, "where is my double cheeseburger, fries, and chocolate milkshake?"

"Looks like you'll be okay," laughed Rick, "because you haven't lost your appetite or your sense of humor."

"I'm now concerned that this house is bugged," said Rick in a low voice. "I've got to call John Lawton, my friend in Rhode Island."

He went outside and called John on his mobile phone. John's service answered, which connected Rick immediately.

"Hello, John. It's Rick Benedict. Are you staying out of trouble? Listen, I know it's late, but I may have a problem out here in Colorado and I sure could use a Frequency Finder Bug Detector. Do you know of someone out here I could borrow one from for a little while?"

"Not to worry," John said. "I'll expedite one for you by overnight courier and you should have it by tomorrow afternoon."

"Thanks, John. Also, is there any type of device you have," Rick asked, "that can track mobile phone locations, like a GPS, for example?"

"Yes, there is," said John. "I'll send that out also."

"When we get all finished here, you need to come out to the ranch for a little vacation. Thanks again," said Rick and hung up.

As he hung up the phone, the doctor pulled up in the front, saw Rick, and asked where Fred was.

"We took him upstairs to his room," Rick said. "Come on. I'll show you."

They went up to Fred's room and after a thorough examination, the doctor said, "He should be okay, as long as he gets some rest. There doesn't appear to be any real damage done. That cream on his wound helped a lot," and the doctor left.

Rick was seeing red and was imagining various ways of revenge.

"I know what you're feeling Rick," said Liz, "but let's think this through."

It was now almost midnight and Rick was agreeing with what Fred said. It was true. They were getting too close to discovering something. But "What?" was still the big question.

"I'm sorry this happened to you," Rick said, "but don't worry. I think I know who did it, and in due time they'll pay for this."

Fred sat up, winced a little from the pain, and tried to smile. "There's a lot of information I put on my laptop," he said, "plus a lot of my own stuff. That's why I had a tracking device installed, in case it ever just *grew legs* and disappeared. All my files are heavily encrypted, so it won't do them any good."

"Maybe it's not what's on your computer," said Rick, "but to slow us down from completing your analysis."

Fred reached into his carry-on luggage and pulled out what looked like a very small mobile phone. "Let's turn it on and see where it leads us," said Fred.

As he did, it suddenly sprang to life, and they saw a red pulsating dot. What was interesting was that it wasn't moving; it was stationary, and it looked like it was close by.

As Rick watched the device, he said, "It says it's only about two hundred yards away, which means it's somewhere on the ranch. I think I know where we'll find it. But right now you need some rest, so we'll see you in the morning. I'm sorry I got you into this."

"That's okay," said Fred. "I was getting tired anyway." He lay back down, nodded off, and within minutes was fast asleep.

He walked out of his room and ran directly into Liz standing in the hallway.

"How's he doing?" Liz asked.

"He'll be okay," answered Rick. "Just a smack on the noggin. He's been in worse fights," and walked to his room.

Liz followed him in and asked, "What do you plan to do?"

"Right now I need a hot shower and some rest so I can think about this some more. There has got to be a lot more to this than we're seeing, but every time I turn around, I run into another problem."

He pulled her into the bathroom and told her not to talk, turned on the shower and said, "I'm afraid the place is bugged, including the telephones. I'm having a package sent to me overnight from my friend in Rhode Island, and I should have it by tomorrow afternoon. After that, I can perform bug sweeps every day if I want to."

He turned off the water, and Liz got close and coyly said, "You want to check me out for bugs, or do you think I'm okay?"

"No, I think you're probably safe," he said smiling, as he peeled off his clothes and jumped in the shower.

Rick wondered why she hadn't followed him. He now felt that maybe her problems ran deeper than what she'd told him so far.

CHAPTER

35

When he got out of the shower, Liz walked back into his room, with her shirttails out of her jeans, with almost all the buttons opened – and with no boots on.

"Now is not the right time," said Rick. "Plus I still want to know about your relationship with Steve."

She was disappointed and pretended to pout. Rick still wasn't comfortable with the situation because Steve was still her bodyguard and might even be lurking around. As he lay there, he was still trying to connect the dots on all the strange things that had happened so far. Liz finally climbed into bed under the covers, and they were both sound asleep in minutes.

Sometime in the morning, while it was still dark, as he was still half-dozing and Liz sleeping, he thought about what had happened so far at the ranch. He felt that the problems had to be more than just a money-laundering scheme. First, he and Grant found six dead cattle in an area of the ranch property that the cattle seldom used, and the next day he accidentally found a mine and was shot at. Then the run-in he had with Billy Haddock, who turned out to be the son of his housekeeper and chef. And on it goes.

He felt drowsy and dozed, now thinking about Liz and Steve. He suddenly woke up, talking in his sleep about their time in Prague last year.

Liz also woke up, calmed him down, and said, "It was only a dream, Rick."

He slept restlessly the rest of the night and finally got up, dressed, and went downstairs. Liz fell back asleep, and he hoped she would sleep longer than he had. He made himself a cup of coffee.

That's when he noticed shadows by the kitchen window. He crept up to the side window and looked out. He saw what he thought was one of the ranch hands, but couldn't tell who it was because the person wore a heavy jacket with a turned-up collar and a large western hat. Rick watched from a distance and decided to follow him. He slowly slipped out the side door and was within hundred and fifty feet of the man.

Suddenly out of nowhere a shorter man, dressed completely in black, rushed out and expertly gave the intruder a swift kick to the head ... and he was down. Rick was watching but with a blink of an eye, the black-cloaked man was gone. Rick rushed over to see who the intruder was, and with the moonlight shining directly on him, he saw it was Billy Haddock. Rick slapped him a few times to wake him up. After a while, Billy finally opened his eyes, obviously wondering what hit him.

When he saw Rick, Billy clenched his teeth and tried to get up, but Rick had the advantage. He gave him a chop to the side of the neck, and he went limp again. Now Rick didn't know what to do with him, because he was sure he was one of the guys who set the fire and beat up Fred in the kitchen. Only problem was ... he couldn't prove it.

He decided to find out how good the local police were with burglars. He went inside and called the Sheriff.

After hearing the situation, the night desk sergeant said, rather dryly, "We'll send someone out right away."

Grant also heard the message.

Meanwhile, Rick went back to where Billy was laying and saw he was gone. A few minutes later, he heard the sirens and a patrol car pulling up to the front door.

Rick went around to the front of the house to tell the Sheriff that Billy Haddock woke up and split.

The Sheriff asked, "You say it was Billy Haddock ... the same guy that you said torched your kitchen?"

"Yeah, I'm almost sure of it. I just can't prove it," Rick answered. "I fired him two days ago, and now he's sneaking around the house, looking for I don't know what."

"Do you want us to issue an arrest warrant for him?" the Sheriff asked.

Rick wondered why he would ask such a question because he thought that was a foregone conclusion.

Rick said, with disgust, "Naw, he's probably long gone and won't be seen around here anymore. I've got more important things to do than to chase after idiots."

The Sheriff said, "Okay .... but it's up to you," and left.

Rick didn't get the feeling that the Sheriff was too concerned, which meant that he might have to take matters into his own hands. Then he remembered that he was Grant's brother -in-law. That suddenly explained some of the things.

By this time, Liz had come downstairs and was standing at the front door, "What's going on?" she asked.

Just then Rick noticed that Aki hadn't come down, so he thought he should see if he was all right.

They all walked up the front stairs, and Rick went ahead to Aki's room and knocked. "Aki, are you awake?"

Aki came to the door, rubbing his eyes, and said, "Good morning. Why were the police here?"

"Is there something we need to talk about or I should know?" Rick asked suspiciously.

Aki said, with a straight face, "Not that I know of. Is there something you wish to ask me?"

Rick thought for a moment and said, "No ... Sorry to have awakened you. See you tomorrow, or rather later today since it's now five o'clock in the morning."

Rick went back to his room and Liz was already in bed waiting for him.

After that little episode, Rick's adrenalin had him pumped up so much, he couldn't go back to sleep. Liz, however, cuddled him and he fell asleep again. He now had another mystery and wondered who his protector was. The more he thought about it, the more it pointed to Steve. On the other hand, maybe it was Aki. He knew and practiced hand-to-hand combat.

He smiled to himself and thought, *That sly Walter. He knew I might have problems out here and could use some help without arousing suspicion.* He lay there for a little longer and decided to get up and start the day.

CHAPTER

36

Grant watched and heard everything that went on. He decided to go out to the mine and find out why Billy was hanging around after the fire was set. He got in his truck and left the ranch on one of the utility roads used to deliver hay and other feed for the cattle. As he was driving, he thought that Billy had probably outlived his usefulness and had become a liability.

It was now getting lighter and the sun was just coming up over the mountains as he got close to the mining area parking lot. He approached it from the other side of the mountain, and as he drove in, he saw his guards standing strategically in various places near pine trees that must be over a hundred feet tall. Some guards stood behind large granite boulders on a hill so they could have an unobstructed view of the area.

He spotted Billy across the road just getting out of his truck and called out to him. "Hey, Billy, wait up for me."

Billy looked startled and turned around to face Grant.

"I thought I told you to lie low. What were you doing back at the ranch?" Grant asked.

Billy, cowering, said, "I didn't like the way Rick treated me, and I was going to show him he couldn't push me around.

I wanted to torch some of the trucks and farm equipment and cause him some more problems."

Grant was now turning red, but controlled himself and said, "Okay, let's go into the mine and see what we can get done."

As he led him into the mine about fifty feet, he pulled out his gun with the silencer and quickly put one shot in the back of Billy's head, making him crumble like wet newspaper. He couldn't let somebody like Billy jeopardize this operation for revenge and have any type of investigation started, much less directed at him. He could jeopardize ten years of planning and his investors were not the forgiving kind, so he had to make sure there were no loose ends. He dragged Billy a little further and threw him down one of the mine holes and tossed his hat down after him.

"Sorry, Billy," said Grant aloud. "Cousin or no cousin, there's just too much at stake."

CHAPTER

37

Grant was at the northern section of the property with a dozen men wearing miner's helmets and respirators. There was low lighting, so they wouldn't attract attention. This part of the mine had drill rods that were two inches in diameter and powered by a generator, with water to keep the drills cool. Three people were drilling new holes and getting ready to blast a few more areas.

"I don't know how long I can keep Rick out of our business," Grant said, "so we need to accelerate the digging. I'm having an additional truck brought in that can carry up to two hundred fifty tons of rock to the smelter."

As Grant was speaking, Dale came out of the shadows of the mine wearing a miner's helmet.

"I agree," she said. "We need to accelerate the dig, because now Rick has copies of all the invoices and bank statements that have been paid, and it won't take him long to figure out what's going on here."

Grant had been surprised to see Dale this early in the morning.

"Dale, those papers have all been destroyed," said Grant. "And by the time they collect another set, we'll be done and long gone from this hick town. Although to tell you the truth, I'm more worried about the Greenland Empire ... the investors from

Las Vegas. They're the other investors, and if this goes sideways, these guys are well connected to the syndicate."

"You've a got a bigger problem if Rick finds out you've been pulling about eighty thousand bucks a month from the Monarch Ranch to help fund this project," said Dale arrogantly.

"Yeah, I know," said Grant, feeling frustrated having to explain to her. "But I'm still not worried about any of the statements, because they all went up in flames at the house."

What Grant was more worried about was the skimming he did from the money his father sent him from Florence. That was his plan "B" exit in case everything else failed. He figured his other nest egg should be about five million dollars by now. He was more afraid of his father because he had the resources and connections, and unless he was dead, his father would find him.

Grant looked outside with pride as one of his new CAT trucks was being loaded to haul boulders from the mine to his smelting factory five miles away. He bought the factory about two year ago with money skimmed from the Monarch Ranch invoices. The factory was off the main highway north of the ranch and hidden from the public by large spruce and pine trees. Other than the occasional puff of smoke, you wouldn't even know they were there. Nobody knew that the smelter was part of the additional ten thousand acres that the previous owner purchased.

The General recommended a mining engineer who had retired from the Army Corps of Engineers named Allen DeWalt to run the smelter. The smelting factory covered about two acres, with only one main road going in and out. The entire perimeter had chain-link fencing, with double rolls of concertina wire on the top that had razor sharp edges, similar to what prisons used. At the other end of the factory, almost hidden from view, was a spur line that hadn't been used in years.

CHAPTER

38

Rick got up early, went downstairs, and saw a message on the kitchen phone. In all the confusion, he hadn't checked for telephone messages. It was from the local employment agency.

Hi, my name is Sandy McNamara. I've found you a kitchen chef that we think you will be very happy with. Please give me a call to set up an interview.

He was overjoyed with this news, because he wasn't fond of cooking, only the eating part. When he was teaching at Brown, he had a great kitchen in his apartment, but usually went out for dinner and generally had lunch in the faculty dining room. When he brought guests over to his house, they often volunteered to cook, and Rick had no problem in letting them.

He could hear stirring upstairs, so he made a big pot of coffee for all. He poured a cup of coffee for himself and one for Liz. When he got back to his bedroom, she was still sleeping but stirring slightly. He put her cup on the nightstand, sat in the chair, and just watched her silky hair slip from side to side on the pillow.

After about ten minutes, she was feeling around the bed to see if Rick was still there and said under her breath, "Oh, no, I scared him off."

Rick stood up, "Good Morning. And, no, I'm still here. I thought you could use a cup of coffee."

She turned slightly, tried to sit up, and the sheet fell down, revealing her firm, round breasts. Feeling shy suddenly, she quickly pulled the sheet up to her neck as if she were modest and smiled impishly.

"Good," said Liz, "you didn't disappear. I was concerned about you."Rick felt he'd waited long enough. "While we have a little time, let's talk about you and Steve and where you are in your relationship with him."

She spent the next fifteen agonizing minutes briefly bringing Rick up-to-date about Steve and her.

Rick reiterated, "I don't want to interfere or be a pawn in some silly love triangle game, if that's what you're thinking."

She lowered her head slightly and when she raised it, she said, with tears rolling down her face, "No, I'm not. I'm just so confused."

In the process, Rick had moved from the chair to the edge of the bed, and when she finally noticed it, she tried to smile. Rick got up from the foot of the bed and walked around to her pillow and gently pulled her toward him and kissed her long and hard. She dropped her sheet, he got back into bed, and they made love for the next hour. They didn't seem to notice that it was daylight and had been for a little while.

When they finally came up for air, they lay back on the pillows, both with big smiles on their faces as if now they could conquer the world.

Rick turned toward her and said, stammering, "Can you cook?"

The statement seemed to catch her off guard, but she eventually said, smiling, "Of course, I can."

They showered quickly, got dressed, and went downstairs.

Rick stopped in Fred's room to see how he'd slept last night, found he was already up and around and smiling.

"I finally had to get up," said Fred, "because you guys were making so much noise. But thanks for asking. I feel fine, but now I want to go find my laptop computer."

Fred found his tracking device and took it with him. When they reached the bottom of the stairs, they noticed that the front door was ajar. The front door was a massive oak door, three inches thick, with double-paned glass that had a special colored leaded glass insert between the clear glass panes. There was a note taped to the outside glass pane, which said, *You need to leave this valley, or the next time we won't be so nice.*

Rick tried to see if there was any other message that he should be reading, but could find none. Soon after that, Aki came down and excused himself for oversleeping.

Rick looked him in the eye. He could see a glimmer, and Rick knew what that meant.

"No apologies necessary," Rick said. "Liz is going to cook breakfast for us. You're welcome to join us."

Aki excused himself. "Thank you, but I would prefer to go look at your cattle. I'll only have a hot tea, if you don't mind."

Rick called out to Fred and Liz, "Let's get some breakfast. Liz volunteered to cook us all some steak and eggs, and I'll make some fresh coffee. Meanwhile, Fred, let's take a look at your tracking device and see if we can figure out where your laptop ended up."

As they walked over to Rick's office, the open door didn't even faze them anymore. As Fred turned on his tracking device, they started watching the signal, which still pointed to the same general area.

"Doesn't look like it's moved since last night," Rick said, "so it must be stationary and maybe in a house."

"Let's sit down and eat," Liz yelled out. "You guys can play with your toys later."

As they sat down, they were amazed at the feast Liz had prepared. There was a mountain of bacon, each had a steak, plenty of toast with real butter and strawberry jam, and that's when Rick remembered he'd forgotten to make the fresh coffee.

"I had decided to make it," Liz said, reading Rick's expression, "just in case you two kids got too involved in your toys."

They both smiled and ate as if they hadn't for days.

When they finished eating, the phone rang and Rick answered. "Hello… Rick Benedict."

"Hi, my name is Sandy McNamara from the McNamara Agency. I called yesterday and left a message on your phone. I'm told you need an all-around individual who can not only cook, but clean up the house, do laundry, and generally act like a house mother."

Rick said, "Yes, that sounds about right. When can I meet her to discuss her actual responsibilities?"

Sandy replied, "How about noon today at your ranch?"

"That would be fine. And by the way, does she have a car, because we're out of town quite a ways?"

"She does have transportation," Sandy answered. "And if you think she's a good fit for you, then she's available to start immediately."

"How much experience does she have in running a ranch house?" Rick asked. "I assume you've checked out her references and feel comfortable."

"Yes, she has excellent references," Sandy said. "She previously worked on another ranch in Colorado Springs. The only reason she left was that the ranch was sold to a developer and so they had to let her go."

"Well, okay, then, I'll see her at noon. By the way, what's her name?"

"Diana Kreutz," said Sandy.

"Thanks so much," Rick said, and they both hung up.

"Sounds like you have a new chef," Fred said, "which means I can stop making my bed in the morning and just do other stuff."

They all laughed and were just finishing breakfast when the doorbell rang. It was the courier service with his package, which came early. He went back into the kitchen, opened up the box, and unpacked the two items: The *Frequency Finder Bug Detector* and the *mobile phone GPS tracker*, wrapped in bubble wrap. Rick put his hand up to indicate that he wanted nobody to talk while he walked around the house looking for listening devices.

He ran across one in the living room by the front door, another in the formal dining room by the bar area, and found four more in his office. He came to the kitchen and signaled them to follow him outside to the front yard.

When they stood on the front porch, he found none.

Rick looked on with a frown and said, "Well, it's as I thought, the house is bugged. But as long as they don't know that I know they're listening, I might want to use that to my advantage. So for now, let's not bring up any findings and limit talking to just small talk."

They all agreed and nodded their heads in agreement..

"However," Fred asked, "who is listening, why, and for how long?"

Rick continued, "This other item will let me track a mobile phone, as long as it's turned on. I'm going to input Grant's mobile phone number, and it should tell me where he is at all times, when it's turned on."

Rick then walked over to his truck and scanned it to see if there were any bugs, and he found one, which he quickly pulled and was ready to destroy.

"Hold on, Rick," Fred said quietly. "Before you do that, let me take a look at it."

Fred opened it and shut it off. Then he said, "This is a high grade military, possibly even a CIA-level listening device, and I've seen these before. The one thing that's great about this is that I can reverse engineer it, make it a homing device, and have it identify the location of the receiver. Do you remember the tracking device I showed you that I have for my laptop? Well, I may be able to use that same device to help me locate the receiver."

Rick raised his eyebrows. "I'm impressed. You may have another side job besides being a forensic accountant." Rick said smiling, "Okay, let's do this. I have a new chef and housekeeper coming over at noon to be interviewed."

Fred got his tracking device and reworked the bug they found in Rick's truck.

"I also remember seeing some of these bugs," Liz said, "when I attended Protection and Intelligence classes in California. These were the latest and greatest. They've installed these in all of the U.S. Embassies around the world. They're difficult to find with the average bug finder, because they're made with a Bakelite material that has no metal and doesn't generate any heat."

Rick smiled at Liz and said, "Now I know I'm impressed."

As Fred worked his magic, he finally got a hit, and it looked like it was just down the road from the house.

"That's odd," said Rick. "It looks like it's coming from the bunkhouse where all the wranglers live during the week. It seems that last night when you tried looking for your laptop, it also signaled in that general direction."

"Let's find out where Grant is with the mobile phone tracker," Rick said. "It came on and looked like it was coming from the same general direction as Fred's laptop finder."

"Hang on a minute," Rick said, and turned around and went into his desk, pulled out his .45 handgun, checked the clip, and pulled an extra clip just in case.

"Okay, now I'm ready." He tucked it into the back waistband of his pants.

They got into the truck and, using Fred's tracking device, slowly made their way to the ranch house where the wranglers would be staying.

"The device is pointing to the right of the wrangler's house," Fred said gesturing. "And it's pointing towards that house."

"That's Grant's house," Rick said. "He has a separate house off to the side of the ranch house."

As they got closer, the device started to beep louder and louder. They stopped at the front door, and just as Rick was going to knock on the door, Grant came out to greet them.

"Well, hello there," he said, smiling at Liz. "I'm Grant Williams, and you are?"

Rick introduced them. "This is Liz Hildebrand, and you remember Fred. Liz is a friend staying with me for a few days. Can we come inside? I've got some questions I need answers to."

"Well, it's kind of messy," Grant said." Really haven't had time to straighten up."

Rick casually pulled out his .45 and said, "We're coming in one way or the other," and pushed himself into Grant's house.

Grant was surprised and found himself at a disadvantage, so he let them in. Fred went in last, adjusted his bug tracking device, and after a few seconds, it pointed to a nearby closet, which he opened. Sitting on the top shelf was his laptop. On a shelf below was a transmitting device for the bugs.

"This is the transmitter," Fred said, "that's being used to record everything from the house."

Rick was now angry and stood in front of Grant, menacingly pointing his gun under his chin.

"First of all," Rick said menacingly, "where's Billy Haddock? Fred has a score to settle with him for giving him a concussion. Second, why are you bugging my house?"

Grant quickly tried to knock his gun away and run for it, but Rick already knew what he was going to do and sidestepped him. He gave Grant a hard right to the chin. Then he kicked him behind the kneecap, and everyone could hear the cartilage breaking. Grant let out a loud cry and fell to the floor, moaning and holding his leg. Blood was spewing from his mouth.

"What's going on here?" asked Rick. "Why are you bugging my house? Why do you have the conversations recorded?"

Grant passed out.

CHAPTER

39

Rick called the Sheriff from Grant's house and said, "Come over here as soon as you can. I have Grant Williams and I want you to arrest him."

The Sheriff frowned when he hung up the phone. He didn't want to arrest Grant Williams – since he was his brother-in-law. But election time was coming up, and he had divorced his sister.

"Hey, Hurley," yelled out the Sheriff. "Go out to Monarch Ranch and arrest Grant Williams."

"Are you kiddin'?" said the Deputy.

"No, I'm not," said the Sheriff. "I'm going fishing."

When Rick hung up, he threw cold water on Grant. Grant stirred and came to.

Rick questioned him again. "Why all the telephone taps? I'm sure that you had Billy Haddock and a couple of your goons come into my house to rough up Fred. That was a bad mistake."

Grant tried to sit up, smiled, and just looked up at Rick.

"Billy set the kitchen on fire and that almost burned down my house," said Rick. "It could have killed Fred, and that's something you'll pay for. There's a lot you don't know about me, and I'm sure you thought that with me coming from Back East, I wouldn't know how to deal with your kind. Well, that was your big mistake. Where is Billy?"

Grant wiped the blood from his mouth and arrogantly said, "You'll never find him. He's long gone. For what it's worth, this thing is bigger than you can imagine."

Rick felt violated, clenched his teeth, and clipped Grant behind the ear with the butt of his gun. Liz looked on in shock and turned her head.

Meanwhile, Fred was busy making sure all of his data was still intact and said to Rick, "They obviously tried, but couldn't get through my encryption security."

Fred looked at a few reels of tape from the lower shelf. He also saw two phones hidden in the closet, one attached to a voice-activated recorder that looked like a standard house phone.

"I'll bet this recording device recorded everything said when you used that line," Fred said. "This way he could listen anytime to your conversation. This other recorder is voice-activated from the bugs in your house, as well as the bug you found in the Jeep."

"That's why Grant gave me this truck to drive," said Rick, "because it was bugged."

Fred called the phone company pretending he was having trouble with this line. They confirmed two phones installed simultaneously with the same phone number. Rick picked up Grant by his shirt collar, dumped him in the chair, and shook him until he opened his eyes.

Rick sensed that Grant wasn't afraid of what was going to happen. Maybe he felt he still had a few cards to play out.

Rick got directly in his face and said, "Grant, you don't know me very well. But there are people in this room who know exactly what I'm capable of doing to you if you don't talk." Rick waited about ten seconds; then he tapped Grant on his nose hard with the handle of his .45, and suddenly blood gushed from his nose.

"What's going on at the ranch?" Rick yelled out. "It's got to be more than just money laundering."

Grant looked up with a surprised look on his face, laughing at Rick. "You think this is about money laundering?"

Grant continued to laugh louder and continued to bleed down his shirt and onto the floor.

Grant was now covered in blood, but only said, "You'll find out soon enough."

"Rick," Liz said, "he's not much good to us if he's unconscious or dead."

Rick didn't say anything and backed off when he heard the Sheriff's car coming up the driveway. He went outside to talk to them and show them where Grant was. The Deputy Sheriff went in and took one look at Grant and cast a suspicious glance towards Rick, but dismissed it.

"Mr. Benedict, we'll take him over to Fort Collins Emergency," said the Sheriff, "and as soon as they're done, we'll transport him over to the county jail."

"I'll be over later this afternoon to file charges against Grant," Rick said.

Rick suddenly realized that the housekeeper he was to interview was probably at the house now since it was past noon.

"Liz … Fred," Rick said, "let's get back to the house. I have an interview to conduct. Bring all the tapes and your laptop so we can continue this later."

But before they got to his truck, several of the ranch hands came over and asked, "What's going on?"

Rick turned around. "Your boss is no longer your boss," he said. "I'll get together with you later this afternoon to let you know what we're going to do."

Sammy, the youngest wrangler, took it personally and walked menacingly towards Rick, but then stopped when he saw the gun tucked in Rick's waistband behind his belt buckle. They all stood there with their mouths open.

"I'll be back later and we'll talk some more," said Rick and left.

They quietly drove up to the main house, and the housekeeper was already waiting for them, sitting on the front porch. As Rick approached her, she held out a hand with a good grip and a smile that said she was ready to work.

"Hello, Mr. Benedict. I'm Diana Kreutz, hopefully your new housekeeper."

"Well, hello there," said Rick. "I'm sorry I'm late. We had to wait for the Sheriff to pick up an individual."

"It's no problem," said Diana. "I saw the Sheriff tearing down the road and was curious why the hurry."

"Just a little problem I had to take care of," said Rick.

Diana was dressed in modest western clothes and carrying a small bag. She was about five foot six and looked like she'd been around kitchens for a while.

Rick introduced Liz and Fred and asked her to come in and sit down.

"I have been in this country for over forty years. I originally came from Croatia with my parents when I was very young. I'm now an American citizen and have worked in several four-star hotels as a chef's apprentice. I can cook almost anything, from the very simple to the more exotic, but my specialty is European cuisine. My husband died several years ago; my children are all grown up and living their lives. Now I think it is my turn to do what I like."

Rick tried not to show much excitement, but after a brief exchange of her responsibilities, his eyes lit up.

"You got the job," said Rick. "And when can you start?"

"I could start tomorrow morning," she said. "I'll be here at the crack of dawn. And if you don't mind, I would like to see my room. Later on this afternoon, I'll move some of my personal things in."

"Terrific," Rick said. "Your room is on this floor in the back, and it's called the *Alder* room."

They walked back to her room, and Diana was surprised how spacious it was.

"That looks great," Diana said. "And thank you so much. You won't be disappointed."

Diana left by the front door, got in her car, and drove back to her apartment, thinking that this time maybe she had found a new home. She would bring all her cookbooks and have a breakfast surprise for Rick and his company in the morning. She would have to send Walter a thank you note for his help in getting this job. Walter knew her husband, Helmut Kreutz, and tried to help them.

"Keep this between us," Walter said. "It isn't necessary to let Rick know, because I don't want him to think I'm meddling in his affairs too much. I'll tell him sometime later."

Diana grew up in Croatia and Germany. She had been a secretary for a large ironworks firm and was doing quite well until World War II broke out. Everyone was scrambling and doing almost anything to feed the family. Like so many other young women in those days, she went to work at Messerschmitt Aircraft as a factory worker assembling the ME 262 airplanes used in World War II. At the time, she and her husband were caught hiding from the Nazis and were both taken to Sachsenhausen Concentration Camp.

Helmut, because of his printing background, went to work with Adolf Berger, the master art counterfeiter. They could see that Diana had office skills and promptly sent her to work in the offices of the camp. She wasn't able to see her husband Helmut for several years. Luckily, they found each other after the Russians came to liberate the camp and all were set free.

CHAPTER

40

As soon as Diana left, Rick asked Aki to go with him to see the ranch hands and introduce him as an expert in developing the finest beef for their restaurants. They headed to the bunkhouse, with Aki's saddle in the back of the truck.

Rick opened the ranch house door and said, "Could I have your attention for a moment? Get up close, all of you, in the center of the room."

The ranch house looked like one very large house. When you entered, you were actually in an immense foyer, with various deer antlers on the wall. From the foyer, you could walk into any of the twenty-five suites assigned to the ranch hands. Each room had a bedroom and bathroom, plus a closet for their work clothes and boots.

"You're probably wondering what's going on," said Rick. "The short version is that Grant is in jail. He and Billy tried to kill my friend and burned quite a few records I was reviewing to try to figure out how this ranch was operating financially. I don't suspect he'll be out visiting you very soon. I told you before about my two-bucket concept. You've all had time to think about it. I want to know right now, which bucket does each of you want to be part of? You have three minutes to decide, and if you lie to me and I find out, I'll fire you on the spot. I'm in no mood to play games."

Shyly, one wrangler shouted out, "Before you came back, we talked among ourselves and want you to know we're all on your team – We just want to make sure we know what the playing field is. Some of us have been on this ranch for over fifteen years and have seen four different owners. Most had no idea about the ranch, and they thought for the most part, this was just a cowboy movie back lot."

Rick smiled and said, "I understand. As you've seen within this last week, I'm a no nonsense guy, and I've a goal which hasn't changed from what I told you at the barbeque.

"I want to introduce Aki Watanabe, who is from Japan and an expert breeder of Kobe cattle. He's going to help us figure out how we can make these cattle healthier and create a much higher quality of beef for our planned restaurants. I'll interview you later today and designate a new ranch foreman. So if any of you are interested, let me know and we'll talk later. Aki is not the ranch foreman and, temporarily, I assume that role. I think most of you know what your jobs are, so let's get to it. Are there any questions?"

Nobody said anything.

"Can someone get Aki a horse," Rick asked, "and show him where the cattle are grazing, how we currently manage, what we feed them, and so on?"

The ranch hands still seemed apprehensive, but one offered to show Aki around.

Rick turned to Aki and said, "It's all in your hands. If you have any problems, call me. Something tells me, though, that you're going to be okay. See you later," and he left.

Rick got back in his truck and drove back to the main house.

"Well, I introduced Aki to the ranch hands," said Rick. "I could see they were a little nervous, but I think it'll be all right. How are you doing, Fred?"

"I'm still feeling slightly woozy with all the excitement," said Fred. "So if you don't mind, I'm going to lay down for nap."

"Okay," said Rick. "We'll look in on you in a little while."

Rick took Liz into the living room, and they sat by the large fire roaring in the immense river rock fireplace. Rick brought out a bottle of his favorite *Sauvignon Blanc* wine and two glasses.

As they sat there, Rick turned to her and asked, "Have you figured out how Steve is going to fit in being your yacht captain and bodyguard? This assumes that we have a life together, of some sorts. Steve's a good guy and I like him a lot."

Liz shrugged and said casually, "I now realize that we never should have tried to get together, and that's why I'm here. I'm not trying to restart our relationship, because I still have personal issues to clear up."

"You know you can spend as much time as you want here at the ranch," Rick said.

"Thanks," Liz said. "But I'm thinking I might want to spend some more time with my mother and try to do some more catching up. But for the moment, I just want to do nothing."

Rick nodded that he understood and said, "Again, stay here as long as you want. But if I know Steve, he's probably lurking about somewhere around here. After all, he is still your bodyguard."

Rick filled her glass with wine and they toasted to better days. They continued to sit and stare into the fire not saying much to each other, and soon Liz, leaning against Rick, dozed off.

Rick was a little disappointed about Liz, so he stayed focused on other things, like trying to figure out why the dead cattle only appeared in one area of the ranch.

He gently laid Liz on the couch, and went into his office. He wanted to look at the personnel files of all the employees working at the ranch. He started with Grant Williams to check out what kind of credentials he had. It appeared that he had no history before 1965. It was now after eleven at night and exhaustion finally set in. He stopped and finally gave in to being tired. He quietly walked over to Liz, tried to wake her, and met with little success. He picked her up and carried her upstairs into his bedroom.

He took off her boots but left her clothes on and just covered her up with a blanket. Before he lay down, he also checked the windows, locked the bedroom door, and parked the back of the chair under the door handle to make sure they weren't disturbed.

CHAPTER

41

The next morning when Rick woke up, he noticed that Liz wasn't in bed but heard the shower was going. He coyly wondered if she needed any help and knocked on the door.

"I was wondering when you were going to wake up," Liz said. "I made so much noise in the room and couldn't wake you, so I finally hopped into the shower.... alone. Would you care to join me? I can't remember when I've had a good back scrubbing."

Rick didn't have to be asked twice. He pulled off his clothes and just before he was going to join her, he heard noises from downstairs. He quickly pulled on his jeans, grabbed his gun, and crept downstairs. He heard more noises from the kitchen. As he quietly approached the door to the kitchen, it suddenly flew open, and there was Diana, carrying two hot pies and placing them on the table.

She looked at him startled because of the gun in his hand and quickly said, "Remember, you said I could start today. You gave me a key and everything. I was going to try to move in last night, but it got to be too late. I'll get settled in after I make breakfast for you and your guests."

Rick was embarrassed, because he looked like a wild man with no shirt on, barefoot, and carrying a gun. In his haste last night, he had forgotten about Diana.

"I'm so sorry," he quickly said. "With all the problems we've had here lately, I guess I got a little jumpy."

She smiled and said, "That's okay. And as soon as you all come down, I'll make you my specialty, spiegel eyer, or in English, mirrored eggs. Somehow it gets a little lost in the translation."

That was when Rick noticed that Diana had a slight accent and wondered if Walter had been helping. He tried to tell himself that Walter wouldn't be bothered with these mundane things. But then again, you just had to wonder. He hadn't talked to Walter in about three days, and bringing him up-to-date with the ranch might be a good lead-in to ask about Diana.

"I'll be right back," Rick said, and ran back upstairs to finish getting dressed.

By that time, Liz was already out of the shower, drying herself off, and looking miffed that he ran off.

"I heard a noise in the kitchen," Rick explained. "It was just Diana making pies and getting ready to make us breakfast."

"You're a little jumpy, aren't you?" she asked. "Because what man in his right mind would give up an opportunity to take a shower with me? However, you'll have another chance to redeem yourself."

Rick winked, finished dressing, went over to Fred's room, and knocked on the door. Fred opened the door shaved, showered, and looking like he was ready to go to a rodeo. Actually, he looked so dressed up that he could pass as a square dance partner.

Rick smiled slightly.

"What's wrong?" asked Fred. "Don't you like my outfit ...... and I almost forgot my hat. I want to blend in and not look like a tourist."

Rick had to laugh and said, "You'll definitely blend in. You look like one of the *Sons of the Pioneers* singing group from the fifties. Now don't get me wrong. They were a great group."

Fred looked at himself in the mirror and said, "So what do I do? You told me to get these clothes, and now you say I don't fit in?"

"I thought it was Dale Honeycutt that dressed you," Rick reminded him, "and I was just waiting at the counter for you. Come on downstairs, and we'll get Diana to wash and dry your clothes while we eat breakfast."

Fred liked that idea and quickly changed and brought all of his new clothes downstairs.

As Fred came downstairs, Diana saw him and laughed slightly because she already knew what she had to do.

"Give that to me," said Diana. "I'll make your clothes look like new but used at the same time. Go sit down and I'll bring you some breakfast."

As they sat down, they noticed a small menu sitting on each plate. Everyone looked at each other, amazed that each could order different things.

Diana said, "This is something I started sometime back with the last family. They seemed to like it."

Rick said, "You typed this out and made copies all this morning?"

"Yes," she said. "You see, I was also a very efficient secretary in my other life, and while I'm not a computer wizard, I can get by."

They each ordered different things and Rick thought to himself, *This is incredible and all without asking.*

Just then the phone rang. It was the Sheriff.

With a long sigh, he said, "I'm sorry to have to tell you this, but we had to let Grant go late last night because he posted his bail. As soon as we got to the hospital, Grant had already called Judge Thornton."

"I haven't even been in to file formal charges yet!" Rick yelled. "And what happened that he was going to be in the hospital overnight and then transferred to your jail the next day?"

"It wasn't me," said the Sheriff. "It was Judge Thornton who decided this. We had no choice but to let him go."

Now Rick was concerned. "And I'm sure that by now he's long gone. What's going on here? Every time I turn around there are strange things occurring, and now the Judge. I guess this means I can't even trust the legal system." Rick slammed the phone down.

Rick turned to the group and said sarcastically, "The Sheriff had to let Grant go, by order of the Judge, because he posted bail."

"You've got yourself a real hornet's nest going on here," Fred said.

"I hate to bring this up," Liz said, "but when Walter bought the business and this ranch was one of the hidden assets, I'm surprised he wasn't aware of some of these things. Or the other possibility is that if he did know, then he's hoping you can straighten it out."

"It appears that almost all of this started just after he bought the company," Rick said. "They may have been planning all of this for years, and maybe even the previous owner didn't know what was going on. But it's now my problem, and I'm going to get to the bottom of this and fix it once and for all."

Suddenly Rick realized he still had the *mobile phone tracker device* with Grant's mobile phone number. He could find out exactly where he was and track his movements. Rick finished eating his breakfast and went back to his office.

CHAPTER

42

Rick was sitting in his office gazing out of the window and thinking about all the events at the ranch. He had to resolve it and figure out what Grant meant when he said, *and this is bigger than both of us.*

"Fred," Rick asked, "how soon do you think you could be finished with your analysis of the books? When you're finished, we should send a copy to Walter and Leonard, so they can see what's been going on here."

"I should be finished in a couple of hours," answered Fred.

"Liz, how about you and I take a ride into town?" Rick asked. "I think you need some more new western clothes."

Diana was listening, and said, "I'm sorry to interrupt, but I couldn't help but overhear your problems. Maybe I can be of some help. I've lived in Fort Collins for about fifteen years and have seen many things going on in this town. About five years ago, a very big chemical company came into town, and they set up a special dinner at the Wagon Wheel Restaurant, where I happened to be the chef at the time."

Rick thought that interesting, because that meant that whatever they were planning, it had been in the planning stage for at least five years.

"One of the dinner hosts," Diana said, "was Grant Williams, your ranch foreman. The other was Dale Honeycutt, who manages Peabody's Mercantile. It turns out they're brother and sister by different marriages, and her great-grandfather was Harry 'Billy' Jackson, the miner who struck it rich but never filed a claim."

Rick heard Diana's story and then wondered again if she had been sent to spy on him. On the other hand, was she just a genuine individual who just had interesting and useful information?

"Thanks for breakfast, Diana. It was great," Rick said, and left. "Are you ready, Liz?"

They got into the truck and didn't say anything until they were well outside of earshot.

"You left in an awfully big hurry," Liz said. "You might have hurt her feelings. She gave you some information that may just possibly help you figure out what's going on, and you didn't even say thank you!"

Rick turned to her and said, "Ever since I came to this ranch, it has been nothing but trouble. Walter thought he was doing me a favor, but it seems like I'm in just another situation like Prague last year. But I'm in it now and I'll fix it. I just have to be careful whom I go to for advice. And I was hoping we would have more time together to sort things out between us, but that's just going to have to wait for now."

"If you think I'm getting in the way," Liz pouted and said, "just tell me. Otherwise let me help you solve this."

He turned back to her and knew he'd hurt her feelings and regretted doing it, but right now he had too much on his mind. He was hoping that Steve was around, because he could really use someone he could trust. He thought about having Liz call him, but knew this might be getting too close to Liz and her problem.

Rick pulled up to the Peabody Mercantile, went in and asked for Dale Honeycutt. "She's out for a few days' vacation," said the salesperson.

Rick didn't look surprised. "Thanks," he said, and left.

As they left the store, Rick said, "No surprise there."

Rick started driving out of town to the mine. This time he brought flashlights and his gun. He also turned the mobile phone tracker on to find out where Grant was.

"I got a reading that says he's about ten miles north of the property," Rick said.

Liz just sat there on the other side of the truck with her arms crossed.

After a few minutes, he reached across and gently pulled her closer to him and said, "I'm sorry if I've hurt your feelings, but please try to understand. I'm glad you called and came out to the ranch, and I promise to make it up to you when this is all over."

She looked over, tried to smile a little, and whispered, "Okay."

As they were driving, they periodically looked at each other, and Rick remembered that Liz could take care of herself in the clinches and was hoping she never had to prove it again. As they got closer to the mine, they pulled off the road and drove through the forest very slowly so as not to attract attention. When he thought he was close enough, he turned off the engine and sat there listening, but only heard crickets and birds chirping in the breeze.

He again looked at the mobile phone GPS tracker, and it showed Grant still about six miles north from where they stood.

"I wonder what he's doing way over there," said Rick. "We'll take a ride over there a little later."

They got out, and Rick came to the passenger side of the truck, opened the door, and said, "I'm sorry. You're the one person in the world that I don't want to offend."

He looked at her, grabbed her, and kissed her squarely on the lips. She responded and seemed glad he finally did kiss her. It was a long, deep kiss. Their lips parted, and she had a wicked smile on her lips. "Thanks, I needed that," she whispered.

"You're welcome," Rick said with a smile.

They both picked up their flashlights, and Rick double-checked to see that his gun was loaded with a full clip.

Liz suddenly pulled out a Colt snub-nosed .38 revolver and said, "Last time you didn't think I needed to carry one, so I brought my own."

Rick cocked his head to the side. "Okay, let's go," he said.

As they walked through the forest into the clearing, he noticed that nobody was in sight and that made him nervous, especially with Grant Williams on the loose. They climbed up a small hill so they could get a better view of the entire area. Still nobody was around.

They climbed down the slope closer to the mine opening. This time more brush had been used to hide the entrance. They crept closer and listened for any machinery noise or anybody talking, but heard nothing. They removed some of the brush and found that the entrance to the mine now had a chain-link gate, with a massive chain and a padlock holding the doors together.

Rick smiled to Liz and pulled out a small case to pick the lock, since bolt cutters weren't available. He pulled two slim. crooked looking pieces of wire, and said, "Watch this."

Within seconds, the lock clicked open.

"Now where did you learn to do that?" Liz asked.

"My good friend John Lawton from Rhode Island," Rick said, "is a private investigator. He gave these to me as a present a long time ago. and I finally got to try them out."

He carefully laid the chain with the lock down on the ground and went into the cave-like structure. They only had to walk about twenty feet when he again saw the massive electrical junction box that probably controlled the entire lighting system. They decided not to turn it on but continued down the pathway using their flashlights.

"We need to be careful," Rick said. "I'm concerned he may have some of his goons scattered throughout the mine shaft."

After another ten minutes, the pathway opened up into a much larger cave that must have been at least thirty feet tall. They looked around and saw pipes of some type hugging the wall opposite them.

"These pipes are still warm," Liz said, "like it was used recently, but for what?" Looking further, they noticed another tunnel going away from them, but the pathway looked like newer walls of the tunnel.

As they walked through the tunnel, they heard in the distance people speaking in a foreign language.

"That sounds like Italian," Liz said, "but I can't hear clearly enough."

"Let's walk a little further," said Rick.

They turned off their flashlights, because it was getting lighter. Rick could now make out the voice of Grant Williams, but he wasn't speaking English. He thought that odd since the tracking device showed Grant still miles away.

CHAPTER
43

Fred continued his forensic analysis and discovered more discrepancies. It appeared that the ranch was generating an income and making a profit, but there were no bills of sale indicating that they ever sold anything. But money continued coming into the Monarch Ranch account through an account in the Cayman Islands. This, it seems, is how the ranch hands received their salaries ... for doing very little.

"I wonder how long this has been going on," Fred said to himself.

As he backtracked, he found that this whole deception started almost five years ago with the original owner of the ranch. It seemed unlikely that he would have just given this ranch up when Walter bought the company. Something was off and Fred was going to find it.

He discovered that heavy-duty mining equipment was shipped from Japan about five years ago. Shortly after, the previous owner bought the ranch. As he looked at the original title search, he noticed that at the time, there were no buildings on the land.

All the buildings except the main house had been built within the last four years. As he went back even further to locate previous owners, he finally found the link. The original deed to the ranch was to Harry "Billy" Jackson, the miner who discovered the gold mine.

As Fred was weaving through the maze of shell companies, he was able to find the origin of the money deposited to the Cayman Islands. It came from the IL Fornai Bank of Italy located in Florence.

He found this most interesting because when he was in the Army attached to division headquarters in Wurzburg, Germany, there was a lot of speculation that several high-ranking Army personnel, and even in some cases generals, had retired in Italy after World War II. They did well selling U.S. Government surplus items on the black market. But Fred had decided to stop the investigation because he was starting to receive death threats. It was all right with him, especially since he only had four weeks to go before he got out of the Army. He always wondered what happened to all the information he collected.

He knew that he was getting into some very sophisticated encrypted databases, but at the same time, he was intrigued that it was so easy to break through their firewall. As he was looking at some bank accounts, suddenly he noticed a red, pulsating dot in the lower right-hand corner of the PC screen. At first he didn't know what to make of it, but as he looked closer, it started to turn a blue color.

He quickly turned off his laptop and yelled out, "Oh, no, this can't be happening to me!"

Diana turned to him and asked, "What's wrong?"

"I think that I've been found out," Fred answered.

"What do you mean?" she asked.

Fred sat down, with his head in his hands, and said, "I was looking at some bank statements at the IL Fornai Bank of Italy, and I think they know I breached their encrypted firewall. I saw this type of recovery before, where the company seems to allow you to get into their master data files, which turn out to be only junk files, so they can track whoever tried to breach their firewall. When the red, pulsating dot turns completely blue, then that means they have my IP address and can find out where I am. I think I was able to turn my computer off in time, but I'm not sure. In any event, if this is what I think it is, then the State Department will be here to haul us, or rather me, off to jail very quickly."

At the IL Fornai Bank of Italy, a call went out to the bank president informing him of what they found out. Fortunately for Fred, the bank didn't want to do anything about it because they happened to have their own irregularities and the last thing they wanted was to cause an international scandal that would surely require an investigation and audit by the highest courts in Italy.

CHAPTER

44

Rick and Liz carefully walked through the tunnel and hid behind some large crates. Rick noticed that the crates looked too new to belong in this old mine. He found a label that said *Kyoto Mining Company*, which had Japanese symbols stenciled on the side of the crates. When he got back to the ranch, he'd have Fred find out who they were.

Liz was still listening to the conversation. "I can hear them better now," she said whispering. "It's Italian. They're saying they have at least another thirty days to dig and then would have to give up this madness."

"I wonder what they mean by *this madness*," Rick said.

They crouched down a little further, and she heard them say: "Are you sure that we'll be able to continue without any more interference from this Rick Benedict?" said Howard. "So far he's cast a dark shadow on this project, and I've already spent millions, with little to show for it."

"Don't worry, Howard," said Grant. "They'll be dealt with."

"I wonder how the Judge is connected to this," Rick whispered.

"We'll be all right," said Grant. "We had to stop using dynamite for a while because the Air Force Space Command's military base records all seismic tremors, which are monitored

185

twenty-four hours a day, three hundred sixty-five days a year. Had it not been for Judge Thornton's relationship with General Alexander, we would have been hard-pressed to keep going. Look, Howard, we all have a big stake in finding the gold, but we have to have some patience."

"Gold!" shrieked Liz in a loud whisper.

Rick turned to Liz and said, "Yep, gold. Evidently, this must be the Pawnee Indian mine and they hadn't mined all the gold when they left."

Howard looked at Grant. "Sometimes I almost wish I never got involved with this. I know of at least ten federal and state laws that have been broken by bringing cyanide into an area that has underground-protected water rights for Colorado and for most of the Western States."

"A new player named Howard," Rick said. "I wonder if this is the same guy that wanted a copy of the Monarch Ranch property boundaries. I hadn't heard that name before. Wonder why Grant is speaking in Italian to the other three people?"

"If you remember, Grant," Howard said, "I was all set to buy the Monarch Ranch for myself, but the previous owner had to sell it as one of the assets of his main business. After all the gold was mined, I would have developed this into a dude ranch for the wealthy and possibly as a sport hunting ranch."

One of the other observers with a thick European accent said, "Look, we will have to call Signore Bustiani in Florence and give him an update. After all, he has supplied almost all of the funding for this project and we owe him that."

Grant gave an exasperated sigh. "Don't you think I know that? I know I have to deliver and soon. My bigger concern is that Bustiani is connected with the Las Vegas syndicate, and if we miss our mark, we could all be sharing space with the desert cactuses."

Grant recalled when he talked to Salvatore Bustiani. He made one trip to the ranch before Walter purchased the company.

"This is Bill Hollander," said Bustiani, "an assayer I had flown in from New York to confirm for myself the gold content."

They met at the ranch and drove out to the mine and, after several tests, confirmed that the mine could yield millions in gold.

"This is great news," said Grant, "but in order to mine the gold, I'll need some money to buy equipment, men, trucks, and a couple of skip loaders."

"We'll set up an account," Bustiani said, "that you can draw from at a bank in the Cayman Islands. I would also like Bill Hollander to periodically perform tests to satisfy myself that we're still on track."

Rick thought this is an interesting turn of events and made a mental note to call Anton Mansard, his friend in Florence, to ask if he knew anything about this person. He told Liz to walk slowly back out of the tunnel. But as she backed away, Liz accidentally knocked over an old miner's kerosene lamp that fell from the crate and hit the ground. What made it worse was the tunnel amplified the sound and that others heard it.

"What's that noise?" asked Howard. "I thought you said nobody was working that end of the mine anymore."

"There shouldn't be anybody in that end of the mine," said Grant. "Stay here. I'll go see who or what it is."

Rick told Liz to start running as fast as she could. Unfortunately, Grant and his men also heard the running. They hurriedly got out. Rick quickly put the chain and padlocks back on the door. Then they ran around the corner and climbed up the hill, out of sight from anybody. They stayed hidden from view for about ten minutes to make sure nobody came out. After some time, they climbed down the hill, ran to his truck, and headed back to the ranch.

Grant glanced through the chain-link fencing, but didn't see anybody. He guessed it was probably Rick.

He smiled and said, "It's a good thing I left my mobile phone at the smelter, so now they can't track me."

Grant walked back to where Howard and the others were still talking.

CHAPTER

45

"I'm going to call Anton in Florence," Rick said, "and ask him if he knows this man named Bustiani. So let's get back to the ranch. I also want to see if Fred found out anything else."

"You know, I still don't understand why they need foreign money to dig out the gold in the hills," Liz said. "You heard that this guy has ties to the Vegas syndicate," Rick said. "It just might be possible that Grant is a major gambler with big losses, and just short of them breaking his legs, he came up with this story about a lost gold mine that I think is on my property. But that's just a WAG."

"What's a WAG," Liz asked quizzically?

"It's a wild-ass-guess," said Rick smiling.

As they drove back to the ranch, Rick was now concerned about the Judge who released Grant.

"Now I know why the Judge let Grant go free," said Rick, "because he also has a stake in this venture. Then there's a General Alexander involved as part of this venture. This whole thing has some major players from both sides of the Atlantic. I'll get Fred to find out about the General and his relationship with the Judge. He can do some research on him and find out how he's connected to all of this."

189

As they were riding in the truck, Liz inched closer and wrapped her arm in his. "I've never ridden in a truck before, and now I know why."

"There are probably a lot of things you haven't experienced," Rick smiled and said, "and this is as good a place as any to experience them."

As they drove up the long driveway, they saw the Sheriff's car in the front of the house.

As Rick got out of the truck, the Sheriff approached him.

"For what it's worth," the Sheriff said, "Judge Thornton passed away early this morning. What's strange is that he was as fit as a fiddle, exercised, and watched what he ate. The coroner can't figure it out."

"I'm going to let you in a little secret, Sheriff," Rick said. "I think someone felt he outlived his usefulness."

The Sheriff looked up with a blank expression on his face, but continued. "For a long time, he was a good and a well-respected Judge. But in the last four to five years, he changed, and we don't know why. Maybe it had something to do with his wife passing. Oh, well, I've gotta get going and catch some bad guys."

"Thanks for the info," Rick said. "But think about what I said." He turned and walked up the steps.

"I really do think they felt he outlived his usefulness and was eliminated," Rick said to Liz. "He did his part and now had become a liability. But that may also mean that they're very close to finishing at the mine and might disappear before long."

They walked into the house, went directly to where Fred was working, and saw he had printed out reams of various forms and charts.

"What have you been doing here?" Rick asked, as he grabbed a cup of coffee from the sideboard.

Fred spent the next half-hour bringing them up-to-date on what he had found.

"By the way," said Fred, "I could go to jail for a very long time if these people at the IL Fornai Bank of Italy ever found out I hacked into their confidential mainframe computer. But I think I covered my tracks well, so I may be okay.

"It looks like the Monarch Ranch has been receiving funds from the Bank of Largo in the Cayman Islands. I then tracked that back to the IL Fornai Bank of Italy in Florence, Italy. That company is a shell company, and one of the companies listed is the Greenland Empire Corporation. Do you know who the CEO of that company is?"

"Never heard of it," said Rick, shrugging his shoulders.

"It's none other than Luigi Gennaro," said Fred, "who is reputed to be the head of the Bacilli crime family in Las Vegas."

"You've got to be kidding," said Rick. "That does explain the connection between Las Vegas and this other guy, Bustiani, in Florence, Italy. With that kind of muscle, maybe it isn't that Grant is a bad gambler, but a great gambler. I'll bet the buy-in must be the gold, and I'm betting it's in the millions."

"Well, that also explains a lot about what we just saw in the mine," Liz said, "although the use of cyanide still has me puzzled."

Fred just couldn't sit still he was so excited. He danced around the desk and finally settled down.

As they went to Rick's computer, they found some information on gold mining specifically related to using cyanide.

Cyanide is used to extract gold and may be used in areas where fine-gold bearing rocks are found. Sodium cyanide solution mixed with finely ground rock, proven to contain gold and/or silver, is then separated from the ground rock as gold cyanide and/or silver cyanide solution. Zinc is added to the solution, precipitating out residual zinc, as well as the desirable silver and gold metals. Once the zinc is removed with sulfuric acid, it leaves a silver or gold sludge that is generally smelted into an ingot, then shipped to a metals refinery for final processing into 99.9999% pure metals.

As they read about the gold mining process, they were both thinking about what they heard in the mine.

"It stands to reason," Rick said, "that they must be using huge quantities of water to chip out the large rock and cyanide, and whatever washes out ends up in the ground. It works its way underground into the water table, and that's why they found dead cattle towards the north side of the property. The cattle were drinking from the small river, which is downhill."

"Unfortunately, he now has a bigger problem," Rick said, "because I'm in his way, and he can't have anyone meddling in his venture, especially since he's so close to being completed."

As Grant walked back to the center of the mine, he made up his mind to eliminate Howard.

"Phil, come on over to the mine," Grant said, on his other mobile phone. "I've got a job for you."

"What kind of problem do you have?" Phil asked.

"See that guy over there?" Grant said. "His name is Howard, and he'll be driving to the airport soon. I want his brakes to give out. I figure that once he starts driving down the hill with very little brake fluid in the system, it should be easy for him to tumble over the cliff and into the ravine."

"I'll take care of it," said Phil.

As Phil left, Grant thought to himself, *I really have to thank my father for insisting I join the German Army, because I got some great training over there.*

CHAPTER
46

Rick wondered how many people were involved in this venture with Grant. There appeared to be several high-level individuals connected to this. It had to be more than just the gold. It didn't sound as though they had found much, with everyone so worried about the investors.

He called Anton in Florence, and even though it was late, he was sure he would be up.

"Hello, Anton. Sorry to be calling you so early, it's Rick Benedict. How are you?"

"Hello, Rick," said Anton, surprised by the call so early in the morning. "I am fine. What can I do for you?"

"I've a question for you." Rick said, "Have you ever heard of a Salvatore Bustiani from Florence?"

There was long pause from Anton.

"He's a very powerful man throughout all of Italy," Anton gulped as he answered. "Some even think he is part of the Italian mafia, but it has never been proven."

"Can you get me any information you have on him?" Rick asked. "And would you please fax it to me ASAP." Rick gave him the fax number to the house. "I need this in a hurry because of some problems I'm having on my ranch in Colorado."

Anton said, "I'll see what I can find out for you," and hung up his telephone.

The name Bustiani made Anton shiver because he knew immediately who he was. He was nervous and rattled by the request. Anton's quiet inner sanctum was just kicked in the stomach. He sat there for a moment, trying to see if he should even get involved. Bustiani seemed to have eyes and ears everywhere, and if Anton asked questions about him to the wrong person, he could end up as fish bait for the fishermen. He decided to call Walter for some advice. As he was dialing, he wondered how he was going to approach him about this delicate matter.

When Walter answered the phone, Anton tried to sound as charming as possible. "Hello, Walter. How are you?"

Anton made small talk so he could build up his nerve.

"Walter, I just received a phone call from Rick asking about Salvatore Bustiani. He seems to be somehow involved in Rick's ranch."

Before he could finish, Walter interrupted him and said, "I'm aware and have been for quite some time about the connections he has with organized crime, but send Rick whatever information he needs. In fact, contact our old friend Marcello Trieste. He should be able to help you with any information you need."

"Thanks for the help, Walter," said Anton.

"Anton, thank you for calling me about this," Walter said and hung up.

Anton was surprised that Walter talked so casually about Salvatore Bustiani, and with no real concern. Anton now knew who to call for information on one of the most feared men in Italy. Anton called Marcello Trieste.

Marcello answered. "Hello, Anton. It is so good to hear from you."

"Would it be all right if we could meet?" Anton asked. "It is of the utmost importance and a very delicate matter."

"Of course. Would you like to come by my house this afternoon," Marcello asked, "and we can have a late lunch if you like. See you around two o'clock?"

"That would be fine," said Anton. "See you then." He hung up the phone.

Anton couldn't rest anymore that day in anticipation of meeting with Marcello.

He left his house in the morning, not knowing if he'd be back. The long drive to Marcello's villa allowed him to think about all of this and what he was going to say. He arrived at Marcello's villa and drove through the guarded gate on a long, straight road to the house, passing through rows of magnificent, mature Cypress trees, which were probably hundreds of years old. They seemed to reach for the sky on both sides of the rough gravel road. The road ended in the center plaza with a beautiful water fountain surrounded by vibrant red and yellow roses. The three-story Italian villa was sitting on a hill with the blue sky and ocean as a backdrop.

Marcello Trieste casually walked down the front steps of his villa to greet him.

"Good afternoon, Signore Trieste," said Anton. "It is good of you to see me on such short notice."

"You are always welcome here," said Marcello. "What is this delicate matter you spoke of?"

Marcello Trieste, a very distinguished man, was dressed casually and appeared to be in his sixties. He had a beautiful wife named Angela and three grown boys. Walter met Marcello during the war in the concentration camp. When the camp was liberated, Walter talked to the Russian Colonel to give them all some money and papers that would get them back home.

Anton noticed that he already had lunch waiting as they entered the courtyard. Anton was nervous about asking for information from Marcello because of his own known ties to organized crime.

Marcello's wife Angela brought out a large bowl of langoustine shrimp, with angel hair pasta, fresh bread with olive oil, and coffee.

As they ate, Anton finally got up the nerve and said, "Signore Trieste, Rick Benedict asked me to get him some information about a Signore Salvatore Bustiani."

Marcello's fork stopped in midair when he heard the name. He put his fork down and told his guards to get out of the courtyard.

After they were sufficiently out of hearing range, Marcello said, with a very concerned look on his face, "Do you know what you're asking?"

"Yes, I do," Anton said, "but I would only ask you because Rick Benedict asked me as a favor."

Marcello rubbed his stubble chin, thought for a minute, and said, "Okay, I'll have something for you."

He called out to his oldest son, Roberto, "Come over here. I have a job for you."

He whispered in his ear, and Roberto was off like a shot.

Marcello, now smiling, said, "Now we can eat and enjoy this meal."

From then on, it was only strained small talk. Anton was still wondering if he had made a mistake, but it was too late to back out.

Anton smiled and started to eat. "I again marvel at how wonderful a cook your wife is. I wish I had someone to cook for me this way."

Marcello smiled. He appreciated the compliment because he could see it was sincere. They ate, drank, and talked about the old days, and before long it was getting dark.

As he sat back in his chair, Anton savored the very last morsel of the sauce with the freshly baked crust bread.

"Enough. I cannot eat anymore," Anton finally said. "This was, again, the most delicious meal I've had in a very long time."

"Please," said Marcello, "have one of my special Cuban cigars, which is one of the last and only pleasures I still indulge in."

Just then his son Roberto came up to him and gave his father, Marcello, several sheets of paper.

He read them and said with a creased brow, "This is the information you requested. I must insist you never tell anyone who you received this from."

Anton was astonished that he received this information so quickly. "You have my word that no one will ever know. I'll tell Walter how helpful you were in this delicate matter," and got up to leave.

"I want to thank you," Anton said, "and your lovely wife, Angela, for your hospitality and wonderful meal."

"You are always welcome at my house," said Marcello.

They shook hands, and Anton walked to his car and drove off.

As Anton drove off, Marcello was looking at Anton's car. He liked it very much and vowed that he would own a car like that one day.

Marcello was curious why Anton wanted this information. He decided to let it go, but not before he told his other son, Angelo, to keep an eye on Anton and to make sure he got home safely. Marcello thought that *opportunities present themselves in extraordinary ways.* He went into his study, sat back, and enjoyed another one of his special cigars. He thought more about Salvatore Bustiani and wondered why people feared him so much.

All the time Anton was driving home, Anton felt as though he were being followed. Maybe it wasn't such a good idea to ask for information from Marcello. But Walter had suggested it, so it must have been all right. It had been years since he was put into a situation like this. He wasn't sure his heart could take this much excitement.

As soon as he entered his house, he locked the door and started to read the two pages he had received from Marcello. Other than what he read in the newspapers, much of it seemed to be the normal information, except an article concerning Bustiani on the subject of a Las Vegas casino he was trying to buy. Since no foreigners could buy a gaming casino license anywhere in the United States, Grant Williams, a U.S. citizen, would manage the casino. Anton knew that the Nevada Gaming Commission would never allow the casino to open if there was any evidence to connect it to organized crime.

It also said that Bustiani had an illegitimate son by one of the caretakers' daughters from his villa. The woman was Katrina Petrofina. He read it again and quickly faxed the information to the number Rick gave him at his ranch.

CHAPTER

47

Rick had a restless night thinking about his problems at the ranch. He woke up early the next morning, walked downstairs into his office, and found the fax that Anton had sent. He told himself that he must call and thank him, but before he could finish, his mouth fell open. He saw Grant's name as the new potential owner or front man for a casino in Las Vegas. Rick almost fell down as he read it.

"Well, that explains quite a few things," said Rick aloud.

The gold that Grant had been mining was going to be a down payment for Bustiani. The connected people in Las Vegas would then allow Grant to become president and manage the casino. But based on what he'd heard yesterday at the mine, it didn't appear that they had gotten much gold out yet.

Just then Liz and Fred came downstairs and Rick shared what he'd just read.

"That makes a lot of sense," Fred said. "Now we know where the trail is going. Last night I couldn't sleep, so I looked a little closer at those Cayman Island accounts. It seems that Grant is actually skimming some of the money off the top when he gets money from Bustiani. He may not have found as much gold as he may be claiming, but he's trying to keep the charade going as long as possible."

"Maybe Grant sold the same gold mine story to several people," Liz said. "I bet if we looked hard enough, we could find that the Judge may have also put money into this venture. Plus he had judicial power to make sure his investment was safe. That also explains why he let Grant go before you were able to press charges."

"Something else has been bothering me," said Fred. "Yesterday I was looking through the title map and noticed that we are around seventy-five miles from the Air Force Space Command's 90th Space Wing Operation. If they were doing any type of blasting in the area, I'd think it would register with the military, since they keep real close track of any seismic activity. That tells me we may just have a military man also involved who has the authority to squash any sort of investigation."

"Maybe Grant is related to Bustiani," said Liz. "If Grant is connected to Bustiani, who is in Italy, he may have those same connections to the Las Vegas casino they want to buy into."

"According to the fax," Rick finally said, smugly, "Grant is the illegitimate son of Salvatore Bustiani."

Rick sat back in his chair and started to connect the pieces of the puzzle. He hadn't given Grant enough credit. He had really underestimated him.

"See what you can find out about Grant Williams in a lot more detail," Rick told Fred. "There must be more to him than what we're seeing, like why would Bustiani trust Grant to manage a casino? There might be another connection."

"That means that Grant is actually Italian," said Liz. "My experience is that these guys don't bring outsiders in, only their blood."

CHAPTER
48

Later on when Fred was in the office printing out information about Grant, he suddenly shouted out to Rick and Liz, "You have got to see this! You think that Grant was just a ranch foreman and punching cattle for a living. He is actually August Adolpho Petrofina. He went to some of the best schools in Europe. It looks as though he was a great student in business and finance."

Fred continued reading. "His father shipped him off to St. Moritz boarding schools in Switzerland. He graduated from Oxford, and he was a *Fellow* with a degree in business and went on to receive his PhD from The Wharton School of Business in Philadelphia. He's not stupid at all, but his father sent him to the United States doing various jobs, and he ultimately landed in Colorado."

"Where did you get that information?" Rick asked, stunned.

"I got this from Leonard Schultz," said Fred quietly. "Leonard always does a complete background check on key people whenever they buy a company or any of the assets' big ticket items. It appears that Grant had no life before 1965. So Leonard dug deeper with the help of a detective agency that took him all the way to Italy. At the time, nobody thought much about it and just assumed he was a foreigner who had changed his name to blend in."

Rick sat down slowly, absorbing all the stunning news.

"Now," Fred said, "that explains the Italian and how he's connected to Florence. He was literally a *sleeper*, and when the time was right, they used him to buy into a Las Vegas casino. But I don't understand why the big mystery with the gold mine?"

"It's possible that Grant wanted to be a bigger player in all of this," said Liz, "and not just *Daddy's* gopher or front man. But I have to think that his father may already be aware of Grant's plan, but may let it play out for a while. You just don't become a celebrity like Salvatore Bustiani without having full control of the situation. It looks like this has been well planned and possibly for quite a few years."

"I think that the ranch was a cover," Fred added. "They were using it to bring money into the United States and just hoarded cash at the bank in the Cayman Islands until they were ready to fully buy in. What threw a monkey wrench into all of this was Walter buying the previous owner's company. Walter said that sometimes he'd pay a little more for a company because he knows it's worthwhile and a good fit for his other business interests."

"We've got to get back to that mine," Rick said, "and find out what Grant is actually planning to do."

At the same time, Rick casually looked at Liz and wondered if she knew where Steve was, because he sure could use his help about now.

"Liz, I know this may be hard," Rick said, "but do you think Steve is around here?"

"I don't know," said Liz, with no change of expression. "Let me find out."

Later that afternoon, Aki knocked on Rick's office door and asked to speak with him.

"Yes, come in, Aki," Rick said. "How do our cattle look to you?"

"Rick," said Aki, "I spent all of yesterday and today with John, your veterinarian, and with some of the ranch hands. I was looking at your herd and feel that these cattle are just okay quality. But by changing how and what we feed them, we could strengthen and develop good strong bulls for breeding. I have created a ten-point plan that is very simple to follow, but would take a good year to fully implement to show any measurable results. Then we will have first-class beef for the restaurants."

Rick liked the sound of that. "Aki, would you help me implement the new process?"

"Yes, I'll help," Aki answered with pride, "but we will also have to train the other ranch hands. But I have one request, if possible?"

Rick nodded.

"I would like to bring my wife out here," Aki said, "and together we can work and develop the prime beef for your restaurant business."

"Sounds fine by me," Rick said. "Have her fly out and join us. I'll also talk to Walter and make sure it's all right with him."

Aki's accent had disappeared and he spoke very formal English that you'd only hear in the finest universities.

Rick came out from behind his desk and asked Aki to walk with him.

"Aki, you've let your accent slip," said Rick.

Aki smiled, a little embarrassed, and turned to Rick and said, "I'm sorry if I have deceived you, but Walter felt it best I downplay my schooling for the time being. I actually graduated with an MBA from Columbia University."

Rick stopped walking and turned to look squarely at Aki. "That was you I saw that night Billy had set the fire."

"Yes, that was me," Aki said. "I'm also proficient in martial arts. My specialty is hand-to-hand combat with special weapons.

"Walter found me at a trade fair and offered me a job to take care of his Kobe. It was an opportunity of a lifetime for my wife and me."

Rick thought, *So Walter continues to do things behind the scenes.* He had to chuckle, because he now knew that Walter was probably well aware of much that had been going on at the ranch. Walter always said that *information is the key in any organization, but you must use it wisely, plan, and act accordingly.*

"That sounds great, Aki," Rick said. "I'll call Walter and pass it by him, but I don't think he'll have a problem."

"Thank you so much," said Aki. "Let me know when you are ready to implement this plan. All the ranch hands need to be on board with the plan or it will fail."

Aki had already had a small scuffle with two of the ranch hands. They thought because of his size, they could push him around, but they soon found out that he was very adept at taking care of himself.

From that point on, they gave him the respect he deserved and tried to learn from him. Nothing further was said about it, and the ranch hands liked it that way. They liked their jobs, and they finally had someone to show them a new and better way to raise cattle.

One individual in particular, Don Smith, made an offer to Aki: "I have a Master's degree from the University of Colorado in ecology and evolutionary biology, which should come in very handy."

"That should be very helpful," Aki said, "but there is more to being a top-notch breeder than just having the right schooling and credentials."

CHAPTER

49

Rick and Aki walked back into his office. "Aki, welcome," he said, "to what must not be very new to you. I don't know what you know so far, but we're going after some people that don't like me meddling in their affairs. They've been using this ranch as a cover to launder money and influence several very high-level individuals. We need to find out exactly who is involved and break up this massive scheme. Keep in mind, these people are ruthless and wouldn't hesitate to kill you. My guess is they've already killed several people, so one or two more would be easy for them. They have a lot at stake financially."

"Thank you for confiding in me," said Aki. "I have been around these types of people for many years."

"Thanks, Aki, for your support," Rick said. "We'll need it."

"Liz, did you find out if Steve is available?" asked Rick.

She looked flushed and answered, "I don't know, but the last time I called him it went directly to his message center. Let me try again."

She called Steve again from her mobile phone and this time he answered.

"Hi, Liz," said Steve. "I got your message and I'm actually already in town, and I'll be there in about ten minutes."

"Thanks, Steve," said Liz. "See you in a few minutes."

"I actually thought I spotted him," Rick said, "the last time we were in town but wasn't quite sure."

They all walked out the front steps. As they stood there making small talk, a taxi drove up the driveway. Steve hopped out and with a big smile yelled out, "You called?"

At this point, Rick looked at Liz, had to smile, and thought, *Of course, he's here; he's her bodyguard.*

As Steve came up the walk, Rick noticed he was already wearing his camouflage gear, carrying a variety of weapons, including his sniper rifle and two holstered .45s.

"How did you get all those weapons through airport security?" Rick asked.

Steve looked at him and winked.

Rick got the message and said, "I guess that was a ridiculous question. Come on up to the house."

CHAPTER

50

Walter was sitting in his office, thinking to himself. He found it refreshing that Rick was using the contacts he had set up to get both information and to get things done. He didn't act as if he was afraid to get his hands dirty, which would come in handy when the time came. So far Rick had met his expectations, which would go a long way in helping make his decision when he finally turned his business empire over to someone.

The only question was, *Did Rick really have the desire to take over his empire*? Responsibility was a funny thing, depending on which side of the table you sat on. Understanding how things work was one thing, but making it work the same or better was another thing entirely.

Walter called Jacob. "Not to put you on the spot, but you've spent time with Rick. What do you think of him taking over my business empire?"

"I may be a little prejudiced," said Jacob, "but from what I have seen so far, he seems to be up for the challenge."

"I know and you know," said Walter," that in our day the world was somewhat barbaric. Today it is even more barbaric, but we use very sophisticated methods to obtain similar or better results. Thank you for your input, Jacob. It is much appreciated."

Walter was also concerned about Elizabeth. While he loved her dearly, she might be a distraction to Rick in running his empire. So far she had been an enormous aid to Rick, as well as a morale booster for him in some ways. But if she truly wanted to keep sailing and be a guest lecturer, that might interfere with his plans. *I want them both to be happy with what they choose in life, except when it interferes with my plans,* he thought selfishly.

Right now both were in that embryonic stage where they were only involved in bits and pieces of his business. Very soon, he thought, *I must see how far I can push both in anticipation of showing them my complete Monarch Empire.*

CHAPTER

51

Rick walked up to Steve, smiling, and shook his hand. "It's great to see you again, Steve."

"Hi, Rick," said Steve. "It's also good to see you again. What a great place."

Rick felt that Walter might have already told Steve what was going on here, but he filled him in anyway.

Rick introduced Steve to everyone, saved Liz for last, and said, "And, of course, you already know Liz very well."

As soon as he said it, he knew it was the wrong thing to say. "I'm sorry, that didn't come out right," said Rick.

Both Liz and Steve shot Rick a quick look, but shrugged it off. Now Rick was in the doghouse with Liz, and he knew it wouldn't be easy to get out of it. He tried to diffuse the situation by inviting them all back into the house for some coffee. They walked up the front porch, and Rick could feel the tension in the air. He looked over at Fred, who just rolled his eyes and shook his head.

Rick pulled Steve aside and said, "I apologize for the comment I made, and I'm really glad you're here. I do understand about you and Liz, and I'm sorry things didn't work out for you two. But I'll always consider you my friend, no matter what happens. I wanted you to know that. I feel that you, Liz, and I are all family, with Walter as our uncle, and I wouldn't change that for the world."

With that, Rick extended his hand, and Steve said, "Thanks. That means a lot to me. Now what kinds of problems do you have at your ranch?"

Rick smiled at Liz as she watched from the top of the landing. They all went into the kitchen.

"Is anybody hungry?" asked Diana. "Maybe a little snack to tide you over until dinner tonight?"

All said, "A little later."

"I want to make sure you all understand," Rick said, "that these guys have a lot at stake and they're playing for keeps. It involves people who would kill you just as soon as look at you. They're going to make sure nothing stands in their way, and I mean nothing, because they've planned this for a very long time. That means we have to be on our guard at all times.

"First, I want to go back to the mine and look for Grant, and hopefully bring him out alive. But I have a feeling he won't go easily, so I want to make sure we don't take any unnecessary chances. I'm sure they're taking the gold to some kind of smelter, and I'm guessing that has to be close by. He may also change his plans and double-cross anyone who has been involved with this project. My guess is he's going to try to skip out of the country. I don't know how much gold he has, so I don't know how he plans to transport it or to where."

CHAPTER

52

Marcello Trieste was sitting in his villa courtyard, listening to the bubbling fountain as the water flowed from the top tray down to the bottom pond. The fountain was over one hundred years old, and the water still flowed using the Roman cantilever system. The water had a very relaxing and soft sound, which allowed him to think clearly. He thought about buying some golden carp to put in his pond so he could feed them.

He was talking to his oldest son, Roberto. "I always wanted to be a *Don* and to be powerful and feared, but also respected. I want people to treat me with the kind of reverence that only the church Cardinals receive. I know of only one way I would get that kind of respect."

Roberto looked surprised. "Father, you already have the respect of the town, and a lot of people look up to you."

"Yes, I know, my son," said Marcello. "But there are people in other towns that could also use my help."

That night, with the full moon shining through his study window, he decided what he was going to do. It would be dangerous, but highly rewarding..... if he succeeded.

The next morning Marcello told his wife he was going on a trip and would be back in a few days. He was taking two of his boys, Roberto and Anthony, with him.

"Pietro, stay here," he said to his youngest, "and protect your mother at the villa."

They headed to Tuscany, where he knew Salvatore Bustiani lived. Roberto, the oldest son, drove. Marcello pulled out a copy of the information he had given to Anton Mansard. He had to develop a plan to eliminate Salvatore Bustiani from the Italian culture.

"Salvatore Bustiani is a bad man," said Marcello to his sons. "Who knows, some people may even thank me. Something you should know my sons is that those doing the deed are not always given credit. In the world we live in today, the right people will know and the less said the better."

He thought about blowing up Bustiani's entire villa, but then he might kill his wife and small children, and he couldn't have that on his conscience. He had to think of a way to kill him and discredit him in the community he ruled. He thought about a friend of his who might be able to help – Adolpho Giornale.

CHAPTER

53

Adolpho Giornale was the Chief Editor of one of the largest newspapers in Florence, Italy – The Corriere Adriatic. He was a boyhood friend of Marcello. They went to school together in Florence and today still kept in touch by an occasional call.

Marcello stopped at a local café and made a phone call to him and, after exchanging pleasantries, told him that he would be in town later that day. He asked if they could meet for dinner.

Adolpho, who was always surprised to hear from his now powerful friend, said, "I would consider it a great honor if you would come to my home for dinner."

"Thank you," Marcello said graciously. "I will see you tonight."

Now he had to consider if Adolpho was pro Bustiani in order for this part of his plan to succeed.

"I want you to stay at a local café," he told his sons, "so I can be alone with him this evening."

"But, Papa," said Roberto, "do you think that's wise? What if he isn't the same man you knew during the war?"

Marcello shrugged and touched his nose and said, "Sometimes you have to trust your instincts."

Marcello started thinking of how to discredit Bustiani and if that was actually enough, because he knew he had powerful friends and could possibly sustain almost any type of attack.

What made it worse was that Bustiani and his family wouldn't rest until they found out who the perpetrator was that created the scandal in the first place. In the end, he figured he would have to kill him and any of his closest soldiers so that no reprisals could be made against anyone. Now all he needed to know was who all the people in his immediate group were. He also needed to find the highest-ranking official in Tuscany that was on Bustiani's payroll.

These people wouldn't stand trial. This required a high-level Magistrate that was honest and could be counted on for his support. This person would be taking a risk but, if successful, would be a hero to the people and feared by other crooks. That name was what he would find out from Adolpho.

As he drove up to the villa, he admired the massive wrought-iron gates and noted that they were much grander than his gates. He also had more guards, and all dressed in three-piece suits. He took note of this for when he returned home.

"I am Marcello Trieste," he said to the guard, "here to see Adolpho Giornale."

The gates opened immediately. Driving on the white, crushed rock driveway on a long, curving road, he stopped by the front door steps. He was somewhat startled at the splendor of Adolpho's magnificent villa. He said to himself that the newspaper business must pay well, too well to live like this, and now he became a little concerned. Adolpho came to greet him on the steps and immediately embraced him as he walked across the terrazzo.

"How have you been, my old friend?" Adolpho asked. "It's so good to see you."

"I am well, and thank you for asking," Marcello responded cheerfully.

As Marcello looked around, he said, "I didn't know the newspaper business paid so well."

"This is my wife's doing," said Adolpho. "She inherited money from her parents which they had received as war reparations. They had also invested wisely."

Marcello felt relieved, because he was almost afraid to ask him about Salvatore Bustiani for fear Adolpho might also be in his pocket.

They stepped inside, and his wife Angelina came forward and greeted Marcello in the customary, warm way. She was beautiful, knew exactly how to wear clothes and jewelry and make a grand entrance.

For the rest of the conversation, Marcello had trouble focusing because she was in the same room, but finally Adolpho said, "Let's have dinner. My wife created a special meal of linguine with white clams, broccoli and a fontina cheese sauce with just a hint of garlic."

"It sounds wonderful," Marcello said smiling. "I must get the recipe for my wife."

They had wine and freshly baked bread dipped in olive oil and balsamic vinegar, which was almost a meal in itself. They talked about the old school days and how each had survived the war. Each told the other what they had been doing for the past ten years.

"I am sad that we haven't kept in closer touch," Adolpho said, "but like so many things, time just seems to slip away."

Dinner was served, and Marcello was sorry he had left his two sons at the café, because they couldn't enjoy this sumptuous feast. They ate quietly, exchanging small talk, and finally finished eating. Angelina excused herself, while the housekeepers cleared off the table.

Adolpho casually leaned over and said, with a serious tone in his voice, "Marcello, you didn't come all this way to break bread with me, did you?"

Marcello finally felt at ease and asked, "What do you know about Salvatore Bustiani?"

At first Adolpho looked mildly shocked, but then said, "Let's go in the garden and have some brandy with one of my imported cigars from Cuba."

"I guess I'm not the only one getting cigars from Cuba," Marcello said smiling, as he pulled one out of his pocket.

Marcello gave Adolpho one of his Cuban cigars, and Adolpho gave him one of his. Each asked for an honest opinion about each other's.

They walked a bit further and sat down in very comfortable wicker chairs. The night air was refreshing, with night blooming jasmine permeating the air. You could hear the waves crashing against the rocks far below the cliffs overlooking the Mediterranean.

As they started smoking their cigars, Angelina came out with two brandy snifters and brandy and said, "I know this is a conversation I shouldn't hear, so I'm going to see our children to bed."

Marcello stood up and said, "I want to thank you for that magnificent meal, and I will have you over to my home very soon."

"Thank you. I look forward to it," she cheerfully said, and left.

As soon as she was out of earshot, Marcello went into a brief explanation of what he wanted to do. It was more fiction than truth. He disliked immensely not telling Adolpho the whole truth, but he felt it was for his own good.

At the end of the conversation, Adolpho said, "Do you know how powerful this man is? What you're asking is almost suicidal."

"That may be," said Marcello, "but I'm going to try. I will need some information, so if you feel you are at risk, tell me now. I will drop the subject and never bring it up again."

Adolpho sat back in his chair and let out a loud and long gasp, as if he had swallowed something he shouldn't have.

He looked at Marcello again, kept smoking his Cuban cigar, and said, "I think I can find a Magistrate that may be willing to stick his neck out to get this individual off the street."

Marcello was smiling, but still wondered if he could trust him.

"How long will you need, because time is of the essence?" he asked.

"Give me until tomorrow afternoon," Adolpho said. "I'll call you to set up a time and where he can meet with you. But no guarantees that he would even want to get involved."

216

"I understand, and I only ask that you try," Marcello said. "Thank you for your hospitality, and please thank your lovely wife Angelina again for me for a magnificent dinner." He said, "Good night," walked to his car, and drove off, still smoking Adolpho's imported cigar.

Adolpho sat back in his chair and had to think long and hard about taking this on. He talked himself in and out of it several times before he decided to go forward. Being a newspaperman, he felt that Marcello may have been holding back the real motive to this plan, but as long as he was very careful, he should be all right. Adolpho, being a good newspaperman, might get to scoop all the other newspapers with this story.

Marcello drove back to the café and told his two sons, "We are going to stay here one, possibly two more days."

The next day arrived and Marcello received a phone call at the hotel from Adolpho around noon. "There's a Magistrate in Florence named Signore Giovanni Terranova who also has connections high in the Government and would be only too eager to help."

"Thank you, my friend. I am indebted to you," Marcello said.

That same day Marcello called the Magistrate and arranged a meeting in Florence for the following day. Marcello was very happy, but now he had to develop a plan that was foolproof so that it would never come back to Adolpho or the Magistrate, or himself. He felt it couldn't be too complicated, because that would take too long to execute successfully.

Marcello met with Signore Giovanni Terranova the following morning. The Magistrate was cautious, but after Marcello conveyed to him his plans in simple terms, he gave him the name of the Magistrate that was in Bustiani's pocket.

"When you read the newspapers," said Marcello, "you can proceed with your investigation. You may want to look at his three villas for starters."

On their way home late that night, he daydreamed of finding a car like Anton's when suddenly he realized Roberto had stopped in front of their own entrance gate.

CHAPTER
54

The next morning Rick was going over his final plan with the group when he heard the fax machine. He wasn't expecting anything, but he walked over and saw a single page that read:

Your problem with an individual in Tuscany is no longer a problem.

It had no signature and no originator's fax number printed on the page. Rick asked Fred to come into his office and showed him the page. "Is there any way we can find out where this fax came from?" he asked.

Fred looked startled, but smiled at the same time as he read the note.

Rick had to nudge him and asked again.

"Oh, yes," Fred answered, "since we have a record in your fax machine with a pin number, we should be able to trace it back at least to the city where it came from. But if they faxed it from a library as an example, then it could be anyone because it's a public place."

Rick was certain who they were talking about, so he called Anton Mansard. He didn't answer immediately, but finally picked up.

"Hello, Anton. This is Rick. I just received a fax from someone. Did you send it?"

"No, it wasn't me," Anton said.

"Have any unusual things happened in Tuscany lately?" asked Rick

"It's interesting that you called," said Anton, "because I was just reading this morning's newspaper, which says:

Salvatore Bustiani was killed in a car bomb along with about a dozen of his top lieutenants. They were crossing the Constantine Bridge in a small caravan of four cars and suddenly they all blew up as if on cue.

"It's all over the news," said Anton, and continued reading aloud:

Twelve people were killed in four cars. In addition, a high-level Magistrate was also indicted as part of the sting operation. He was living too well for a simple Magistrate. Signore Giovanni Terranova is the prosecutor.

"That's all it says in the newspaper."

"Thanks for the info, Anton," said Rick and hung up.

Rick turned around and said, "It looks like our Las Vegas anonymous connection from Italy seems to be dead."

They all looked in Rick's direction and shook their heads in disbelief.

Rick smiled and said, "I don't know what happened, but this may work to our advantage. Fred, I wonder if Grant Williams knows that his father is dead?"

"I doubt it," Fred said, "since you just got the fax and it seems to have happened only today. Furthermore, unless someone else contacts him, he's going to go on with his project. On the other hand, if we notify him that his father and some of his close henchmen are also dead, he may relish the idea and feel the pressure to get into the casino business is off him temporarily."

"On top of that," Rick said, "he put up millions of dollars for this venture and had no one to be accountable to, except his father. Grant may also just keep the money he's been skimming, including the gold. Maybe he'll buy himself an island somewhere and just disappear."

Liz nodded in agreement. "I can't believe he would just give up so easily. My guess is that the casino business was his main target all the time, because everything had been set in motion.

The idea that he could be an owner, without his father pulling any strings anymore, may just have given him the edge he's been looking for."

"I wonder how this will work with the Las Vegas syndicate?" said Fred. "I'm guessing they were going to make sure the deal goes through. They may even have money in this venture. I know the mafia can get pretty unhappy when they discover they've been taken."

Rick thought that made a lot of sense. "That means we must find him and shut him down before he finds out about his father, assuming he doesn't already know. Remember, he's not afraid to kill someone to get what he wants. I want to get back to the mine and see what he's up to and find out where they've been taking the ore to process the gold they find."

"By the way," said Fred, "when I was digging into the financials of Grant, I found that there were other deposits made by another dummy corporation. When I finally tracked that down, it came from the Greenland Empire Corporation in Las Vegas."

"That's interesting," said Liz. "That could mean that Grant might have sold the same gold story to them and they have both been financing Grant's little venture."

"I hate to be a wet blanket," said Fred, "but I'm still concerned that this gold mine may legally still belong to the Pawnee Indians. I'll do some more research and tell you where the new Pawnee Indian Reservation is located and who we could talk to in the tribe. Just give me a minute or two."

"We don't have time right now," said Rick, "but when we get back, I'll call them."

Rick turned around and realized that he only had three other people to help him with this and only a vague plan. He was sure that Grant must have at least fifty heavily armed men around him. But Rick figured he had the element of surprise on his side.

"Aki, Steve, and Liz," Rick said, "let's take a ride out to the mine. In the meantime, Fred, I also need you to see if you can find out if there are any precious metal smelting companies in the area. I doubt that Grant and his crew would go very far, and

I have to think that he may also be the owner somehow of the smelter."

"If you don't mind," Aki asked, "I would rather meet you there on horseback. I have a few things to pick up."

Rick looked at him with a sly grin and said, "Okay. But take a mobile phone with you in case you get lost."

Aki smiled and said, "Thanks," and left.

As they got into the Jeep, Rick started wondering how he was going to stop Grant. As far as he knew, he hadn't actually broken any laws ...yet. In addition, he wasn't sure he could count on the local police to help in this, because this whole thing was so complicated.

"Do you think we should take any of the ranch hands with us?" asked Liz.

"Not at this time," answered Rick, "because at this point, I don't know where their loyalties lie. I also think it's too dangerous, and I wouldn't want any of them to get hurt. They didn't sign up for this."

CHAPTER

55

The smelter was about five miles to the north of the Monarch Ranch property. It was part of the newly purchased ten thousand acres that Grant talked the previous owner into buying. It was completely fenced in with a row of double concertina wire on the top of the fence. It had been abandoned over thirty years ago, because the mine had outlived its value. Grant accidentally stumbled on the smelter about eight years ago when he was out looking for strays. There was one large building, Quonset hut style, with another smaller building for all the trucks and equipment.

Grant was busy at the smelter when he got a phone call from Dale Honeycutt.

"Hi, Grant. It was a good thing you had me hang around the ranch. It looks like Rick, two other guys, and a girl are taking off – probably heading for the mine."

"That's okay," said Grant smiling. "When they get there, I've got a few surprises in store for them. You better head back to the general store so you don't create any suspicion."

"Okay," Dale said. "But you'd better not take off and leave me with this mess to deal with. First, I'll follow Rick and his group and find out exactly where they're going."

"Watch out," barked Grant, "or you'll get caught and spoil everything." He hung up the phone.

Unbeknownst to Dale, Aki was traveling through the hills, spotted Dale, and called Rick to let him know she was about a mile behind them.

"Thanks for keeping an eye on her, because I definitely think she is involved. That was a great idea of yours taking your horse," Rick said. "Talk to you later."

As they got closer to the mine, they approached it from a different direction in case they were spotted. They parked in a grove of dense Aspen trees. Rick looked through his binoculars, but saw no movement around the mine entrance.

"Steve, you go around to the other side," Rick said, "where the original mine opening is. Liz and I'll approach it from this side."

Steve took off like a shot and found the mine opening easily, with the heavy chain-link fence. He easily picked the lock and, with careful and calculated steps, walked into the mine, looking for any booby traps that may have been set. He walked in about a hundred yards and saw the tunnel split off into two directions. He went into each tunnel but found each to be blocked.

He thought it very odd that the tunnels were blocked off. He could only surmise that they wanted to trap someone from the other side. Suddenly it came to him. Rick and Liz were going into the mine from the other side and they had set traps for them.

He quickly rushed out and ran past the gate to the other side. As he did, he heard a small explosion behind him, with smoke and water rushing out of the mine opening. He knew he had tripped one of the booby traps set by Grant. He watched for a few seconds, then quickly left.

Steve now realized that Liz and Rick were walking into a trap set by Grant to eliminate any witnesses and tie up loose ends. As Steve was running back to the other opening, he spotted Dale Honeycutt hiding behind a tree, getting ready to use her mobile phone. Suddenly she was out of sight. In her place was a man dressed in black with several swords strapped to his back and waist. Only his eyes were showing through the slits. He waved and Steve took that as a sign he was friendly.

When Dale regained consciousness, she looked startled at seeing the man dressed in black. He stared at her with piercing eyes, and suddenly, with a wild terrified look in her eyes, she tried to scream, but no sound came out.

"I put a small pin in your throat," Aki said quietly, "similar to those used in acupuncture. The pin dipped in a special solution I prepared paralyzes the vocal cords. But if left in too long and pushed in farther, it will go into the bloodstream and further paralyze you from the neck down ... permanently."

Dale thought that today would be her last day on earth.

Aki looked at Dale, slowly pulled out the needle, and calmly asked her, "What are you doing here spying on these people? And don't forget that I can put this pin back in and walk away."

Dale, with a panicky look, caught her breath and said, with a voice that was barely audible, "Who are you people?" She could barely hear herself talk. "This was going to be simple," she again tried to talk, "but all of you have made it so complicated."

"I'll give you one more chance to answer me," Aki said, coming closer to her.

She was still barely able to talk, so Aki gestured as if he was going to push the pin in again, but she shook her head.

Dale coughed a little. "They're taking the gold out of the mountain," she said, "that the Pawnee Indians had left behind.

Grant convinced the previous owner to purchase the land before the ranch was sold two years ago."

"Where are they taking the gold for processing?" Aki asked.

Dale had a frightened look on her face but knew that this was not what she had bargained for.

Still coughing she said in a whisper, "The smelter factory is about five miles from here just off Highway 120. But there are lots of guards, so you won't get within three hundred yards of the fenced in area. Plus it's almost hidden from any roads."

"Thank you," said Aki. "You became a very cooperative captive, and as your reward, I will let you sleep."

With that Aki again pushed the pin into her throat, and as he did this, she had a strange and horrified look as though she knew she was going to die. She passed out, and Aki untied her and pulled out the pin. He remembered what his master told him when he was in training, *that sometimes the thought of death is worse than actually dying.* She would wake up in about two hours, but with a terrible headache.

Aki got back on his horse, rode to the original entrance of the mine, and spotted two sentries on a hill. He silently rode within a hundred yards of them, quietly dismounted, and hid in the shadows. He carefully walked within fifty feet of the sentries, pulled out his blowgun with a tranquilizer dart and shot. He hit his mark with deadly accuracy. They never saw him coming.

As he crouched over the guards, he turned his mobile phone on. Rick was calling to see if everything was all right.

Aki said, in his flawless English accent, "Everything is okay here." Then Aki told Rick what Dale had said.

"That's interesting," said Rick. "That means they're not far away. Thanks, Aki."

With that, he closed the mobile phone, jumped onto his horse, took one last look around for any other guards, and rode back.

CHAPTER

56

Steve continued running towards the other entrance, certain that Liz and Rick had already gone inside the mine. He rushed through the front gate opening and called out to them, but nobody answered. He walked in slowly and came to a massive opening in the mine. Looking around for other booby traps, he found none – and that made him nervous.

He picked up some of the fine sand from the ground and threw it in the air. He thought, sure enough, there are plenty of laser beams, but only going across two of the four openings. That meant that Liz and Rick had walked through one of the openings that had no triggered laser beam, and that meant to him that this particular shaft was the main booby-trapped area. Now he had to find the source of the laser beam to shut it off. Unfortunately, there were too many to track.

What he was afraid of was that the previous tunnel had triggered an explosion, which would send a mountain of water flowing into the tunnel. He had no doubt that this would be a similar type of trap.

Liz and Rick were walking through the tunnel when they heard faint voices, which grew louder as they continued walking. They saw another large opening in the tunnel, but it was dripping with water. They could see lights and heard a generator humming.

"There's something wrong," said Liz. "I just know it. Why would they still be here, unless ..."

At that exact moment, Rick spotted a small red dot on the side of a box that seemed out of place and realized it was a laser light. He held up his hand and motioned her to freeze, while he tried to see where this beam was coming from. Liz whispered that she thought it was coming from overhead, pointing just to the left of them.

Rick carefully picked up some fine sand and threw it at the light. It quickly showed that there was not only one, but four beams. Any one of these could either alert Grant that he had intruders or trigger some type of explosion and possibly seal them in this mine forever.

Rick was worried about the dripping water and said, "I hadn't noticed before, but we've been gradually descending and could be several hundred feet below the surface. You can easily lose your bearings when there's no outside light to direct you. I think this water might be part of a stream or river overhead that was used in the mining of the gold."

"It looks like the point of origin is up on that ledge," Liz said. "That won't be easy to get to, but it would've been difficult to install without some type of ladder."

Using their flashlight, they looked high and low for another opening and finally found what they thought to be the access to the top shelf of the cave.

"I'll crawl over to the opening," Rick said, "and see if I can get around to the other side and come up the back way to disarm the laser beam system."

As Rick climbed up and was carefully crawling over to the other opening, Liz leaned forward trying to listen to what the others were saying deeper in the mine. She was careful not to trigger any of the laser beams. As she listened, it seemed that the conversation wasn't about business but more like general conversation. She soon realized that she was hearing the same conversation repeated, and it had to be a tape recording. She yelled to Rick, but he was out of range and she couldn't move. It would have to wait until he got back.

CHAPTER

57

Steve slowly crept into the mineshaft and finally got close enough to see Liz crouched behind a large rock. As he walked closer, he hadn't noticed that he triggered a laser light that was close to the ground and difficult to see. Suddenly an explosion occurred and rocks were flying everywhere.

With the force of a double-barrel shotgun, one of the flying rocks glanced off Steve's shoulder, and he fell back against a large wall. Blood was running down his shoulder.

Liz turned towards the explosion and saw Steve. Liz called out to Rick, fearing the blast might have buried him as well. She started to panic, questioning what she was doing here. She had traded being on her yacht and sunning in the Mediterranean for almost being killed – again.

She made a beeline towards Steve and quickly tore part of her shirt to bandage Steve's shoulder.

"Don't worry, Liz," Steve said. "I've had worse injuries when I was in Viet Nam. Where's Rick?"

"He crawled up to an opening," she said, "and is trying to shut off the laser beam controls. Right now I don't know if he's buried under rocks on the other side. You stay here. I'll try to find him."

Steve got up. "We'll both go. We'll need to watch out for other low level laser beams, because that's what I just triggered."

Rick heard the blast, but was almost at the ledge where he thought the laser controls might be. As he crawled onto the ledge, he spotted the main controls, and that's when he saw Steve and Liz running back into the tunnel.

He quickly switched the system off, looked down, and said, "It looks like it's off. I'll be right down. Is anybody hurt from the blast?"

Rick saw that Steve had a bandage on his shoulder. Just beyond Steve's shoulder, he spotted another way down to the bottom and into the same cavernous area.

"Are you all right?" Rick yelled out.

"Yeah, I'm fine," Steve, answered. "Just a little scratch. What have you found out so far?"

"Wait a minute," Liz interrupted. "While I was waiting for you guys, I noticed the voices we heard kept repeating the same conversation about every ten minutes. I'm almost sure it must be a recording."

"They must have anticipated we were coming," Steve said. "This was a trap, and we need to get out of here pronto."

Before they could take a step, another huge explosion occurred at the entrance, and water was gushing into the mine at a horrific pace.

"What was that?" yelled Steve.

"I'm guessing another little reminder from Grant," yelled Rick.

Rick pointed upward. "I'm guessing that when I turned off the laser beam system, it must have started a countdown to set off another explosion. We need to get to higher ground, and I know the perfect spot. Follow me."

As the three of them started to run, Steve could see small trickles of water coming down the path as they ran for higher ground.

"We need to get going," Rick shouted. "Run for it!"

Rick rounded the corner, pushed Liz up to the first step of the ledge, and told her to crawl up as far as she could go. Rick made Steve go next, so he could watch out for the water. He pulled his flashlight and aimed it towards where he thought the water was coming from, and yelled, "A huge ten-foot wall of water is coming right at us."

"It looks like the whole lake is being emptied into the mine," Steve said.

Rick climbed up behind Steve. Liz had crawled to a ledge about twenty-five feet from the ground. Rick was climbing as fast as he could, but the water was already up to his waist.

"Go on, Steve, you can make it," shouted Rick over the roar of the water.

"I'm trying, with only one good arm," said Steve, "but I'm almost there."

But the water was too strong and pulled Rick into the rushing water. Rick grabbed onto a crevice with one hand and found some footing so he was able catch his breath. Suddenly the water caught Rick again and washed him further down the tunnel.

"Rick," yelled Liz, "hold on."

"The water is slowing down a bit now," said Steve." I'm going to get Rick, but you stay here where you'll be safe."

Steve lowered himself into the water and swam into the mineshaft toward Rick.

CHAPTER

58

Aki was riding the ridge to the other side of the mine when he heard the blast. He saw a huge, billowing gray cloud of dust and was afraid he might be too late. He rode closer and noticed that the gray cloud wasn't at the mine opening, but rather closer to the top of the mountain. That meant there might be a large air hole on top.

He rode up the side of the mountain until he got to the opening. He grabbed the rope from his saddle and carefully crept closer to where the smoke was coming from. He yelled down the opening several times, but no one answered. He tied the rope to his saddle horn, pulled his mask over his mouth, and climbed down the opening.

He let himself down the hole, but the smoke was so thick he couldn't see more than a few feet below him. He was almost to the end of the rope, when he felt a flat stone under his feet, and the smoke was slowly dissipating. He again called out, and this time he thought he had heard some sounds like someone moaning, so he called again.

As he was walking, he suddenly felt water and wondered where it was coming from. He saw a shadow, ran towards it, and saw it was Steve.

Another small explosion and Aki's horse was frightened and took off with the rope still tied to his saddle.

"Steve," asked Aki. "is everybody okay?"

"Liz is safe and I'm okay," said Steve, "but Rick was sucked in by the rushing water. I know he floated down this way, and it looks like the water is subsiding. There must be an exit where this water is going."

"Come up here. I'll find Rick," said Aki. Before Steve could say anything, Aki dove into the water to look for Rick. As Aki was swimming, he saw Rick clinging to a rock, with his head hanging to one side. He quickly swam over to him, grabbed him by his jacket collar, and towed him back to where Steve was waiting.

Rick finally opened his eyes, shook his head and said, "I thought I was a goner."

"I'll go get Liz," said Steve. "I'll be right back."

By this time, the water was about four feet high, and Liz had already started coming Steve's way.

"I see you found Rick," Liz said anxiously.

"Don't be afraid," he said aloud. "It's me, Aki."

She was startled, because she was looking at a man dressed in black, with swords strapped to his back, and a black mask."

"Where did you come from?" Liz said.

"I found an air hole at the top of the mountain," said Aki, "and just lowered myself down. Unfortunately my horse got frightened and left."

"Looks like everybody made it," said Rick, trying to feign a smile.

"Thanks, Aki," Rick said. "Now I know why Walter sent you out here to the ranch, besides helping us upgrade the beef. He must have known we might have some trouble. In any event, I'm glad you're here."

"Thanks to Steve," said Rick, looking exhausted trying to get up. "I owe you guys. How about I invite you out to the ranch for some steaks and a couple of beers … I'm buyin', of course."

They all tried to smile, but they knew they were in a difficult position.

As Rick finally stood up, he shook the water from his clothes. "Okay, enough of this," said Rick. "Let's get out of here. I have a score to settle, and I'm not going to be nice about it."

He looked at Aki and smiled. "It looks like you'll always be a Samurai warrior."

Aki bowed to Rick.

Aki climbed down the side of the cave. As he did, he noticed the various pictures drawn on the cave walls. He interpreted that this was a sacred cave for the Indians. This now convinces me that this was probably the Pawnees' gold mine

"The water must be going somewhere," said Rick, "since we're downhill from the main opening."

Aki led the way and they all followed. They lit a match and saw that the flame was pointing in the direction they were heading.

"Rick," Steve said, walking next to Rick, "it seems that I wasn't much help to you this time."

"Don't worry about it," Rick said. "I'm still glad you're here. Don't let any of this bother you. We just underestimated the enemy a bit. The fact that we're still alive is all that counts."

"I see a small shaft of light in the distance," Aki said.

He walked forward and found that the opening was too small. But as he pointed his flashlight at the cave walls, he noticed a glimmer.

"Everybody, come here," Aki shouted. "I think I found some of the gold that they were mining for."

They all rushed forward and looked. "I think you're right," said Rick, "but right now we need to find a way out of here."

Aki nodded. "I saw an opening, but as I got closer, it was too small to get out. I'll crawl down to the opening and see if I can see where we are."

As he crawled down, he said to Rick, "Tie a rope to my ankles in case I get stuck so you can pull me back out."

He got to the opening, which was about two feet in diameter, and tried to look out.

He called back to the group and said, "Pull me back. This is not the way to get out."

Rick then pulled Aki back from the opening.

Aki dusted himself off and said, "I cannot believe all the water went out through this small opening so quickly. There must have been something we missed coming down this way."

"I think you're right," said Rick. "We were all in such a hurry to see daylight we may have missed something. Anybody have a lighter with them or matches?"

"If we are out of matches," Aki said, "and don't have a lighter, I can start a fire with some other things I have with me."

He pulled out a black silk handkerchief-sized cloth and opened it up to show the group. In it, he had a small piece of flint. He picked up a piece of granite and quickly had a flame going. This time he picked up the flame in his black cloth and held it high, so they could see which way the breeze pointed the flame. They noticed the flame was pointing up above them. They were all astounded at how Aki carried the flame in his black cloth. He dropped his flame and put the black cloth back in his pocket. Aki scaled the short wall of granite like a Springbok in the Alps.

He saw a much larger opening and called down to them, "This may be the way out."

He went closer to the opening, looked out, and saw that the hill had a gradual slope, with trees along the hillside, perfect to walk down the hill.

"This is how we get out and go down," he called out.

"That's easy for you to say," Liz said smiling, and slowly climbed up to the ledge where Aki was waiting.

Within minutes, all were ready to start their descent down the hill.

Rick stopped to get his bearings. "We're facing east, so the entrance to the mine is on the other side of the mountain and that's where my truck is parked."

They slowly climbed down the rocky slope, relieved to be breathing fresh air.

As they walked, Liz noticed two Indians sitting on horses at the top of the facing hill.

"I didn't know Indians were still riding horses these days," she said, with a surprise in her voice. "I thought they all drove cars and trucks nowadays."

As soon as she said that and turned back, they were gone from sight.

"I wonder if these are the ghosts of the Pawnee Indian descendants," Rick jokingly said, "that used to mine the gold back in 1865."

"Hard to imagine," Liz said, "they'd still be watching this plot of land."

CHAPTER
59

As they got closer to the base of the hill, Rick could see everyone was tired and hungry, and so they sat down to rest.

Rick pulled out his mobile phone and noticed he had lost his gun in all the excitement. He was happily surprised that his phone was still working and called the ranch house. Diana answered.

"Rick, we were so worried about all of you." Diana asked, "Is everyone all right?"

"Hi, Diana," Rick said. "Yeah, we're fine, but our vehicles are all on the other side of the mountain and we sure could use some help."

"I'm not sure who to call to come and get you," said Diana.

"Call John Hammond," Rick said. "Tell him we're on the other side of the hill on the northeast corner of the ranch, close to where he picked up the dead cattle earlier this week. He'll know where to find us. Also tell him to bring some water with him."

"Okay, I'll call him right away," said Diana and hung up.

"John should be here in about forty-five minutes," said Rick, "so get some rest."

Rick went over to look at Steve's shoulder and saw it had finally stopped bleeding.

Rick then turned to Liz and said, "I don't think I'm cut out for ranch life, but now the question is what to do with the ranch, since it's actually a good investment."

Liz shrugged her shoulder. "I think that's a decision you'll have to make. I know you'll work this out .... you always do."

Rick looked over at Liz and thought about the comment she just made, and she was right.

With the sun shining on their faces, Rick began to snooze. No sooner had he drifted off than he heard a truck horn. It was John in his Vet truck. He saw them, stopped his truck, and ran out to greet them. He gave them all cold water.

"Where have you guys been?" John asked. "We were getting ready to call out the Army to try and find you. There were explosions, and someone from the Army came around trying to find out what was going on. They knew generally where it came from. Did you see any of them?"

"We haven't seen anybody," Rick said, "because we've all been stuck inside this mountain for the last four hours. I'm curious why the Army suddenly took an interest in this particular explosion, because I'm sure they've been using dynamite for quite some time. It doesn't seem to have bothered anyone before. Now I'm suspicious at how high up the cover-up goes, because we know a federal Judge was involved, and then he mysteriously died of a heart attack."

"It was a Captain Peterson from the Air Force 90th Air Tactical Wing Division over in Cheyenne, Wyoming," John said.

"Isn't he a little far from home?" asked Rick.

"He said he'd been suspicious because of all the seismic readings in this general area," said John. "He knew that his commander, General Alexander, must have been covering up something because he never got any feedback from him about any of the reports he'd submitted for the past year or so."

Rick shook his head in disbelief. "That means they must have been using a lot of dynamite over the same time period. They may have a lot more gold mined than we originally thought. This explains why Grant's been so concerned about not leaving any witnesses behind. He must be closer to shutting everything down and loading up and getting ready to leave."

"Gold," John said. "You mean Grant's been mining for gold all this time?"

"Yeah, he has," said Rick. "Don't talk to anybody about this though."

"Then that explains a lot of things," said John, "and why he really hasn't paid much attention to the ranch itself."

CHAPTER
60

Grant was surveying the surrounding mountainside with his binoculars when he saw several explosions. There were gray clouds as if a small volcano had just erupted. He felt confident he had seen the last of Rick and his merry men.

He turned around and saw Dale Honeycutt get out of her truck and stagger sluggishly towards him rubbing her head. Gone were the fancy western clothes and boots that were her signature ensemble at the Peabody Mercantile. She was now wearing jeans and a leather jacket.

Dale, almost screaming and crying at the same time, said, "Are you aware that they have some guy running around here wearing black clothes, seems to be some kind of martial arts expert? He pushed a pin into my neck, and for about a minute, I couldn't speak or move. He gave me some type of sedative, and I thought I was going to die. But I woke up about a half-hour later and with a headache that just won't quit."

Grant looked at her with cold, menacing eyes and thought, *It's too bad it didn't kill you.*

Massaging her temple, she sarcastically said, "You know, of course, we still have a few loose ends in town, like Eldon Johnson, the manager of Peabody Land Management, and Judd

Stewart from the City Clerk's office. We may also want to check on this guy Fred Tremane, who's probably still at the ranch. Rick brought him in to go over all the financial records of the ranch."

Grant thought for a moment, then with an arrogant grin said, "That's already being taken care of, so you don't have to worry your pretty little head about that."

He was also thinking that Dale had become a liability and outlived her value to the project. If she were ever caught again, she just might spill the beans about this operation or may have already – *and that's something I can't have.* The only regret he had was that in another life she might have made a great wife. But recently she had grown too possessive, and he wasn't ready to share all of his wealth.

It's a good thing I never told her, he thought, *who my father really is. That probably would have been a deal breaker, but then again she may already know.*

"Let's go over to the furnace," Grant said, "and see how they're doing. By tonight I should be pretty much complete."

"Why did you say *I*?" Dale asked. "Aren't I included in your plans anymore?"

"I remember about ten years ago," said Grant overlooking her comment, "when I was in your store and read the story about how Harry 'Billy' Jackson had accidentally stumbled on a small gold mine while looking for the old Pawnee mine. It turned out to be a much larger find than he had anticipated."

As they were walking towards the back, Grant grabbed his hard hat and walked Dale to the furnace area, pulled out his gun equipped with a silencer, and without any fanfare, expertly placed two shots in her head. She was dead before she hit the ground. There was an empty fifty-five gallon drum that he dumped her in and filled the rest with small rock chips that had been sitting close by. He put the lid on, sealed it, and had one of his men push it into the far corner of the building, out of sight. Nobody would notice it until he was long gone. He smiled to himself as he came around the corner of the office .... *another loose end eliminated, which also means less to share.*

CHAPTER

61

"When we're finished," Grant told Ralph Middleton, his plant manager, "we'll have approximately a hundred and fifty thousand pounds of pure gold. I'll have a flatbed truck ready to load with special pre-stressed 'I' beams running the length of the truck bed to support the weight so we can truck it to its final destination."

"Grant," said Ernie, "when do I get the rest of the money you owe me for the job?"

"Soon, Ernie," Grant said. "Why don't we meet at the Carriage House tonight around eight, have a drink, and I'll give you your money?"

"That sounds great," Ernie said.

Grant also had a surprise for him.

Grant thought that the gold he mined would go a long way to buying a casino. By tomorrow morning, a truck would be heading towards San Francisco right onto the grounds of the Italian Embassy. It took a bit of doing, but he was able to replicate the seal from the Italian Government to make sure that truckload would be on a ship bound for Florence, Italy.

"So far all is going as planned," said Grant to Jerry, his lead guard. "Of the twenty guards, some will accompany my gold shipment and the rest I will pay off. All of the customs papers and the special containers were delivered that I had manufactured in Sacramento. The customs papers will identify that this container has furniture belonging to Signore Adolfo Siglione, the retired Italian Consulate from San Francisco. He is returning to his villa in Italy to retire. Since he has diplomatic immunity, no branch of any government can open the containers."

Grant prided himself on the precision and expert execution of the plan, and it seemed that he had thought of everything, even how he took care of Rick Benedict and his group.

Grant called Ernest Smith on his mobile phone to check on his progress with the three people he was to eliminate.

At first he didn't answer, but someone finally did. Grant stood up, alarmed – It wasn't Ernest.

"Who is this?" Grant demanded.

"It's me, Fred Tremane. I wonder if this is *the* Grant Williams and former ranch manager of the Monarch Ranch?"

Fred's sarcasm wasn't lost on Grant, who quickly hung up the phone. Grant was now concerned that Ernest hadn't taken care of Eldon Johnson and Judd Stewart. He called their office and was told they hadn't come in yet. Ernest may have been eliminated .... or they may have skipped town ... or gotten themselves arrested.

Fred put the phone down and laughed. He was looking at Ernest and Phillip tied to a chair with blood trickling from the sides of their head.

"They'll have a heck of a headache when they wake up," said Fred to Diana.

Right about that time, he heard sirens driving up the hill. Diana let the Sheriff in the front door, with his guns drawn.

"Sheriff, these men tried to kill me," Fred said. "I also found a note in his pocket about visiting Eldon Johnson, and Judd Stewart, and I don't think it was to have a beer. You need to find these two guys and arrest them also, because they were part of a much larger scheme to defraud this ranch and this state to the tune of several million dollars."

"I'm a forensic accountant," he went on to explain, "with special clearance from the government. I've spent the best part of two weeks going over the books of Monarch Ranch. Eldon and Judd were paid off by Grant Williams to look the other way on certain matters. If you'll take these two people with you and find those other two guys, we'll be in town tomorrow to close this case. By the way, you may also want to take a second look at how Judge Thornton actually died."

The Sheriff was listening to all of this, as he handcuffed Ernest and Ralph.

He said, with a determined look on his face, "Thanks. We've wanted to put these guys away for a long time. I will also look into the Judge's death again."

As they were getting in the patrol car, the Sheriff called into the office and said, "Issue an arrest warrant for Eldon Johnson and Judd Stewart immediately."

After the Sheriff left, Fred turned to Diana and said, "Now we've got to find out where Rick and the gang are."

He called and Rick picked up after the first ring.

"Hi, Fred. Are you keeping busy?" Rick asked.

Fred told him what had transpired with the two people. "The Sheriff was just here to take them to jail. They said that this time no judge was going to let them go."

"That's some good news. Is Diana all right?" Rick asked.

"Yeah, she's okay," said Fred. "She stayed very cool. Something tells me she's been through this kind of situation before. But I gotta say, you sure know how to show a fella a good time. I got beat up, had to beat someone else up, and all just for

249

some fresh mountain air. And by the way, you still owe me a double cheeseburger, fries, and chocolate shake."

Rick laughed aloud and then told him about some of what had been happening. Suddenly Fred felt his story wasn't as exciting anymore.

Fred got up from his chair surrounded by paper stacked two feet high and asked, "Is there anything else I can do for you?"

"No, not right now," Rick said. "John came out with some water, but we've rested enough, and now we're going over to the foundry."

"Yeah, that's what I was going to tell you," said Fred. "This may interest you. I found some paperwork for an old iron ore smelter that's located just northeast of where you are. It was included with the additional ten thousand acres they bought about two years ago. It's been abandoned for a long time, but it evidently still had the capability and capacity to work."

"Yeah, I know." Rick said, "Aki got that info from Dale when he threatened to kill her. That's where Grant is probably processing the gold. I'll ask John if he knows exactly where that is. He's familiar with this area. Thanks."

He turned to the group and told them what had been going on up at the house.

"Do you know," Rick asked, "where an old iron ore smelting operation is located around here? It makes sense that it would be close to the mine and wouldn't attract much attention."

"Yeah," John said quietly, with an embarrassed expression on his face, "I know where it is."

He paused, then looked up at Rick. "I think there's something else you should know about Grant. A while back, I overheard him talking on the phone to somebody about buying into a casino in Las Vegas. The Judge then introduced him to a General Alexander of the Air Force. Grant was able to hire some ex-Army Rangers to act as armed guards to escort a flatbed truck to an Italian Embassy. I drove around one day and stumbled on the foundry."

"Why didn't you tell me this before?" demanded Rick.

"I didn't know what he was planning," said John, "but when he started bragging to some of the ranch hands, I figured he was planning to leave. I don't know what his schedule is, but my guess is with you poking around, they might just shut down soon. I overheard him say he has all types of diplomatic paperwork and seals."

"What's the significance of the diplomatic paperwork?" asked Rick.

"I don't know, but Grant said that when he gets done," John said, "he plans to retire, and he'll promote me to be the next ranch foreman. But he wasn't expecting someone like you to take such an interest in the ranch and the business. He pretty much had free rein from the previous owners to do whatever he wanted to do."

"I never figured Grant was such a calculating individual," Rick said, "and with all these connections."

"As far as I know," John replied, "he went to the best schools in Europe and also did a tour with the German Secret Police. When he came to the ranch, he later found out that Judge Jack Thornton and General Alexander were cousins, and that helped him lay the groundwork for whatever he was planning, which now appears to be mining for gold."

"How much gold can he possibly get out of the mine?" Rick asked. "I thought the Pawnee Indians had left because it was panned out."

"Something doesn't make sense here," Liz said. "If that's the case, why did the Indians give up the mine? I thought it was always on their reservation land. I'd have to think that they would still own it."

"I think that's where Judge Jack Thornton came into the picture," said John. "As I understand it, since he was a federal Judge for Colorado, he had the reservation boundaries changed by a friend of his at the Bureau of Land Management in Washington, D.C. That's how he talked the previous owners into buying the property."

"Dale must have known some of this," Rick said. "I'll bet Grant has spent years going through all the historical records he could find."

"Remember, he'd been the foreman of this ranch for over ten years, and in that time, he'd had a lot of time on his hands," said

John. "The other owners didn't mind as long as they were taken care of when they brought visitors for a business vacation. I'm sorry I didn't tell you sooner, because with new owners coming and going, I didn't know who to trust or talk to."

CHAPTER
62

"John," Rick said, "for now just go back to the ranch, and we'll talk about this later."

"Okay. But please don't fire me," John said. "All that my wife and I have is working on this ranch."

"Don't worry about that now," Rick said. "Right now I need you at the ranch helping Don Smith, the temporary ranch foreman."

Rick and the group piled into John's truck, and he drove them around to the other side of the mountain so they could use their own transportation. Rick was now more determined than ever to stop Grant and his mercenaries.

John dropped them off by Rick's truck and said, "Call me if you need anything else." Then he drove off.

As John drove back to the ranch, he called his wife and said, "Hi, honey. I'm gonna stay at the ranch tonight. Rick asked me to help Don Smith, the new ranch foreman. I'll talk to you tomorrow," and hung up.

As he continued to drive back to the ranch, he stopped the truck and looked around. He was hoping this was not his last view of the ranch.

CHAPTER
63

Grant could finally see the culmination of his ten exhausting years of planning, and now he didn't even have to buy into a Las Vegas Casino. Everything was still going according to plan. But he was now concerned about Ernest, especially since the Judge was not around to fix his problems anymore. He was still a little worried about the Vegas partners. Even though they didn't contribute much to the project, he knew they were on the hook to the Bacilli family in Las Vegas. He actually didn't care anymore because he couldn't do anything about it. He was just going to disappear.

They were starting to load the balance of the forty-two containers onto the flatbed truck. He would pay each of the key guards fifty thousand dollars, shoot the rest, and leave them in the back of the building.

He wanted to thank his Italian partner for getting him all the necessary forged papers to ship these containers on a freighter bound for Italy. It was too bad he had to kill him, because he rather liked the guy. Now that his father was dead, he could make other plans that didn't include the hotel and casino business – at least not in the United States.

Grant had received a call last night from his mother in Florence to let him know his father was killed yesterday in a bombing. She had called to let him know about the funeral arrangements.

"I may be there if all goes well here, Mother," said Grant. "I'll see you soon."

He still spoke to his mother occasionally and even sent her money from time to time. He figured he was at an age he could do what he wanted. His father didn't see him that much, so he figured he didn't owe him a thing.

Grant sat in his makeshift office and pulled out a list of people who were part of this operation. He noted who to pay off and who to eliminate.

"Hey, Grant," Ernie called out, "I've been thinking. Is there any way you could pay me at least a partial now?"

"Sure, Ernie." Grant looked up and said, "Come on in."

Grant opened a cabinet and saw there was a safe inside.

Grant pulled out twenty thousand dollars and said, "Is this enough to tide you over until tonight?"

Ernie was surprised but happy and said, "Yeah, that will be fine," and took the money.

"Let's have a drink on it," said Grant.

He poured two glasses of scotch. They toasted and Ernie downed his drink quickly – but Grant didn't. Ernie started to cough and gag.

"You didn't think I'd just let you walk out of here knowing what you know, did you?" Grant said. "My guess is that you probably wouldn't have come to the restaurant anyway. Sorry, Ernie, but I couldn't risk that you might *slip* and tell somebody about this."

Ernie fell with a crash and a puzzled look on his face. Grant picked up Ernie by the arms, dragged him into the small bathroom, and closed the door. Grant took back the money he gave him and took his wallet and other ID.

"Sorry, Ernie," said Grant, "but you've become a liability to me."

Some of his ex-rangers were skilled in the art of killing and making it look like an accident or death by natural causes. It came in handy with Judge Thornton. Grant covered his tracks by not telling too many people about the complete operation, and in that way, it would be much more difficult to connect it to him. He was a little concerned with how much Judge Thornton had told General Alexander about the overall plan. Even though the Judge had limited information, he wasn't a stupid man.

He was sorry about Dale, but she was getting too arrogant regarding her value to this operation. He had become concerned when they all met at the Cheyenne Country Club last week. But a missing general would require much more careful planning.

He decided to call the Las Vegas family to see how they'd react.

"Hello, Sully," he said. "Things are going well here, and we may even be a little ahead of schedule. Hey, listen, I just heard that the General is retiring soon and wants to be a partner in the casino as payment for his service over the past couple of years. Is there any truth to that rumor?"

He heard the phone slam down and didn't get an answer. He had already anticipated their answer, and now he knew they would take care of his other problem.

CHAPTER

64

Liz was hoping that when this was all over, she could spend some time with Rick to see if there was still a future for them. She daydreamed about sailing in the Mediterranean with just Rick. She also knew that because she had already given Rick up once for Steve, he might be reluctant to get involved again. But she felt she had to try. So far Rick had responded, but he was clearly hesitant. He was also not his usual self due to these problems.

They got back to their own truck. Nothing looked suspicious at the mine entrance, but Rick noticed several eagle feathers scattered around the truck that seemed out of place. He looked around but saw nothing and decided that it was just a coincidence.

"These are the coordinates where the old abandoned iron ore smelter is located," Rick said, "and it's not far from here."

"Don't you think we should contact the local Sheriff to assist us in this?" Liz asked. "I'll bet that Grant has plenty of guards with weapons."

Rick frowned but said, "Right now we have the element of surprise, because they think we're either dead or trapped in the mine. The local cops aren't equipped for this type of engagement."

"I agree with Rick," Steve said. "But before we bust in there, we ought to do a little reconnaissance to see how much fire power they actually have."

Aki nodded in agreement.

It was now about three in the afternoon. Rick was driving and could see everyone was tired. They were getting close to the abandoned foundry located in a valley and hidden from regular highway traffic.

They drove within two hundred yards and stopped. Looking through his binoculars, Rick saw where the guards were all posted.

"Let's get a little closer," Rick said.

They used the surrounding trees and bushes as cover. Suddenly Steve motioned for them to stop in their tracks. He pointed to a red dot on a tree trunk, which meant that there were traps set up in the woods. He picked up some dirt from the ground and tossed it at the beam so he could tell where it was coming from.

"I see three beams, all crisscrossing," said Steve. "If you get by one, then the others will probably catch you. My guess is these aren't for explosive purposes, but to notify them at the factory they have company. Rick, can you see where the source is?"

Rick nodded his head. "Yeah, it looks like it's coming from that direction."

"These are sophisticated devices," Steve said, "because with commercial devices you need a corresponding beam *catcher* in order to complete the circuit. But these seem to require none. They look like military grade laser beams."

"Let's find an alternate route," Rick said, "like cutting through these bushes where you wouldn't normally try to walk."

As they cut and waded through the bushes, Steve said, "Let's stop at the clearing. I spotted at least four guards and all carrying HK33 automatic assault rifles. Plus there was a guard in each of the watchtowers. They were all dressed in black camouflage gear and each carrying a Browning .50 caliber machine gun. None looked like he would have a problem using it."

"We absolutely have no cover between here and the factory entrance gate," Liz said.

Aki chimed in, "Let me create a diversion for you."

Before anyone could say anything, he was behind the guard in the watchtower. As Rick watched with binoculars, he saw a very quiet puff of smoke, and then the guard went down. Aki ceremoniously took out all of the guards in the watchtower, and the four guards patrolling the fence perimeter … all went down. It was all over in less than two minutes.

Rick looked hard but couldn't see Aki. He knew he was around. Once all the guards were down, he showed himself to Rick and the others and motioned to them that it was safe. Rick looked at Steve and thought, *Aki needs to show us how he does that smoke thing and disappears.*

Steve said he was still reluctant to cross the open clearing without any cover, but he went anyway.

As they crept closer to the entrance to the building, they heard voices. Rick was hoping that Grant wouldn't look for the guards for the next ten minutes or so. Suddenly a flatbed truck came roaring out of the factory, broke through a section of the chain-link fence, and was on Highway 25 as if it were on fire.

The tinted windows on the cab of the truck made it hard to see who or how many people were in the cab.

Rick cursed himself and yelled, "Grant must have been alerted somehow that we were coming and figured to hightail it out of here. I guess I didn't give Grant enough credit, because it looks like he may have pulled this off."

"Let's get in our truck and follow them," he yelled out to Steve and Liz.

As Rick was getting into his truck, he stopped. "Something is wrong here. Maybe Grant isn't as crafty as we think he is," he said. "Steve, I'm going to stay here and look around the factory. Something just doesn't add up. If he had the gold on board and tore out like that, the gold could shift and tear that trailer apart.

On top of that, his truck couldn't outrun our truck. Call me on my mobile phone and let me know where he's going. We'll snoop around here and see if we can find out anything."

"Okay, I'll let you know shortly," Steve said, and drove off as if he was in a NASCAR race.

CHAPTER
65

As they walked into the factory, they saw that some of the equipment was still running and littered with a few of the ingot forms left behind. By the size of the forms, Rick figured about a ten-pound bar. What was especially interesting was the impression and seal for the ingots.

He saw several large canisters with a label that said, "CYANIDE USE WITH CAUTION."

"This must be how the cyanide got into the water system," said Rick, "and killed the cattle I saw earlier this week. I need to shut off the laser light switches, but I don't see any switches."

Rick, looking confused, turned to Liz. "This looks like an Italian bank logo. But if he was going to buy a casino in Las Vegas, why would he need an Italian Government logo? Why not simply hand the gold bars over to the people he's buying them for?"

"Three things come to mind," Liz said. "First, he needs the gold bars to look legitimate to the buyer. There's an extensive process to determine the actual gold content. It may say it's 99.99% pure gold, but those are only markings. A real buyer would still want to assay at least some of the bars randomly to make sure they were pure gold. Second, since he's not a legitimate gold bullion reseller, they may want to re-assay it themselves. Lastly, that much gold in the U.S. would set off alarm bells everywhere. The U.S. Government would want to know where it came from."

"And another thing," Liz said. "He could take these directly to another country and let them be responsible for the authenticity. Remember, once he has the gold in that country, he could easily re-melt the gold bars with different markings."

"There may also be another option," Rick continued. "He's not going to buy the casino at all and instead just disappear in Europe. Maybe he's planning to double-cross everyone. If this is true, there's considerable weight involved and transportation would require a ship of some kind. Let's find out where the flatbed truck is heading and if there are any ships leaving the West Coast within the next twenty-four hours."

Grant was in the shadows listening and impressed by what they knew about his plans. It appeared he had grossly underestimated Rick. He was angry that they hadn't taken the bait to go after the other truck. It was actually a decoy, filled with lead bars and rocks for weight. In addition, he thought he had gotten rid of them with the mine explosion. He'd now have to eliminate them himself.

He signaled to his small army to flank them from the rear and block the gate exit in case they tried to leave.

Aki slowly crept back into the shadows. As he did, Liz spotted him, and he signaled her to be quiet. He was going to look around. As Aki left, Grant came out from behind some large barrels carrying another HK33 machine gun in his hand. Rick spotted him and froze.

"Hello, Rick," said Grant, walking towards Rick with a limp. "It's too bad you discovered our little operation. But not to worry, it will all be over shortly, and this time it'll be final. You've shown amazing resilience by staying alive all this time."

"The shows over, Grant. Give it up," Rick said menacingly.

Suddenly twelve of Grant's mercenary soldiers showed themselves from the shadows, wearing their black camouflage outfits and with their guns drawn. They all looked serious, and each looked meaner than the next.

"Your little band of merry men have found out a lot in a short time," said Grant. "Tell me, what gave us away?"

Rick wanted to buy some time and thought, *Why not.*

"First, when we heard you speak Italian and you mentioned Bustiani. I had a friend check, and he found that Bustiani had been bankrolling you for the last several years. You're his illegitimate son. You're cozy with Dale Honeycutt, who also happens to have a degree from Dartmouth. She wrote her thesis on the Pawnee Indians in Colorado, which was how she discovered that there might still be gold on that property."

"Very clever," Grant said with a sarcastic grin.

"You used Dale until you were done with her. I don't see her around, so I suspect she's not available to talk to anyone … permanently."

Suddenly Grant's grin disappeared and his jaw clenched; a genuine loathing was starting to show.

Rick smiled slightly and continued, "You got Judge Jack Thornton to help you move the Pawnee Indian Reservation property line, and then you bought the property for next to nothing, to appear legitimate. Since the Judge did what you had asked, you had no more need of him. He conveniently had a heart attack.

"I suspect the Air Force is also involved, because how could you possibly get around using explosives for well over a year so close to a major military base, since one of their missions is to record all seismic activity. It had to be kept quiet. How am I doing so far, Grant?"

Grant was now getting red and angrier by the minute.

"Again, my guess is that both Dale and the Judge outlived their usefulness," said Rick, "and you killed them or had them killed. You're absolutely psychotic if you think you can get away with this."

"You think you have things figured out pretty well, don't you?" Grant arrogantly said. "Well, I've been planning this for over ten years. My plan is foolproof, and so far everything has happened just as I'd planned. We had small hiccups, but they were dealt with, and nothing important has changed. Right now it looks like I may just play my last trump card."

Grant suddenly looked around. "Where is the other guy that was with you?"

"I don't know," Rick said, smiling and looking around at his options, "but he'll find you soon enough."

CHAPTER

66

Suddenly one of the guards moaned and collapsed to the ground. He had a Ronin Throwing Star in his upper chest. A few seconds later, two more guards fell down. All you heard was a slight *swooshing* sound and a moan. The next guard had an arrow in his chest that had come through the opening from the large gate. Rick turned around and saw a lone Indian sitting on horseback at the top of the hill about two hundred yards away.

Everyone looked towards where the arrow came from, but nobody saw anything.

Grant, frustrated, said, "This wasn't supposed to happen." He ducked down behind a drum barrel and yelled out, "Kill them …. kill them all …now."

But before they could start shooting, three more guards went down, without a shot fired. Some of the remaining guards were looking around nervously, because they couldn't see anybody shooting. After a few seconds, three of them turned around, took cover, and left through another building exit. Grant decided it was time to leave.

He had planned for contingencies and quietly sneaked out the side window to a waiting ambulance. He got into the driver's side and came face to face with Aki.

'I'm sorry, but you can't leave yet. Get out," said Aki, smiling underneath his black ninja bandana.

As Grant got out of the ambulance, he pulled a small pistol from his boot and shot at Aki. It missed him, but the bullet ricocheted in the cab and grazed Aki's right temple. Aki fell out of the passenger side of the ambulance door, as Grant clumsily got back in the ambulance and took off. He didn't waste any time crashing through the chain-link fence onto a dirt road. He was cursing because his leg was never set properly after Rick kicked him in the knee back at his house. Now his head was throbbing and he was reliving the pain in his leg. He vowed to one day get even with Rick.

Rick heard the shot and rushed outside to see Aki on the sidewalk slightly bleeding from the forehead. Liz ran over to Aki, while Rick was still shooting at the remaining guards. After several more rounds, the other guards felt it was time to leave and made a quick exit. Rick saw that Liz was bandaging Aki.

Aki shook his head. "I failed you, and I let him escape."

"Don't worry about that," Rick said. "We'll find him. I think I have a pretty good idea of where he's going."

Just then Steve drove up and hopped out of the truck.

"That truck was just a decoy," said Steve. "I took out the guy, locked him in the back, and called the local police to come and get him. What happened to Aki?"

"He took one for the team," Rick said, trying to make light of the situation.

"Liz, can you stay with Aki for a few minutes? We're going to see if there are any clues in the office as to how and where he's shipping the gold."

She nodded. Just as they went into the office in the back of the building, she noticed that two of the guards were hugging the wall, hoping not be seen. As they were about to fire at Rick and

Steve, she pulled out her gun and quickly shot each guard in the chest.

"Rick," yelled Liz, "are you guys okay?"

Steve quickly turned around in time to see the two guards crumble to the floor, with blood spewing from their chest. Rick rushed out to see what Liz was shooting at.

"Good thing I brought my own," said Liz, standing up.

"Are you all right, Liz?" asked Rick.

"Yeah, I'm fine," Liz said. "But I've never shot anybody before. I guess all that training I had has finally paid off."

"Looks like it did," said Rick, and went back into the office.

In the office, they found papers scattered everywhere. They found a crumpled fax sheet dated just that morning that said, *Grant Williams agreed to a ten percent handling fee to convert the gold to Swiss Francs*. It was from Bern, Switzerland, and signed by Mr. Jacque Marcie, Vice President at the Bank of Bern.

"It looks like he may be transporting this gold all the way to Switzerland," said Steve.

"Yeah, I agree," said Rick. "But I wonder just how much gold he actually has in those containers. I'm curious though. If the truck you followed was empty – and I don't think the ambulance could have carried much – then where is the gold?"

As they kept looking through some of the paperwork, they checked the trash cans by one of the desks. Rick discovered several Embassy passes to the Italian Embassy in San Francisco.

"He may have been transporting the gold over the past several days or even weeks," said Steve. "It seems that he's been moving small amounts of the gold bars, using the ambulance for cover, and storing it on the Embassy grounds. I can't believe that the Italian Government would allow this, unless they were in on the whole thing."

"I also see a visitor's pass for General Alexander," Rick said. "I know that he and the Judge are cousins. He must have been in it from the beginning, because Fred said this military base tracks all seismic disturbances. Using dynamite in the mine must have set off the seismic tracking devices."

Just then Liz walked back inside with Aki and jokingly said, "It looks like he's going to live. By the way, did you guys get a glimpse of an Indian on a horse about a couple of hundred yards up the hill?"

"Yeah, I saw him," Rick said, shrugging his shoulders. "But even an expert marksman couldn't shoot that well with a bow. I think he may have been a decoy and someone else closer to us made the shot. My guess is they're long gone by now.

"A thought just occurred to me. If Grant Williams is really an Italian citizen and somehow his father actually pulled some strings and has him attached to the Italian Embassy as some type of attaché, then we can't touch him. If he does get it out, neither he nor the containers with the gold can be touched, because he would have diplomatic immunity."

"That may be true," Steve said. "But he wasn't expecting us. But judging by the number of guards he still had around, he must have some unfinished work to do before he actually leaves. My guess is he's on his way to the Embassy now as we speak."

"The Italian Embassy in San Francisco," Liz reminded them, "is over a thousand miles away. It will take him over fifteen hours to get there if he's driving all the way."

"You're right," Rick said, "but I'm thinking he won't drive all that way. He'd take a helicopter or a private plane. We need to look at a map and see if there are any private airports close by that can carry a large payload."

"I'm on it," Steve said, and left.

CHAPTER

67

Steve called Jeb Morrow, a friend of his at the FAA in Cheyenne. He'd met Jeb when stationed in Viet Nam while a Huey Helicopter pilot.

"Hi, Jeb ... Steve Weisen. Remember me, from Nam?"

"Well I'll be," Jeb said, "if it isn't the guy that I used to help out of more scrapes in Nam."

"Yep, it's me," Steve said. "I need a big favor, and it won't cost you your job. And it's also nothing illegal."

Jeb just laughed. "Are you kidding? I live for those days. What can I do for you?"

"Could you check for any private airports in the Fort Collins general area that could carry large payloads and fly over twelve hundred miles without refueling?"

He came back within minutes and said, "There are no private airstrips close by, but there's an airstrip used by the military about forty miles from your location. It hasn't been used in quite some time, but from time to time, we do get special requests for clearance to a variety of places. As you know, they still have to tell us when they're taking off."

"Thanks for the information," Steve said. "I owe you one."

"You still owe me for when I picked you up in the rice paddies, not just once, but four times," Jeb reminded him. "You never did tell me what you were doing there all by yourself." He chuckled.

"I'll tell you what," Steve said, "how about when I finish this assignment, we get together over dinner and I'll tell you some stories. But I gotta warn you, as soon as I tell you, I'll have to kill you." Steve laughed, said "Thanks," and raced back to the building.

"I found a receipt for specially-made containers," Rick said. "But what's interesting is he ordered ninety of these, which cost about fifteen hundred dollars apiece. Each container was made specially to carry an estimated thirty-five hundred pounds."

Just then Liz yelled out, "I think I found one of the containers," and they rushed over to see where she was looking. She lifted a large tarp and found the empty canister.

"Let's take a look at the gold ingot form that he used and see how big they actually are," Rick said.

Steve looked at the ingot form and said," It looks like about six by three by two, which, if my memory serves me correctly, is the general size of a typical Fort Knox size *brick*. They weigh about ten pounds each."

"If they stacked them carefully inside the custom-made containers," said Rick, "they could probably get about three hundred fifty bars in each container.

"Don't forget that the flatbed I stopped," said Steve, "had forty-four canisters on board. However, it was filled with just rocks. I'm gonna guess he must have some or all of the gold already moved."

"I don't think so," said Rick. "If he did, he'd be long gone by now. Of the ninety containers he had made, at least half were planned as a diversion if he needed it. That means that each container must weigh about thirty-five hundred pounds. Do you realize he must have about a hundred and fifty thousand pounds of gold? Last time I looked, gold was selling for around three hundred and forty-five dollars an ounce. If my math is correct, he has somewhere in the neighborhood of over eight hundred million in gold."

They looked at each other, stunned at what they'd just found out.

"Holy smokes," Rick said, getting louder. "Do you know what that means? If all he did was hold onto the gold and it went up by ten cents an ounce, he'd make an additional twenty-four million dollars!"

They all walked back to the foundry area, still stunned by the amount of gold Grant was able to take out of the mine. That's when they noticed another arrow stuck in one of the metal barrels, but this time blood was running down the side of the barrel. They opened the barrel and saw it was loaded with small rocks, but they also found Dale inside. They looked outside and again saw an Indian, with his full headdress, quite a ways away just sitting on a horse on top of the ridge.

"I'll bet he's a Pawnee Indian," Liz said, "coming to warn us about something."

"Can't worry about him now," Rick said. "We need to focus on finding where Grant's going."

"I did find out," Steve said, "that there's a small old military airstrip about forty miles north of Fort Collins, which gets very little use, but is still managed by the Air Force because they still own it. That may be where they plan to take off."

"Don't forget," said Aki, "there were two canisters in the ambulance. Carrying seven thousand pounds will also slow him down a little."

Yeah, that's right, Aki," said Liz.

Rick nodded. "That also explains General Alexander's involvement in this little venture. He has enough authority to get him and Grant clearance to fly in and out, because nobody would question him. We need to get there but fast and driving won't do it. We need a helicopter."

"Let me see what I can do," Steve said.

❖ ❖ ❖

Steve called his friend Jeb again. "Hey, Jeb. It's Steve again. Do you still have that Huey Helicopter in your backyard and is it still flyable?"

"Are you kidding?" Jeb answered. "I keep it in tip-top condition, and I even have it stored in a hangar right here at the airport. Why do you ask?"

"I need another really big favor, but I need it right now. Can you come pick us up? We have a total of four passengers that need to get to that abandoned airport you told me about, but fast."

"You got it. I'll be there in twenty minutes. But this will cost you big time," said Jeb.

"When this is all over," Steve said, "you're going to have the best meal in town. See you soon."

CHAPTER
68

Grant was now racing against time to get out of town and to the airfield with his last two containers. Suddenly he heard a loud popping noise and the ambulance started to veer to the right. He applied the brakes and slowly stopped. He hobbled out of the ambulance and found he had a flat tire on the right front.

Off all the crappy luck, Grant thought. *This had to happen to me when I needed to be out of here. I sure hope they have a spare.*

He had no choice but to change the tire, since there wasn't any time to have someone come and get him. Fortunately, he was on a small road going out of town and not traveled much. As he started using the heavy-duty hydraulic jack, he could feel the strain with the weight of the canisters in the back. At one point, he was worried that if he wasn't careful, the whole ambulance could tip over on its back, because it was back heavy.

As Grant was changing the tire, he slipped and fell backwards into a small ravine. In the process, he disturbed a large rattlesnake sunning itself. Grant fell within five feet of it, when it started to raise its head, and its tail started to rattle. He knew that he needed to stay still for a moment and the snake would go away. But it didn't go away. Before Grant could move, it struck him in the ankle and then slithered away. Luckily for Grant, it bit into his boot, missing his flesh.

"Go on and git," said Grant, yelling at the snake. "Go find a rabbit to eat."

Grant climbed up from the ravine, his knee aching badly, and finished changing the tire, including bruising a few knuckles, and cursing the whole time.

He left the old tire and jack on the road and hopped gingerly back into the ambulance and thought, *Thank God it was only the front tire. With the canisters in back weighing almost seven thousand pounds, I couldn't have ever changed the tire.*

He now had to make up for lost time.

CHAPTER

69

General Alexander finished packing and was on his way to the private military airstrip, where he and Grant were flying to Italy with the gold. He didn't trust Grant to send him his share of the money, so he was going with him to be there when they offloaded the containers. He got into his car and drove off. As he started his drive to the airstrip, he noticed in the rearview mirror a car following him.

He made several turns into streets, just to quell his nerves, but they were still following him. He wondered why anybody would be following him. He still had his uniform on, and they must know who he is. After another ten minutes, he pulled into a small street, over to the curb, and waited.

The car stopped behind him. Two men dressed in dark suits, wearing dark glasses and hats, got out of their car and approached from both sides.

As they did, the General rolled down his window and asked, "Why have you been following me?"

The individual on the passenger side showed him identification and said, "We're from the Adjutant General's Office, and we've been told to escort you back to the base for some questioning concerning the death of Judge Jack Thornton."

"I knew of him," the General said, "but I understand he died of a heart attack a few days ago, and that's all I know."

"I'm sorry, sir, but we have our orders."

The General was now worried about being detained too long and possibly missing his flight with Grant. Knowing Grant, he would use any excuse to leave without him.

The individuals looked like CIA operatives, with all the right credentials, so he thought he had to go with them. He got into the backseat of their car, and they drove off. They quickly pulled off the street, faced him, and gave him one shot to the side of the head, using a silencer.

They put papers in his inside jacket pocket that included a suicide note, along with some pictures of him in very compromising positions. They turned around, drove him back, and put him back in his car, and left him. They put the gun in his hand as if he committed suicide.

As they left the scene, they called and said, "The job is done," and hung up.

The individual on the other end smiled. "He thought he was going to get part of our casino business? Where would he get an idea like that? One more loose end eliminated." He said to his boss sitting across the desk, "It's done. What do you want to do with Grant Williams?"

"That's already being taken care of," Luigi said to Sully. "I just know that crook somehow had my uncle killed in Florence, and he's going to pay for it. I still think he had a hand in killing his father. I suspect he was also upset that they never accepted him as part of the family."

"Get our friends in Denver on the phone," said Sully.

CHAPTER

70

Jeb Morrow circled the field where Steve was standing and made a perfect landing.

Jeb jumped out, gave Steve a big bear hug, and said, "Hi, Steve. I'm here just as I promised."

"Hi, Jeb," said Steve. "It's so good to see you after all those years. It looks like the years have been good to you."

They all came rushing out to the parking lot. Steve introduced everyone, and Rick asked, "Can your copter hold us all?"

"It held sixteen men," Jeb said proudly, "with full combat gear. We airlifted them from the Mekong Delta and flew them all the way to Hanoi. Two had to hang on the outside foot rails, but we did it."

"Steve, tell him where the airfield is," Rick said, "so we can get there the quickest way possible."

Before he could answer, Jeb held up his hand and said, "I already know where it is. I had a friend of mine do a little research to find out more about it. You do know that this is still military property and there may be guards on duty. But I did find out they have a C-130H airplane located there, but the funny thing is that it has Italian Air Force markings on it."

"Can that plane carry about one hundred and fifty thousand pounds?" Rick asked.

"Normally, no," said Jeb.

"How big a cargo can that plane normally handle?" Rick asked.

"I'd say around ninety thousand pounds," Jeb said. "But if the interior was completely gutted and they installed extra fuel tanks in the wings and in the cargo hold, my guess is it could probably fly and could carry an additional forty to fifty thousand pounds. It could fly over ten thousand miles before having to refuel. Why do you ask?"

"I think the plane will still be grossly overweight," Steve said, "with that much weight on board. He might not use the additional fueling pods and refuel more often, before they get to Switzerland. And if he has legitimate diplomatic immunity papers, then he doesn't have to tell anyone what's inside."

"They've had the plane parked on the base's tarmac," Jeb continued, "for about a week and have been loading containers of some kind almost every day. It's all very hush-hush, because there's a General Alexander with special papers from the Italian Consulate, and so nobody can get near it. They're just waiting for two more passengers, and they'll be on their way."

Rick was now even more worried because he knew that if Grant and the General got airborne, they wouldn't stand a chance of catching them. They would be in international airspace, and their cargo could not be touched.

As they took off in Jeb's helicopter, Rick looked down. They circled once and saw another big eighteen-wheeler flatbed sitting idle in the far backside of the property. As they rose higher, he also saw what he thought was an Indian sitting on his horse, wearing a full headdress similar to the chief of a tribe. He looked again, and he was gone. Rick told himself he needed to get his eyes checked when they get back.

❖　❖　❖

Grant was now late, but he was hoping the General was either already there waiting for him or his friends in Las Vegas had taken care of him. He decided to call the pilot on his mobile phone, but couldn't get a signal because of the surrounding mountains. As he drove along the road, he heard the faint noise of a helicopter overhead, but didn't pay much attention to it and just kept driving. He now had to make up for lost time so he could be in Bern, Switzerland, for lunch the next day to celebrate.

Rick spotted Grant driving on the road and pointed down to him. "Let's just get to the airfield and wait for him, because now we know for sure that's where he's going."

They all agreed.

"I just thought about something," Rick said. "Once we get there, if he has the canisters marked with *property of Italian Embassy*, then legally we can't touch the canisters or Grant."

It suddenly sank in that he was right.

"What's in those canisters that he needs a C-130H to carry it?" Jeb asked.

Rick said casually, "It's classified, but was stolen from my property, or I think it's on our property."

"Who does it actually belong to?" asked Jeb.

"We aren't quite sure," said Liz. "It legally belongs to Rick since he's the new owner of the Monarch Ranch."

Rick looked over and suddenly realized Liz might be right. Up to this point, he just wanted to catch Grant because he was a crook and probably responsible for several killings. He decided to call Walter and see if Leonard Schultz could help.

Rick called Walter and quickly brought him up-to-date. "Is there anybody in Italy you can call to find out if Grant actually has consulate attaché privileges? That may help to stop him."

"I'll make a call right away, Rick," said Walter.

CHAPTER
71

As Grant sped away in the ambulance with his last two containers of gold, he was feeling very confident that he had beaten them. He left enough clues for them to think that he was on his way to the Italian Embassy in San Francisco. But he had his plane just about twenty miles from here. and within forty minutes. he'd be loaded and on his way to Bern, Switzerland.

He'd worked out a deal with the Italian Air Force and the Italian Consulate to use their C-130 cargo plane that he had refurbished to carry the heavy load. The plane would transport forty-two containers labeled as expensive furniture for the retired Consulate to Rome, Italy. But as soon as he was in the air, he was going to commandeer the plane and fly it to Bern, Switzerland.

As Jeb's copter approached the airfield, the base Commander contacted Jeb and said, "You are in violation of U.S. military airspace. You need to turn around and leave immediately."

"This is retired Colonel Jeb Morrow of the 101st Airborne Division requesting permission to land. I have some wounded on board."

The air traffic controller came back and said, "Jeb, is that really you? This is Wily Jenson. We served in Nam together. What's the problem?"

"Wily," said Jeb, "well I'll be. What have you been up to? Sorry I haven't called you, but I've been busy in Cheyenne. Listen, we gotta problem here. Is there an Italian C-130 sitting on the tarmac waiting to take off?"

"Yeah," said Wily. "She's been sitting here all week, and they've been loading boxes with Italian Consulate seals every day for about the last three days. They're supposed to be coming with the last load today and flying out of here as soon as they're loaded. They've been waiting on the tarmac for the last four hours, and we weren't to touch or go near them and just let them go through. It's supposed to be a hush-hush operation."

"That's not quite true," Jeb said, "but I understand you have orders. Has anybody boarded yet?"

"Just the two pilots so far," Wily said, "and they're getting a mite nervous because they've been waiting here since this morning. I understand that Lieutenant General Alexander is supposed to be taking off with another person from the Italian Embassy. That's all I know about this. But I still can't let you land here. It's against orders."

"I knew this would happen," Rick said. "And that's because Grant has diplomatic immunity. Somehow we have got to land and be on the ground before Grant comes and tries to get on that plane."

As he said that, he saw the airplane on the runway, with the four engine props straining to take off. The massive rear cargo door was open like a giant whale ready to eat. In the distance, Rick saw a rider on horseback coming over the ridge and moving at a very fast pace. He noticed as the rider got closer that he was dressed in black clothing, and right then he knew who it was … it was Aki.

The old airstrip wasn't very large. It was left over from the Second World War, with only perforated metal sheets used as the tarmac for takeoff and landing. The CIA used it occasionally for *black ops* assignments.

Grant was still driving feverishly. He was now within twenty miles of the airstrip and by now feeling euphoric, because he was going to be airborne soon. He looked out and still saw a helicopter hovering, but it finally disappeared over the ridge. He decided again not to pay any attention to it. Instead, he thought about sitting on his new villa's veranda overlooking the sea and enjoying himself, with a few women close by. On the other hand, maybe he should consider buying a yacht and just live on it without having any restrictions.

He grinned and said aloud, "The decisions we have to make in order to find true happiness."

Jeb was now circling the field trying to convince the tower they must land and told everyone he had an idea.

"I'm going to circle the airfield to see which direction Grant will be entering," Jeb said. "In the meantime, have you figured out what we're going to do when we land, since we're going to try and take back what's actually considered Italian sovereign property?"

"Here's what I think," Rick answered. "In order for him to land, wherever that is, it must be an Italian military airfield, because he can't just land anywhere."

"That's not actually true," said Steve. "It's because he has a military plane and whoever has an alliance with Italy would have no problem allowing them to land, refuel, and take off again. There are plenty of countries in both South America and Africa that would allow that."

CHAPTER

72

When Walter heard the estimated weight of the gold, he jumped out of his chair, stood up, and quickly looked at the stock market quotes for gold. He then calmly said he would call Leonard to see what he recommends. Walter called Leonard and relayed the story from Rick.

"There are several things we can do," Leonard said, "but I think that given the short notice, I would try to claim it for the Monarch Ranch as property that was stolen. But as a sign of good faith, you may want to give the Pawnee Indians a nice share. They don't pay taxes on their reservation, but you'll be paying many taxes. On top of that, it may open up a Pandora's Box, with people asking a lot of questions, which I don't think we want … do you?"

"You're right," Walter agreed. "We don't want to create a bigger problem. Thanks, Leonard. I'll call you later."

He then quickly made a call to his friend Signore Giovanni Terranova, the Signore Magistrate in the city of Florence, to see if he would help with this delicate matter. After several transfers, he was finally connected.

"Hello, Giovanni. This is Walter Donleavy. How are you and your family doing?"

"Just fine, Walter," Giovanni answered. "Thank you for asking. And your family as well?"

"As well as can be expected, given these difficult times," Walter answered." I have a question for you concerning a rather delicate matter, and I hope you can help me or guide me to someone who can."

"If an individual is considered an attaché from the Italian Embassy," asked Walter, "and is bringing in stolen cargo, does the individual still have diplomatic immunity?"

"It's a difficult question to answer," Giovanni said. "Much depends on who it is. But I have a high-ranking friend in the Italian Parliament I can ask. If this individual were doing something illegal, then it would be easier to revoke his attaché privileges, and then he could be prosecuted by any country. What's the individual's name?"

"You may not recognize his name ... Grant Williams. But you may recognize his father's name. You see, he's the illegitimate son of Salvatore Bustiani from Florence, who I'm certain you're familiar with."

Giovanni stood up from his chair, smiling. "I'll look into this myself and find out if he's actually registered as an attaché to the Italian Government and will let you know shortly."

"How long does something like that take," Walter asked, "because time is of the essence?"

"I will make a call immediately," Giovanni said. "My friend is a senior Member of Parliament, and I know he would be very happy to look into this for me."

"Thank you so much for your assistance in this delicate matter," Walter said. "Please call anytime, day or night."

Giovanni decided to call his friend, the assistant Prime Minister of Italy – Alberto Bartolome.

"Hello, Giovanni," Alberto said. "How are you, my old friend?"

Giovanni and Alberto exchanged pleasantries and Giovanni relayed what Walter requested.

Alberto paused a moment after reading his file and said to Giovanni, "We have nobody in our files by those names listed as an attaché, either here or in the United States," Alberto said. "I hope this helps you, my friend."

"Thank you for the information," Giovanni said. "We need to get together for dinner soon. Since moving to Florence for this new position, we have not seen each other. I live in Florence and you're living in Rome. We must make time for old friends to stay in touch."

He agreed and said, "Until next time."

Giovanni called Walter at the number he gave him, which Walter picked up immediately. "Hello, Walter. I checked with my friend, and he assures me that there's no one by either of those two names considered an attaché to the Italian Government."

"Thank you so much for the information," Walter said. "I hope it wasn't too much trouble."

"No, not at all, my friend," Giovanni said. "But I should tell you that he's the Assistant Prime Minister of Italy and seemed almost relieved he didn't find the name."

"Thank you so much," Walter said and hung up.

The Assistant Prime Minister looked over the document quietly and swore under his breath. A document did exist making the request. He signed it when he was just a Chief Prosecutor and had forgotten all about that period of his life. He took this time to correct the files, because there was a petition for an attaché for San Francisco in the United States requested by Salvatore Bustiani. Now that he was dead, there was no reason to keep it active. He quickly shredded the document and said to himself, *another problem resolved that has haunted me for years.*

He also faxed a note to the San Francisco Embassy to destroy any papers containing Grant Williams' or Salvatore Bustiani's name.

CHAPTER

73

Delighted with the new information, Walter called Rick.

"Rick, I went to the second highest authority in Italy," said Walter, "and there wasn't anybody by that name registered as an attaché to the Italian Embassy either in Italy or in the United States. It appears all those papers were forged."

"This changes everything." Rick said. "That's great news, because I couldn't believe that he actually had those rights. Thanks, Walter. I'll let you know what happens."

He hung up and told Steve and Liz what Walter said. Both had big smiles on their faces.

"Well, that takes care of the legal side of the problem," Liz said, "but he still has forged documents plus a pilot and co-pilot and an Italian military airplane on the tarmac waiting to take off. As far as the pilots and even the U.S. military traffic controllers are concerned, Grant is legitimate, and they will have to protect him."

"I've got an idea," Jeb said, "that may give us some more time, but I gotta land this, and you guys can't come out until I say it's okay."

"Okay," Rick said.

Jeb called back to the tower. "I need to make an emergency landing at the base because I have a fuel leak problem."

The military traffic controller, Wily Jenson, said, "You have permission to land, but as soon as you land, you need to come up to the tower and fill out form DOD-897A. You're a civilian landing on a military airfield."

Jeb landed his helicopter and within minutes was out and running up the stairs, two at a time. Sergeant Benjamin Hawthorne, who looked at him suspiciously, met him at the top of the stairs and showed him to the office. Jeb showed him his credentials indicating that he was a retired Colonel having flown in both Korea and Viet Nam. A few minutes later, he came back downstairs and got back into his helicopter. Suddenly the Italian airplane shut its engines down. The pilots got out of their C-130 airplane and walked over to the tower.

As soon as the pilots got to the foot of the stairs, Jeb ran back to his helicopter and said, "Now we get our cargo."

As they were about to board the Italian aircraft, Grant came tearing around the corner and smashed through the chain-link gate, driving like a maniac to get to the plane. He only had about three hundred yards to go and knew that once he got on his plane, nobody could touch him because of his diplomatic immunity credentials. He looked down the runway and was angered that the Italian pilots had shut off the engines and disembarked and were heading towards the tower. Then he spotted a helicopter to the left.

Suddenly a group of people started to board his airplane through the rear cargo hold. He now drove wildly over the clattering metal tarmac towards the plane, but they were already inside and raising the cargo bay door.

"I'm going underneath the plane," Steve said, "and shoot out the tires, so even if they come back and cause trouble, they can't go anywhere until they change the tires."

"Let's do it," Rick said. "I may be in a lot of trouble before this is all cleared up, but you know what they say, *it's easier to ask for forgiveness than to ask for permission."*

Steve had to stand back far enough so the blowout wouldn't hit him. He shot with precision, but the tires wouldn't blow.

He just kept shooting at the same spot at least ten times. Finally one of the tires blew, and he said, "Just a couple more."

It finally happened just as he planned. By shooting out several of the tires, the rest blew out from the sheer weight of the cargo. The plane was not going anywhere, at least not for a while.

CHAPTER

74

Grant was now in a wild rage. He pulled out a small caliber machine gun and was ready to use it.

Suddenly the air traffic controller from the tower called out to him on the outside speaker. "This is Major William Jenson. You must stop your vehicle. You have no authority. This is a U.S. Government military-controlled airport."

Grant just kept driving, as if he hadn't heard anything. The Major repeated his command. "I ask you once again to stop your vehicle or we'll use force to stop you."

Grant heard him, but felt that all he had to do was get to his airplane and he would be safe. He had diplomatic immunity, and they wouldn't want to cause an international incident. They would have to stand down.

MP soldiers arrived and shot out the tires of the ambulance. After a heavy volley of rifle shots, the ambulance lurched to one side and tipped over on its right side. It slid a hundred feet, creating a trail of sparks in its wake, before finally stopping just fifty feet from the back of the rear cargo door.

Grant was delirious and rambling, with blood running down his right side and from his head. "I need to get to my gold, and as long as I'm on the plane, you can't touch me."

The air traffic controller from the tower called out to him on the outside speaker. "This is Major William Jenson. Put your weapon down. You have no authority to be on this base."

Grant crawled out of the top of the ambulance and slowly lowered himself down to the tarmac. Blood was flowing from his mouth, and his left arm was bleeding through his jacket. But he kept walking towards the plane, dragging his left leg slightly.

Just then Rick came out of the shadows of the cargo door plane, with a gun in his hand.

Grant stumbled and fell. When he got up, he looked in horror and disgust seeing Rick.

Speaking in a desperate whisper, Grant said, "It's you. What the hell are you doing here? This has nothing to do with you. I've got diplomatic immunity, and my father is well connected in Italy."

He tried to get up again and pointed his machine gun towards Rick.

Just then the military MPs yelled out, "Look out! He has a gun!"

The MPs got closer, and Grant turned, as if he was going to shoot his way out. He tried to stand up and brought his gun to waist level. The MPs took aim and shot him five times in the chest, and he slowly fell backwards. He lay there with a look of shock and desperation on his face.

"I was so close ..." Grant said, whispering his lasts words, "to being one of the richest people in the world. My plan was perfect. I don't understand ... I have diplomatic immunity ......" His garbled words trailed off.

CHAPTER

75

Liz came out to look and put her hand over her mouth. "It could only have ended this way," she said.

The Lieutenant of the MP squad placed two fingers on Grant's neck to see if there was a pulse, then said to everyone, "He's dead."

Major Jenson by this time had come down from the tower and had driven his Jeep to the tarmac where the airplane and ambulance were parked. "Who is Rick Benedict?" he asked.

Rick stepped forward. "I'm Rick Benedict, sir, and if you give me a few minutes, I can explain all of this to you."

The Major put his hand up, interrupted him, and said, "We need to spend more than a few minutes, son. I have two Italian Air Force pilots with containers of illegal drugs on board that have Italian Embassy papers attached, and now an ambulance with some lunatic driver wielding a machine gun trying to get on board this plane. The truth is that all of this is way above my pay grade and I need to call my superior, Lieutenant General Alexander, and let him sort this mess out."

"I'm sorry to tell you this, sir," Rick interrupted him, "but he's probably dead. My guess is he left the country or is dead, and this guy had a hand in it," pointing to Grant. "In addition, he may have also been involved in this conspiracy. Let me make a phone call to somebody I think can help this situation."

Rick turned around and, looking at Steve and Jeb, said, "We need two flatbed or container trucks with a forklift so we can offload these containers."

"I think I can handle that for you," Jeb said. "I'll be right back."

Jeb made a few calls and within minutes reported to Rick and Steve. "We should have something here in about half an hour."

Rick, in the meantime, called Walter and told him what happened. "We're in a real sticky situation here. We need someone here to help explain things without having to open all the containers and show them what's inside."

"Let me make a call and see what I can do," Walter said.

Rick looked at the Major and said, "You may be receiving a call shortly that will explain this, Major."

Within ten minutes, Major Jenson received a call from the Vice Chairman of the Joint Chief of Staff in the Pentagon, who said, "This is General Theodore DeWitt. Major Jenson, let these people have the containers. They're working on a special assignment for the Pentagon."

"Yes, sir," Major Jenson said. "I'll take care of it."

"Mr. Benedict, I just got an interesting call from the Vice Chairman of the Joint Chief of Staff in Washington telling me to give you the containers and help you get out of here."

Rick looked at Steve and Liz with a surprised expression. He didn't know Walter knew the Vice Chairman of the Joint Chief of Staff at the Pentagon.

The Major told the MPs to tow the ambulance away.

"Sir, there are two containers on that ambulance," Rick said, "that we also will need to retrieve."

Fortunately, even though the ambulance slid sideways on the metal tarmac, the containers hadn't broken open. Two eighteen-wheelers came around the corner, with a forklift strapped to the back of one of the trailer's flatbeds, and stopped at the gate. The drivers showed their credentials, drove in, and parked close to the cargo plane. They started moving the containers from the cargo hold to the flatbed trucks. Rick jumped up to the truck bed and pulled off all evidence of the Italian Embassy certificates. Everything was loaded on the new trucks within an hour and ready to go.

"Steve, why don't you ride with the first driver," Rick said, "and just drive it up to the ranch. We'll sort all this out when we get there."

The two Italian Air Force pilots just stood there trying to figure out what had happened. But since the U.S. military was removing the containers, they weren't going to object.

Liz quickly went over to them and translated for them. "They say they don't know what to do, with almost all their tires blown out and their cargo taken off their plane."

"Tell him not to worry," Major Jenson said. "We'll help them get some new tires and have them out of here in no time."

He told his Chief Maintenance Officer to give them a hand.

He turned back to Rick and said quietly, "I assume I can send you the bill for new tires for this plane?"

"Yes, sir," Rick nodded. "Send me the bill at the Monarch Ranch just outside of Fort Collins and I'll take care of it."

"This is somewhat strange," the Major said, "but on par for typical *black ops* assignments."

With that, Rick and Liz got back into Jeb's Helicopter and took off back to the smelter to get their vehicles and head home. Aki, watching from a distance, got back on his horse and rode back to the ranch.

"I know this has been a lot of fun for me," Jeb asked grinning, "but I gotta ask, what's actually in those containers anyway?"

Rick looked at him and said, "It's classified; so if I told you, I'd have to kill you. But when you come out to the ranch in two weeks, I'll tell you the version I'm allowed to tell."

"Yeah, sure," Jeb said. "If that's what you want to go with, that's okay with me."

Liz took this opportunity to wrap her arms around Rick. "I can't remember when I've had so much fun," She said. "Not since we were in Prague, that is. You sure know how to show a girl a good time."

CHAPTER
76

The following week, Rick flew back to Rhode Island to bring Walter up-to-date with the ranch.

"By now, you've read all the reports I sent you," said Rick, "and what's been going on at the ranch. Firstly, as you can see by the assaying reports how much gold was mined for this first effort."

"What do you mean first effort?" asked Walter.

"As we were trying to get out of the tunnel," Rick responded, "we noticed what looked like another vein of gold. In order to be sure, we should get a geological engineer out there to confirm it. There could be a lot more gold still in the mine. I know that Grant would still be mining had we not come along. How much gold is there, I don't know. All the mining equipment is there and already paid for, so we don't have to buy any more. I would think that at least some exploratory drilling would be worthwhile.

"However, if we do find something, I think that the only way we can make this work is to share it with the Pawnee Indian Reservation."

"That sounds fine," said Walter. "When you're ready, I'll get someone that I know to come out and make an assessment."

"Secondly," said Rick, "I think that a ranch for wayward boys and girls might be a good thing for Colorado. Fred did some preliminary number crunching and created a business plan for that part of the ranch to pay for itself. I'd like to devote two thousand acres of the total twenty thousand acres to a newly created *White Feather Camp for Children*. The ranch gets the tax write-off and Colorado gets a new ranch for kids.

"Have Fred send these figures to Leonard," Walter said smiling, "and let's see how we can make it happen."

"We can establish a special trust fund," Rick continued. "The camp could pay for itself for at least the next hundred years or more.

Walter held up his hand, smiling, and said, "You had already sold me at the *White Feather Camp for Underprivileged Children*."

"The other eighteen thousand acres," Rick said, "will be devoted to raising the beef for the restaurants that we're going to open. I've been talking to Aki, and he thinks we have a great chance to create that higher grade of beef we originally talked about for the restaurants."

Walter was smiling with enthusiasm. "I wholeheartedly approve of your plans."

Walter asked Rick to walk with him in the garden. "Rick, you have again surprised me with your wisdom, strength, and leadership to resolve another problem for us and make money in the process."

"Well, I must admit it was a challenge," Rick said. "And there were times I was very frustrated, but I was lucky that I had some great people to help me through all of this."

"You have learned," said Walter, "how to use the tools and the people around you wisely."

"Now, Walter," Rick said, "I still have trouble believing that this ranch was an accident, but finding gold on the property was a nice touch."

Walter smiled and continued, "Rick, I told you that this ranch was always part of the assets when I bought the company. That was always true."

The next day Rick flew back to his ranch in Colorado.

CHAPTER

77

Rick located the Chief of the Pawnee Indians, Chief Black Bear, and the tribe that had owned the land where the gold mine was located.

Rick called and introduced himself, but before he could finish, the Chief said, "I know who you are. I have been expecting your call."

"I'd like to invite you," Rick said, a little surprised, "to the Monarch Ranch in two weeks on Saturday. There are some things I would like to discuss with you that we need to clear up."

"We'll be there," the Chief said, "and thank you for the invitation."

Rick hung up and was happy that the Chief accepted his invitation, but wondered if he would really come.

Around noon on the day of the celebration, a stretch limo pulled up to the ranch. Walter, Liz and Rick's parents, and Aki's wife all got out of the limo. They had flown in together in Walter's private plane. Both Liz and Rick were excited and very happy that they could join them.

Rick went over to his dad, hugged him, and said, "Hi, Dad. I'm sure glad you could come out to the ranch."

"I'm very happy for you, my son," said Jacob, beaming with pride. "We heard from Walter that you've been very busy lately."

"That's an understatement," said Rick.

Liz also went over to see her mother, Hilda, and said, "Hi, Mom. I'm so glad to see you. How about next week when I'm back in Rhode Island, I'd like to spend more time with you. Maybe we can get out on my boat and sail along the coast."

"That would make me very happy," said Hilda. "I know you may still not have forgiven me, but we did the best we could with what we had."

"I forgave you a long time ago," said Liz, her eyes glistening.

Rick walked over to Walter. "Hi, Walter. It's good to see you again.

Later that day, another stretch limousine drove up to the front of the house.

The Chief of the Pawnee Indians got out first and went directly to Rick. "I am B lack Bear , Chief of the Pawnee Nation. These are my four sons, White Cloud, Red Eagle, Red Wolf, and Three Eagles, and my daughter, who we named White Feather."

Chief Black Bear, and his four sons and daughter were dressed in full Native American Indian headdresses and looked as though they just walked off a high budget western movie set.

Rick shook hands with each person and walked back to the Chief and said, "I am so happy to meet you and your family."

After all introductions were made, the Chief turned and signaled to his son Red Eagle. He stepped forward holding a large, highly polished mahogany case with polished brass hinges and clasps, and presented it to Rick.

"We have seen what greed can do to people," the Chief said, "and we have also seen people that are truly our friends. We wish you to have this as a token of our appreciation."

Rick opened it and couldn't believe his eyes. He was looking at an original pair of 1860 Colt Army six-shooters, with gold embellishments on the barrel. The handle was hand-carved from an Elk horn.

"Thank you so much," said Rick astonished. "This is truly an honor, and I will cherish this always. I don't know what to say."

Walter was standing next to Rick, when he tugged on Rick's sleeve and said, "Don't you have something for the Chief."

He had almost forgotten, surprised by the gift from the Chief. Rick said, "I also have something for you. In fairness to your people, here is a check that I hope will help the Pawnee Indian Nation."

The Chief looked at it, and now he had a surprised look on his face.

The Chief nodded at Rick and Walter – each said nothing, but all understood.

"That was quite a present the Chief gave you," said Liz.

"It was great, and I'll treasure it always," said Rick. "Let's get something to eat."

Rick, holding Liz's hand, wandered over to the barbecue pit.

They walked towards John Hammond, and Rick said, "Hi, John. Having a good time?"

"Hi, Rick. Yeah, we are," said John. "This is my wife, Imelda."

"How do you do," said Rick. "It's great to meet you."

"It's a pleasure to meet you also," said Imelda. "John has told me so much about you."

"I hope he hasn't exaggerated too much," said Rick smiling.

John walked up closer to Rick and whispered in his ear, "Are we square?"

"Yeah, we're fine," said Rick. "Go and enjoy yourselves, and we'll talk on Monday."

Steve watched from afar and finally walked up to Rick and Liz and said, "I've got to go, but we'll keep in touch."

"Thanks an awful lot for your help," Rick said, "and let's plan to sit down somewhere and just have a drink and soak up the sun. You know you're always welcome here anytime."

"I'd like that," Steve said. "I'm flying back to Rhode Island to spend some more time with my parents."

Steve walked over to Walter and told him, "Things are okay with Rick, Liz, and me."

"That's good, but don't go too far," said Walter. "We have other things still to do."

Steve gave Liz a big hug and whispered to her, "See you soon."

Rick and Liz watched Steve get into a waiting taxi and drove off.

Liz held onto Rick's arm ever so tightly, as if she never wanted to let go.

He looked at her and smiled. "We still need to talk. How about tonight, after everybody goes home, we take a shower and you let me scrub your back for an awfully long time, and then you can tell me all about what you'd like to do."

She smiled at him and said, "Great. I'll just say good-bye to Walter and my mother and get the water started."

EPILOGUE

Walter was in great spirits, especially since his investment just paid him a dividend of three hundred million dollars. He was already thinking about a new building for Colorado State. It would work together with the scholarship Rick would be administering.

Walter walked over to Chief Black Bear and said, "I would like to stay in touch with you and see if there is anything else that would be beneficial to both of us."

"It would be my great pleasure," the Chief said, "and thank you for your generosity and hospitality."

The Chief had been very happy to receive a check for five hundred million dollars. He now felt it was time to retire. He had come to the ranch, along with five of his tribe in full Pawnee Indian headdresses. It was a special occasion for all. They provided entertainment and performed a special ceremonial Pawnee Indian dance, complete with drums and tribal chanting. This was to bless and take care of the children on the new *White Feather Camp for Children*. He now felt he had completed what his ancestors had started.

"Aki," Walter said, "I understand you have a plan where you will stay on about three months and train the ranch hands to breed better cattle?"

"Yes, I do," said Aki. "We should have no problem in achieving your goal. You were right, Mr. Donleavy; I have grown, and you have given me opportunities that went beyond anything I could have ever anticipated." Aki bowed to Walter.

"Aki," said Walter, "people can develop magnificent plans, but it takes magnificent people to execute them successfully. I told you a long time ago, you and I would do great things together – this is just a start."

He again bowed to Walter, turned, and went back to the festivities with his wife.

Rick was watching Fred enjoying himself, because he finally got to parade around in his brand-new duds. Rick looked at him and didn't have the heart to tell him that now he looked like Howdy Doody.

"Hi, Don," said Rick. "How does it feel to be the new ranch foreman?"

"It feels great," said Don to Rick. "You won't be disappointed. This is my sister, Danielle, who's been dancing with Fred."

Rick had to admit that one of the things that Grant did right was to buy the smelter foundry. The great part is that the property had a spur line that was connected to the regular railroad line. This was a perfect place for a slaughterhouse. This would go a long way to getting their beef to the local restaurants in the other states.

Rick then walked up to Chief Black Bear and pulled him to the side and asked him, "Chief, I have to ask you. When we were at the foundry, we kept seeing several Indians in full headdresses sitting on their horse on top of a hill. Was that you we saw last week?"

The chief winked and said, "No, it wasn't, but it may have been our forefathers, because you know we still watch how the land is being treated."

After that, the Chief thanked all for the invitation and drove off with his five children.

The newly formed Monarch Mining Company continued mining the gold and made an agreement to split the profits fifty-fifty with the Pawnee Indians.

The Chief knew their ancestors would be proud of how everything turned out for their tribe. They could now pay to have their sons and daughters go to some of the finest schools in the country. Walter had said he would help him with that when they were ready.

"Walk with me a little, Rick," Walter said. "Now that you have this organized, I would like you and possibly Liz to help me on another project. I recently purchased a llama ranch in Bolivia."

Rick spun around and said, "A llama ranch? Are you kidding?"

"No, I'm not," said Walter, "but hear me out. I would like to transport llamas to the United States and breed them, along with the alpaca ranch I already have established in New Mexico. They have the greatest wool and when made into yarn, has a very high resale value."

"There are still a great many things you don't know yet," said Walter. "In time, you will understand and embrace what I have created as my Monarch Enterprise business."

The next day back in his home, Walter was sitting in his office when he received a phone call from Anton Mansard.

"Walter," Anton said, "I have Signore Giovanni Terranova, who wishes to speak with you."

"Hello, Mr. Donleavy. I want to thank you for your support," Giovanni said, "in accomplishing my goal of becoming the Signore Magistrate in the city of Florence."

"I'm only too happy to help," Walter said. "I see you have succeeded in reducing crime in your country. Congratulations. And again, I was glad to help in my small way."

Shortly thereafter Anton became an advisor to Signore Giovanni Terranova on political matters in Florence.

Marcello Trieste, with the help of Anton, found another Mercedes like the one that Anton had. He now took his wife to church every Sunday in it, with his youngest son driving them. Word spread quickly of how Bustiani died. If you were privy to be in the inner circle of Marcello's friends, you were aware of the new *don*.

Look for the next exciting and spellbinding adventure.

THE NEW MEXICO CONNECTION

An organization called The Balducci Couture developed control of the textile industry used to support the global fashion industry. One of their sources of the fabric comes from Peru and Bolivia – from llamas and alpacas. Many in the fashion industry prize the wool from these beautiful animals. Over the past several years, a secret process surfaced that takes that wool and processes it to an almost silk-like quality. The organization had to find that formula and eliminate any competition that would potentially destroy their lock on this lucrative industry.

Soon after Walter Donleavy purchased his llama and alpaca ranch in New Mexico, he received a call from a close friend from his past in South America and asked him to visit him in Bolivia. Walter never dreamed that this would take him on a perilous journey that would force him to rethink his life goals and could potentially expose his multi-million dollar empire.

Rick went to Carrizozo, New Mexico to manage Walter's new San Lorenzo Llama and Alpaca Ranch. However, from the moment he arrived, he could already feel there were problems – he just didn't know how much. Rick went to Bolivia with Walter to purchase another, but larger ranch. However, within twenty-four hours they were entrenched in a war that had global consequences if they were to succeed. In the process, Walter was kidnapped by the Cartel, who demanded a secret from him that had been handed down from the Chief of the Quechua Indian tribe in the early 1500s. Rick flew to Tel Aviv to meet with the person who was holding Walter hostage. Walter's financial empire was in jeopardy, because certain people had found out about Walter's life before he came to the United States.

THE PRAGUE DECEPTION

Throughout history, many dictators developed a primeval almost sadistic view of society and felt that power was for the taking. Some of these dictators went to the finest educators in the world and learned how to mesmerize their citizens, converting them to their own twisted ideologies. They began the process by corrupting the military generals who controlled the workforce and weapons that could control their people.

One individual during World War II set in motion a contingency plan in the event he wasn't successful in accomplishing his goal of ruling the world – and that was Adolf Hitler. Toward the end of the Second World War, Hitler ordered his Army to enter Prague. He moved his munitions factory from Berlin to Prague's underground city, because the Russians were getting too close to the city.

To temper his paranoia, he created a backup plan. That's when he created – The Doomsday Device. As such, he planned an apocalypse so devastating it was beyond description, one from which the world might never recover.

Thirty-five years later, a letter surfaced reminding five people that the device could still be a real threat to the world and had to be disarmed.

Rick Benedict was a professor at Brown University at the time. Little did he know that soon he was going to be embroiled in a world of betrayal and deceit that would shake the very foundation of his own beliefs.

BIOGRAPHY - VIC SWATSEK

Vic Swatsek is also the author of **The Prague Deception**. **The Colorado Conspiracy** *is the second in a series of novels that follow several primary characters into thrilling adventures throughout the world. He was born in Austria, and when he was six years old, the family immigrated to the U.S. He did a tour of duty for the U.S. Army in Europe and used this experience in some of the stories. As the Senior Vice President of Production Operations for a major aerospace company, Vic managed over a thousand employees to produce a product for airlines used around the world.*

He is the first to agree that writing a novel has many additional, interesting, and very challenging facets. His prior business experience has helped him to organize and effectively present very imaginative ideas. He grew up and still lives in Southern California with his wife, Liz.